Constant

Recollections of the Private Life of Napoleon

Volume 2

Constant

Recollections of the Private Life of Napoleon
Volume 2

ISBN/EAN: 9783337349783

Printed in Europe, USA, Canada, Australia, Japan

Cover: Foto ©Andreas Hilbeck / pixelio.de

More available books at **www.hansebooks.com**

NAPOLEON 1814.

RECOLLECTIONS

OF

THE PRIVATE LIFE

OF

NAPOLEON

BY

CONSTANT

PREMIER VALET DE CHAMBRE

TRANSLATED BY WALTER CLARK

ILLUSTRATED

VOLUME II.

NEW YORK
THE MERRIAM COMPANY
67 FIFTH AVENUE

TABLE OF CONTENTS.

VOLUME II.

CHAPTER I.

CHAPTER II.

CHAPTER III.

CHAPTER IV.

CHAPTER V.

CHAPTER VI.

CHAPTER XIX.

CHAPTER XX.

CHAPTER XXI.

CHAPTER XXIV.

CHAPTER XXV.

CHAPTER XXXI.

LIST OF ILLUSTRATIONS.

RECOLLECTIONS OF NAPOLEON.

CHAPTER I.

I left the Emperor at Berlin, where each day, and each hour of the day, he received news of some victory gained, or some success obtained by his generals. General Beaumont[1] presented to him eighty flags captured from the enemy by his division, and Colonel Gérard[2] also presented sixty taken from Blücher at the battle of Wismar. Madgeburg had capitulated, and a garrison of sixty thousand men had marched out under the eyes of General Savary. Marshal Mortier occupied Hanover in the name of France, and Prince Murat was on the point of entering Warsaw after driving out the Russians.

War was about to recommence, or rather to be continued, against the latter; and since the Prussian army could now be regarded as entirely vanquished, the Emperor left Berlin in order to personally conduct operations against the Russians.

We traveled in the little coaches of the country; and as was the rule always on our journeys, the carriage of the grand marshal preceded that of the Emperor. The season, and the passage of such large numbers of artillery, had rendered the roads frightful; but notwithstanding this we traveled very rapidly, until at last between Kutow and Warsaw, the grand marshal's carriage was upset, and his collar-bone broken. The Emperor arrived a short time after this unfortunate accident, and had him borne under his own eyes into the nearest post-house. We always carried with us a portable medicine-chest in order that needed help might be promptly given to the wounded. His Majesty placed him in the hands of the surgeon, and did not leave him till he had seen the first bandage applied.

---

[1] Comte Marc Antoine Beaumont de la Bonnière, born in Touraine, 1760; served 1795–1809; peer, 1814; died 1830. — TRANS.

[2] Etienne-Maurice Gérard, born at Damvilliers, 1773; served 1794–1815; minister of war 1830, and marshal 1831, commanding the expedition to Belgium; died 1852. — TRANS.

At Warsaw, where his Majesty passed the entire month of January, 1807, he occupied the grand palace. The Polish nobility, eager to pay their court to him, gave in his honor magnificent *fêtes* and brilliant balls, at which were present all the wealthiest and most distinguished inhabitants of Warsaw.

At one of these reunions the Emperor's attention was drawn to a young Polish lady named Madame Valevska, twenty-two years of age, who had just married an old noble of exacting temper and extremely harsh manners, more in love with his titles than with his wife, whom, however, he loved devotedly, and by whom he was more respected than loved. The Emperor experienced much pleasure at the sight of this lady, who attracted his attention at the first glance. She was a blonde, with blue eyes, and skin of dazzling whiteness; of medium height, with a charming and beautifully proportioned figure. The Emperor having approached her, immediately began a conversation, which she sustained with much grace and intelligence, showing that she had received a fine education, and the slight shade of melancholy diffused over her whole person rendered her still more seductive.

His Majesty thought he beheld in her a woman who had been sacrificed, and was unhappy in her domestic relations; and the interest with which this idea inspired him caused him to be more interested in her than he had ever been in any woman, a fact of which she could not fail to be conscious. The day after the ball, the Emperor seemed to me unusually agitated; he rose from his chair, paced to and fro, took his seat and rose again, until I thought I should never finish dressing him. Imme-

diately after breakfast he ordered a person, whose name
I shall not give,[1] to pay a visit to Madame Valevska, and
inform her of his subjugation and his wishes. She proudly
refused propositions which were perhaps too brusque, or
which perhaps the coquetry natural to all women led her
to repulse; and though the hero pleased her, and the idea
of a lover resplendent with power and glory revolved
doubtless over and over in her brain, she had no idea
of surrendering thus without a struggle. The great personage returned in confusion, much astonished that he
had not succeeded in his mission; and the next day when
the Emperor rose I found him still preoccupied, and he did
not utter a word, although he was in the habit of talking
to me at this time. He had written to Madame Valevska
several times, but she had not replied; and his vanity was
much piqued by such unaccustomed indifference. At last
his affecting appeals having touched Madame Valevska's
heart, she consented to an interview between ten and eleven
o'clock that evening, which took place at the appointed time.
She returned a few days after at the same hour, and her
visits continued until the Emperor's departure.

Two months after the Emperor sent for her; and she
joined him at his headquarters in Finkenstein, where she
remained from this time, leaving at Warsaw her old
husband, who, deeply wounded both in his honor and his af-
fections, wished never to see again the wife who had abandoned him. Madame Valevska remained with the Emperor
until his departure, and then returned to her family, constantly evincing the most devoted and, at the same time,

---

[1] It was Murat, Marshal and Grand Duke of Berg, and later King of
Naples. — TRANS.

disinterested affection. The Emperor seemed to appreciate perfectly the charms of this angelic woman, whose gentle and self-abnegating character made a profound impression on me. As they took their meals together, and I served them alone, I was thus in a position to enjoy their conversation, which was always amiable, gay, and animated on the Emperor's part; tender, impassioned, and melancholy on that of Madame Valevska. When his Majesty was absent, Madame Valevska passed all her time, either in reading, or viewing through the lattice blinds of the Emperor's rooms the parades and evolutions which took place in the court of honor of the château, and which he often commanded in person. Such was her life, like her disposition, ever calm and equable; and this loveliness of character charmed the Emperor, and made him each day more and more her slave.

After the battle of Wagram, in 1809, the Emperor took up his residence at the palace of Schoenbrunn, and sent immediately for Madame Valevska, for whom a charming house had been rented and furnished in one of the faubourgs of Vienna, a short distance from Schoenbrunn. I went mysteriously to bring her every evening in a close carriage, with a single servant, without livery; she entered by a secret door, and was introduced into the Emperor's apartments. The road, although very short, was not without danger, especially in rainy weather, on account of ruts and holes which were encountered at every step; and the Emperor said to me almost every day, "Be very careful, Constant, it has rained to-day; the road will be bad. Are you sure you have a good driver? Is the carriage in good condition?" and other questions of the same kind, which evidenced the deep and **sincere** affection he **felt** for Madame Valevska. **The** Emperor was not wrong, besides, in urging me to be careful; for one evening, when we had left Madame Valevska's residence **a** little later than usual, the coachman upset us, and in **trying** to avoid a rut, drove the carriage over the edge of the road. I was on the right of Madame Valevska; and the carriage fell on that side, in such **a** position that I alone **felt the** shock of the fall, since Madame Valevska falling on me, received **no** injury. I was glad **to** be the means of saving her, and when I said this she expressed her gratitude with a grace peculiarly her own. My injuries were slight; and **I** began **to** laugh the first, in which Madame Valevska soon joined, **and** she related **our** accident **to** his Majesty immediately **on our** arrival.

I could not undertake to describe **all** the **care** and attentions which the Emperor lavished upon her. He **had** her brought to Paris, accompanied by her brother, **a very** distinguished officer, and **her** maid, and gave the grand marshal orders **to** purchase for her a pretty residence in the Chaussée-d'Antin. Madame Valevska was very happy, and often said **to me,** "All my thoughts, all my inspirations, come from **him, and return to** him; **he is** all my happiness, my future, **my** life!" **She never** left her house except **to come to the** private apartments at the Tuileries, and when this happiness **could** not be granted, went neither **to** the theater, the promenade, nor in society, but remained at home, seeing only very few persons, and writing to the Emperor every day. At length she gave birth to **a** son,[1]

---

[1] Count Walewski, born 1810; minister to England, 1852; minister of foreign affairs, 1855-1860; died 1868. — TRANS.

who bore a striking resemblance to the Emperor, to whom this event was a source of great joy; and he hastened to her as soon as it was possible to escape from the château, and taking the child in his arms, and caressing him, as he had just caressed the mother, said to him, "I make you a count." Later we shall see this son receiving at Fontainebleau a final proof of affection.

Madame Valevska reared her son at her residence, never leaving him, and carried him often to the château, where I admitted them by the dark staircase, and when either was sick the Emperor sent to them Monsieur Corvisart. This skillful physician had on one occasion the happiness of saving the life of the young count in a dangerous illness.

Madame Valevska had a gold ring made for the Emperor, around which she twined her beautiful blonde hair, and on the inside of the ring were engraved these words: "*When you cease to love me, do not forget that I love you.*" The Emperor gave her no other name but Marie.

I have perhaps devoted too much space to this *liaison* of the Emperor: but Madame Valevska was entirely different from the other women whose favor his Majesty obtained; and she was worthy to be named the La Vallière of the Emperor, who, however, did not show himself ungrateful towards her, as did Louis XIV. towards the only woman by whom he was beloved. Those who had, like myself, the happiness of knowing and seeing her intimately must have preserved memories of her which will enable them to comprehend why in my opinion there exists so great a distance between Madame Valevska, the tender and modest woman, rearing in retirement the son she bore to the Emperor, and the *favorites* of the conqueror of Austerlitz.

CHAPTER II.

THE Russians, being incited to this campaign by the remembrance of the defeat of Austerlitz, and by the **fear** of seeing Poland snatched from their grasp, were not deterred by the winter season, and resolved to open **the** attack on the Emperor at once; and as the latter was **not** the man to allow himself to be forestalled, he consequently abandoned his **winter quarters, and quitted Warsaw at the**

end of January. On the 8th of February the two armies met at Eylau; and there took place, as is well known, a bloody battle, in which both sides showed equal courage, and nearly fifteen thousand were left dead on the field of battle, equally divided in number between the French and Russians. The gain, or rather the loss, was the same to both armies; and a *Te Deum* was chanted at St. Petersburg as well as at Paris, instead of the *De Profundis*, which would have been much more appropriate. His Majesty complained bitterly on returning to his headquarters that the order he had sent to General Bernadotte had not been executed, and in consequence of this his corps had taken no part in the battle, and expressed his firm conviction that the victory, which remained in doubt between the Emperor and General Benningsen,[1] would have been decided in favor of the former had a fresh army-corps arrived during the battle, according to the Emperor's calculations. Most unfortunately the *aide-de-camp* bearing the Emperor's orders to the Prince of Ponte-Corvo had fallen into the hands of a party of Cossacks; and when the Emperor was informed of this circumstance the day after the battle, his resentment was appeased, though not his disappointment. Our troops bivouacked on the field of battle, which his Majesty visited three times, for the purpose of directing the assistance of the wounded, and removal of the dead.

Generals d'Hautpoult,[2] Corbineau,[3] and Boursier were

---

[1] Count Levin August Benningsen, born at Brunswick, 1745, headed the conspirators who put to death the Emperor Paul; commanded the Russian army at Eylau; died 1826. — TRANS.

[2] Jean Joseph d'Hautpoult-Salette, born 1754, of a noble family in Languedoc; general of division under Moreau, distinguished himself at Austerlitz and Jena. Senator, 1806. — TRANS.

[3] Claude Louis Corbineau, born at Laval, 1772; general of brigade, 1806. — TRANS.

mortally wounded at Eylau; and it seems to me I can still hear the brave d'Hautpoult saying to his Majesty, just as he dashed off at a gallop to charge the enemy: "Sire, you will now see my great claws; they will pierce through the enemy's squares as if they were butter!" An hour after he was no more. One of his regiments, being engaged in the interval with the Russian army, was mowed down with grape-shot, and hacked to pieces by the Cossacks, only eighteen men being left. General d'Hautpoult, forced to fall back three times with his division, led it back twice to the charge; and as he threw himself against the enemy the third time shouted loudly, "Forward, cuirassiers, in God's name! forward, my brave cuirassiers!" But the grape-shot had mowed down too many of these brave fellows; very few were left to follow their chief, and he soon fell pierced with wounds in the midst of a square of Russians into which he had rushed almost alone.

· I think it was in this battle also that General Ordener[1] killed with his own hands a general officer of the enemy. The Emperor asked if he could not have taken him alive. "Sire," replied the general with his strong German accent, "I gave him only one blow, but I tried to make it a good one." On the very morning of the battle, General Corbineau, the Emperor's *aide-de-camp*, while at breakfast with the officers on duty, declared to them that he was oppressed by the saddest presentiments; but these gentlemen, attempting to divert his mind, turned the affair into a joke. General Corbineau a few moments after received an order from his Majesty, and not finding some money

---

[1] Michel Ordener, born in department of the Moselle, 1755; made general of division at Austerlitz, 1805; died 1811. — TRANS.

he wished at Monsieur de Méneval's quarters, came to me, and I gave it to him from the Emperor's private purse; at the end of a few hours I met Monsieur de Méneval, to whom I rendered an account of General Corbineau's request, and the sum I had lent him. I was still speaking to Monsieur de Méneval, when an officer passing at a gallop gave us the sad news of the general's death. I have never forgotten the impression made on me by this sad news, and I still find no explanation of the strange mental distress which gave warning to this brave soldier of his approaching end.

Poland was relying upon the Emperor to re-establish her independence, and consequently the Poles were filled with hope and enthusiasm on witnessing the arrival of the French army. As for our soldiers, this winter campaign was most distasteful to them; for cold and wretchedness, bad weather and bad roads, had inspired them with an extreme aversion to this country.

In a review at Warsaw, at which the inhabitants crowded around our troops, a soldier began to swear roundly against the snow and mud, and, as a consequence, against Poland and the Poles. "You are wrong, Monsieur soldier," replied a young lady of a good bourgeois family of the town, "not to love our country, for we love the French very much." — "You are doubtless very lovable, mademoiselle," replied the soldier; "but if you wish to persuade me of the truth of what you say, you will prepare us a good dinner, my comrade and I." — "Come, then, messieurs," said the parents of the young Pole now advancing, "and we will drink together to the health of your Emperor." And they really carried off with them the two soldiers, who partook of the best dinner the country afforded.

The soldiers were accustomed to say that four words formed the basis of the Polish language, — *kleba? niema;* " bread? there is none; " *voia? sara;* " water? they have gone to draw it."

As the Emperor was one day passing through a column of infantry in the suburbs of Mysigniez, where the troops endured great privations since the bad roads prevented the arrival of supplies, " Papa, *kleba,*" cried a soldier. "*Niema,*" immediately replied the Emperor. The whole column burst into shouts of laughter, and no further request was made.

During the Emperor's somewhat extended stay at Finkenstein, he received a visit from the Persian ambassador, and a few grand reviews were held in his honor. His Majesty sent in return an embassy to the Shah, at the head of which he placed General Gardanne, who it was then said had an especial reason for wishing to visit Persia. It was rumored that one of his relations, after a long residence at Teheran, had been compelled, having taken part in an insurrection against the Franks, to quit this capital, and before his flight had buried a considerable treasure in a certain spot, the description of which he had carried to France. I will add, as a finale to this story, some facts which I have since learned. General Gardanne found the capital in a state of confusion; and being able neither to locate the spot nor discover the treasure, returned from his embassy with empty hands.

Our stay at Finkenstein became very tiresome; and in order to while away the time, his Majesty sometimes played with his generals and *aides-de-camp*. The game was usually *vingt-et-un;* and the Great Captain took much pleasure in cheating, holding through several deals the cards necessary to complete the required number, and was much amused when he won the game by this finesse. I furnished the sum necessary for his game, and as soon as he returned to his quarters received orders to make out his account. He always gave me half of his gains, and I divided the remainder between the ordinary *valets de chambre*.

I have no intention, in this journal, of conforming to a very exact order of dates; and whenever there recurs to my memory a fact or an anecdote which seems to me deserving of mention, I shall jot it down, at whatever point of my narrative I may have then reached, fearing lest, should I defer it to its proper epoch, it might be forgotten. In pursuance of this plan I shall here relate, in passing, some souvenirs of Saint-Cloud or the Tuileries, although we are now in camp at Finkenstein. The pastimes in which his Majesty and his general officers indulged recalled these anecdotes to my recollection. These gentlemen often made wagers or bets among themselves; and I heard the Duke of Vicenza one day bet that Monsieur Jardin, junior, equerry of his Majesty, mounted backwards on his horse, could reach the end of the avenue in front of the château in the space of a few moments; which bet the equerry won.

Messieurs Fain, Méneval, and Ivan once played a singular joke on Monsieur B. d'A——, who, they knew, was subject to frequent attacks of gallantry. They dressed a young man in woman's clothes, and sent him to promenade, thus disguised, in an avenue near the château. Monsieur

B. d'A—— was very near-sighted, and generally used an eyeglass. These gentlemen invited him to take a walk; and as soon as he was outside the door, he perceived the beautiful promenader, and could not restrain an exclamation of surprise and joy at the sight.

His friends feigned to share his delight, and urged him, as the most enterprising, to make the first advances, whereupon, in great excitement, he hastened after the pretended young lady, whom they had taught his *rôle* perfectly. Monsieur d'A—— outdid himself in politeness, in attentions, in offers of service, insisting eagerly on doing the honors of the château to his new conquest. The other acted his part perfectly; and after many coquettish airs on his side, and many protestations on the part of Monsieur d'A——, a *rendezvous* was made for that very evening; and the lover, radiant with hope, returned to his friends, maintaining much discretion and reserve as to his good fortune, while he really would have liked to devour the time which must pass before the day was over. At last the evening arrived which was to put an end to his impatience, and bring the time of his interview; and his disappointment and rage may be imagined when he discovered the deception which had been practiced on him. Monsieur d'A—— wished at first to challenge the authors and actors in this hoax, and could with great difficulty be appeased.

It was, I think, on the return from this campaign, that Prince Jérôme saw at Breslau, at the theater of that town, a young and very pretty actress, who played her part badly, but sang very well. He made advances, which she received coolly: but kings do not sigh long in vain; they place too heavy a weight in the balance against discretion. His

Majesty, the King of Westphalia, carried off his conquest to Cassel, and at the end of a short time she was married to his first *valet de chambre*, Albertoni, whose Italian morals were not shocked by this marriage. Some disagreement, the cause of which I do not know, having caused Albertoni to quit the king, he returned to Paris with his wife, and engaged in speculations, in which he lost all that he had gained, and I have been told that he returned to Italy. One thing that always appeared to me extraordinary was the jealousy of Albertoni towards his wife — an exacting jealousy which kept his eyes open towards all men except the king; for I am well convinced that the *liaison* continued after their marriage.

The brothers of the Emperor, although kings, were sometimes kept waiting in the Emperor's antechamber. King Jérôme came one morning by order of the Emperor, who, having not yet risen, told me to beg the King of Westphalia to wait. As the Emperor wished to sleep a little longer, I remained with the other servants in the saloon which was used as an antechamber, and the king waited with us; I do not say in patience, for he constantly moved from chair to chair, promenaded back and forth between the window and the fireplace, manifesting much annoyance, and speaking now and then to me, whom he always treated with great kindness. Thus more than half an hour passed; and at last I entered the Emperor's room, and when he had put on his dressing-gown, informed him that his Majesty was waiting, and after introducing him, I withdrew. The Emperor gave him a cool reception, and lectured him severely, and as he spoke very loud, I heard him against my will; but the king made his excuses in so low a tone that I could not hear a word of his justification. Such scenes were often repeated, for the prince was dissipated and prodigal, which displeased the Emperor above all things else, and for which he reproved him severely, although he loved him, or rather because he loved him so much; for it is remarkable, that notwithstanding the frequent causes of displeasure which his family gave him, the Emperor still felt for all his relations the warmest affection.

A short time after the taking of Dantzig (May 24, 1807), the Emperor, wishing to reward Marshal Lefebvre for the recent services which he had rendered, had him summoned at six o'clock in the morning. His Majesty was in consultation with the chief-of-staff of the army when the arrival of the marshal was announced. " Ah!" said he to Berthier, "the duke does not delay." Then, turning to the officer on duty, " Say to the Duke of Dantzig that I have summoned him so early in order that he may breakfast with me." The officer, thinking that the Emperor had misunderstood the name, remarked to him, that the person who awaited his orders was not the Duke of Dantzig, but Marshal Lefebvre. "It seems, monsieur, that you think me more capable of making a count [*faire un conte*] than a duke."

The officer was somewhat disconcerted by this reply; but the Emperor reassured him with a smile, and said, "Go, give the duke my invitation, and say to him that in a quarter of an hour breakfast will be served." The officer returned to the marshal, who was, of course, very anxious to know why the Emperor had summoned him. " Monsieur le Duc, the Emperor invites you to breakfast with him, and begs you to wait a quarter of an hour." The marshal, not having noticed the new title which the officer gave him, replied by a nod, and seated himself on a folding chair on the back of which hung the Emperor's sword, which the marshal inspected and touched with admiration and respect. The quarter of an hour passed, when another ordnance officer came to summon the marshal to the Emperor, who was already at table with the chief-of-staff; and as he entered, the Emperor saluted him with, "Good-day, Monsieur le Duc; be seated next to me."

The marshal, astonished at being addressed by this title, thought at first that his Majesty was jesting; but seeing that he made a point of calling him Monsieur le Duc he was overcome with astonishment. The Emperor, to increase his embarrassment, said to him, "Do you like chocolate, Monsieur le Duc?" — "But — yes, Sire." — "Well, we have none for breakfast, but I will give you a pound from the very town of Dantzig; for since you have conquered it, it is but just that it should make you some return." Thereupon the Emperor left the table, opened a little casket, took therefrom a package in the shape of a long square, and handed it to Marshal Lefebvre, saying to him, "Duke of Dantzig, accept this chocolate; little gifts preserve friendship." The marshal thanked his Majesty, put the chocolate in his pocket, and took his seat again at table with the Emperor and Marshal Berthier. A *pâté* in the shape of the town of Dantzig was in the midst of the table; and when this was to be served the Emperor said to the new duke, "They could not have given this dish a form which would have pleased me more. Make the attack, Monsieur le Duc; behold your conquest; it is yours to do the honors." The duke obeyed; and the three guests ate of the pie, which they found much to their taste. On his return, the marshal, Duke of Dantzig, suspecting a surprise in the little package which the Emperor had given him, hastened to open it, and found a hundred thousand crowns in bank-notes. In imitation of this magnificent present, the custom was established in the army of calling money, whether in pieces or in bank-notes, Dantzig chocolate; and when the soldiers wished to be treated by any comrade who happened to have a little money in his pocket, would say to him, "Come, now, have you no Dantzig chocolate in your pocket?"

The almost superstitious fancy of his Majesty the Emperor in regard to coincidences in dates and anniversaries was strengthened still more by the victory of Friedland, which was gained on June 14, 1807, seven years to the very day after the battle of Marengo. The severity of the winter, the difficulty in furnishing supplies (for which the Emperor had however made every possible provision and arrangement), added to the obstinate courage of the Russians, had made this a severe campaign, especially to conquerors whom the incredible rapidity of their successes in Prussia had accustomed to sudden conquests. The division of glory which he had been compelled to make with the Russians was a new experience in the Emperor's military career, but at Friedland he regained his advantage and his former superiority. His Majesty, by a feigned retreat, in which he let the enemy see only a part of his forces, drew the Russians into a decoy on the Elbe, so complete that they found themselves shut in between that river and our army. This victory was gained by troops of the line and cavalry; and the Emperor did not even find it necessary to use his Guards, while those of the Emperor Alexander was almost entirely destroyed in protecting the retreat, or rather the flight, of the Russians, who could escape from the pursuit of our soldiers only by the bridge of Friedland, a few narrow pontoons, and an almost impassable ford.

The regiments of the line in the French army covered the plain; and the Emperor, occupying a post of observation on a height whence he could overlook the whole field of battle, was seated in an armchair near a mill, surrounded by his staff. I never saw him in a gayer mood, as he conversed with the generals who awaited his orders, and seemed to enjoy eating the black Russian bread which was baked in the shape of bricks. This bread, made from inferior rye flour, and full of long straws, was the food of all the soldiers; and they knew that his Majesty ate it as well as themselves. The beautiful weather favored the skillful maneuvers of the army, and they performed prodigies of valor. The cavalry charges especially were executed with so much precision that the Emperor sent his congratulations to the regiments.

About four o'clock in the afternoon, when the two armies were pressing each other on every side, and thousands of cannon caused the earth to tremble, the Emperor exclaimed, "If this continues two hours longer, the French army will be left standing on the plain alone." A few moments after he gave orders to the Count Dorsenne,[1] general of the foot grenadiers of the Old Guard, to fire on a

---

[1] Jean Marie François Dorsenne, born in the Pas de Calais, 1773; general of division, 1809; commanded in north of Spain, 1811; died 1812. — TRANS.

brick-yard, behind which masses of Russians and Prussians were intrenched; and in the twinkling of an eye they were compelled to abandon this position, and a horde of sharp-shooters set out in pursuit of the fugitives.

The Guard made this movement at five o'clock, and at six the battle was entirely won. The Emperor said to those who were near him, while admiring the splendid behavior of the Guard, " Look at those brave fellows, with a good-will they would run over the stone-slingers and pop-guns of the line, in order to teach them to charge without waiting for them; but it would have been useless, as the work has been well done without them."

His Majesty went in person to compliment several regiments which had fought the whole day. A few words, a smile, a salute of the hand, even a nod, was sufficient recompense to these brave fellows who had just been crowned with victory.

The number of the dead and prisoners was enormous; and seventy banners, with all the equipments of the Russian army, were left in the hands of the French.

After this decisive day, the Emperor of Russia, who had rejected the proposals made by his Majesty after the battle of Eylau, found himself much disposed to make the same on his own account; and General Bennigsen consequently demanded an armistice in the name of *his* Emperor, which his Majesty granted; and a short time after a treaty of peace was signed, and the famous interview between the two sovereigns held on the banks of the Niémen. I shall pass over rapidly the details of this meeting, which have been published and repeated innumerable times. His Majesty and the young Czar conceived a mutual affection from the first moment of their meeting, and each gave *fêtes* and amusements in honor of the other. They were inseparable in public and in private, and passed hours together, in meetings for pleasure only, from which all intruders were carefully excluded. The town of Tilsit was declared neutral; and French, Russians, and Prussians followed the example set them by their sovereigns, and lived together in the most intimate brotherhood.

The King and Queen of Prussia soon after joined their Imperial Majesties at Tilsit; though this unfortunate monarch, to whom there remained hardly one town of the whole kingdom he had possessed, was naturally little disposed to take part in so much festivity. The queen was beautiful and graceful, though perhaps somewhat haughty and severe, which did not prevent her being adored by all who surrounded her. The Emperor sought to please her, and she neglected none of the innocent coquetries of her sex in order to soften the heart of the conqueror of her husband. The queen several times dined with the sovereigns, seated between the two Emperors, who vied with each other in overwhelming her with attentions and gallantries. It is well known that the Emperor Napoleon offered her one day a splendid rose, which after some hesitation she accepted, saying to his Majesty with a most charming smile, "With Magdeburg, at least." And it is well known also that the Emperor did not accept the condition.

The princess had among her ladies of honor a very old woman, who was most highly esteemed. One evening as the queen was being escorted into the dining-hall by the two Emperors, followed by the King of Prussia, Prince Murat, and the Grand Duke Constantine, this old lady of honor gave way to the two latter princes. Grand Duke Constantine would not take precedence of her, but entirely spoiled this act of politeness by exclaiming in a rude tone, " Pass, madame, pass on ! " And turning towards the King of Naples, added, loud enough to be heard, this disgraceful exclamation, "The old woodcock ! "

One may judge from this that Prince Constantine was far from exhibiting towards ladies that exquisite politeness and refined gallantry which distinguished his august brother.

The French Imperial Guard on one occasion gave a dinner to the guard of the Emperor Alexander. At the end of this exceedingly gay and fraternal banquet, each French soldier exchanged uniforms with a Russian, and promenaded thus before the eyes of the Emperors, who were much amused by this impromptu disguise.

Among the numerous attentions paid by the Russian Emperor to our own, I would mention a concert by a troop of Baskir musicians, whom their sovereign brought over the Niémen for this purpose, and never certainly did more barbarous music resound in the ears of his Majesty; and this strange harmony, accompanied by gestures equally as savage, furnished one of the most amusing spectacles that can be imagined. A few days after this concert, I obtained permission to make the musicians a visit, and went to their camp, accompanied by Roustan, who was to serve as interpreter. We enjoyed the pleasure of being present at a repast of the Baskirs, where around immense wooden tubs were seated groups consisting of ten men, each holding in his hand a piece of black bread which he moistened with a ladleful of water, in which had been diluted something

RAPP.

resembling red clay. After the repast, they gave us an exhibition of shooting with the bow; and Roustan, to whom
this exercise recalled the scenes of his youth, attempted
to shoot an arrow, but it fell at a few paces, and I saw a
smile of scorn curl the thick lips of our Baskirs. I then
tried the bow in my turn, and acquitted myself in such a
manner as to do me honor in the eyes of our hosts, who
instantly surrounded me, congratulating me by their gestures on my strength and skill; and one of them, even more
enthusiastic and more amicable than the others, gave me a
pat on the shoulder which I long remembered.

The day succeeding this famous concert, the treaty of
peace between the three sovereigns was signed, and his
Majesty made a visit to the Emperor Alexander, who
received him at the head of his guard. The Emperor
Napoleon asked his illustrious ally to show him the bravest
grenadier of this handsome and valiant troop; and when he
was presented to his Majesty, he took from his breast his
own cross of the Legion of Honor, and fastened it on the
breast of the Muscovite soldier, amid the acclamations and
hurrahs of all his comrades. The two Emperors embraced
each other a last time on the banks of the Niémen, and his
Majesty set out on the road to Koenigsberg.

At Bautzen the King of Saxony came out to meet him,
and their Majesties entered Dresden together. King Fred-
erick Augustus gave a most magnificent reception to the
sovereign who, not content with giving him a scepter,
had also considerably increased the hereditary estates of the
elector of Saxony. The good people of Dresden, during
the week we passed there, treated the French more as
brothers and compatriots than as allies.

But it was nearly ten months since we had left Paris;
and in spite of all the charms of the simple and cordial
hospitality of the Germans, I was very eager to see again
France and my own family.

CHAPTER III.

Death of the young Napoleon, son of the King of Holland. — Lovely disposition of this child. — Weakness of the nurse, and firmness of the young prince. — Submissiveness of the young prince to the Emperor. — His affection for the Emperor. — An attractive family portrait. — The shoemaker, and the portrait of *my Uncle Bibiche.* — The gazelles of Saint-Cloud. — The King and Queen of Holland reconciled by the young Napoleon. — The Emperor's affection for his nephew. — The designated heir of the Empire. — Predictions of misfortune. — First ideas of divorce. — Grief of the Empress Josephine on the death of the young Napoleon. — Despair of Queen Hortense. — The suggestion of a chamberlain. — Universal sorrow caused by the death of the young prince.

It was during the glorious campaign of Prussia and Poland that the imperial family was plunged in the deepest sorrow by the death of the young Napoleon, eldest son of King Louis of Holland. This child bore a striking resemblance to his father, and consequently to his uncle. His hair was blond, but would probably have darkened as he grew older. His eyes, which were large and blue, shone with extraordinary brilliancy when a deep impression was made on his young mind. Gentle, lovable, and full of candor and gayety, he was the delight of the Emperor, especially on account of the firmness of his character, which was so remarkable that, notwithstanding his extreme youth, nothing could make him break his word. The following anecdote which I recall furnishes an instance of this.

He was very fond of strawberries; but they caused him such long and frequent attacks of vomiting that his mother became alarmed, and positively forbade his eating them, expressing a wish that every precaution should be taken to keep out of the young prince's sight a fruit which was so injurious to him.[1]   The little Napoleon, whom the injurious effects of the strawberries had not disgusted with them, was surprised to no more see his favorite dish; but bore the deprivation patiently, until one day he questioned his nurse, and very seriously demanded an explanation on this subject, which the good woman was unable to give, for she indulged him even to the point of spoiling him.   He knew her weakness, and often took advantage of it, as in this instance for example.   He became angry, and said to his nurse in a tone which had as much and even more effect on her than the Emperor or the King of Holland could have had, " I will have the strawberries.   Give them to me at once." The poor nurse begged him to be quiet, and said that she would give them to him, but she was afraid that if anything happened he would tell the queen who had done this.   " Is that all ? " replied Napoleon eagerly.   " Have no fear; I promise not to tell."

The nurse yielded, and the strawberries had their usual effect.   The queen entered while he was undergoing the punishment for his self-indulgence; and he could not deny that he had eaten the forbidden fruit, as the proofs were too evident.   The queen was much incensed, and wished to know who had disobeyed her; she alternately entreated and threatened the child, who still continued to reply with the greatest composure, " I promised not to tell."   And in spite of the great influence she had over him, she could not force him to tell her the name of the guilty person.

[1] Strawberries produced the same effect on the King of Rome.   More carefully watched or more docile, he stopped eating them when Madame de Montesquieu, his governess, forbade him. — CONSTANT.

Young Napoleon was devoted to his uncle, and manifested in his presence a patience and self-control very foreign to his usual character. The Emperor often took him on his knee during breakfast, and amused himself making him eat lentils one by one. The pretty face of the child became crimson, his whole countenance manifested disgust and impatience; but his Majesty could prolong this sport without fearing that his nephew would become angry, which he would have infallibly done with any one else.

At such a tender age could he have been conscious of his uncle's superiority to all those who surrounded him? King Louis, his father, gave him each day a new plaything, chosen exactly to suit his fancy: but the child preferred those he received from his uncle; and when his father said to him, "But, see here, Napoleon, those are ugly things; mine are prettier." — "No," said the young prince, "they are very nice; my uncle gave them to me."

One morning when he visited his Majesty, he crossed a saloon where amid many great personages was Prince Murat, at that time, I think, Grand Duke of Berg. The child passed through without saluting any one, when the prince stopped him and said, "Will you not tell me good-morning?" — "No," replied Napoleon, disengaging himself from the arms of the Grand Duke; "not before my uncle *the Emperor.*"

At the end of a review which had taken place in the court of the Tuileries, and on the Place du Carrousel, the Emperor went up to his apartments, and threw his hat on one sofa, his sword on another. Little Napoleon entered, took his uncle's sword, passed the belt round his neck, put the hat on his head, and then kept step gravely, humming a march behind the Emperor and Empress. Her Majesty, turning round, saw him, and caught him in her arms, exclaiming, "What a pretty picture!" Ingenious in seizing every occasion to please her husband, the Empress summoned M. Gérard, and ordered a portrait of the young prince in this costume; and the picture was brought to the palace of Saint-Cloud the very day on which the Empress heard of the death of this beloved child.

He was hardly three years old when, seeing his shoemaker's bill paid with five-franc pieces, he screamed loudly, not wishing that they should give away the picture of his Uncle Bibiche. The name of Bibiche thus given by the young prince to his Majesty originated in this manner. The Empress had several gazelles placed in the park of Saint-Cloud, which were very much afraid of all the inhabitants of the palace except the Emperor, who allowed them to eat tobacco out of his snuff-box, and thus induced them to follow him, and took much pleasure in giving them the tobacco by the hands of the little Napoleon, whom he also put on the back of one of them. The latter designated these pretty animals by no other name than that of Bibiche, and amused himself by giving the same name to his uncle.

This charming child, who was adored by both father and mother, used his almost magical influence over each in order to reconcile them to each other. He took his father by the hand, who allowed himself to be thus conducted by this angel of peace to Queen Hortense, and then said to him, "Kiss her, papa, I beg you;" and was perfectly overjoyed when he had thus succeeded in reconciling these two beings whom he loved with an equal affection.

How could such a beautiful character fail to make this angel beloved by all who knew him? How could the Emperor, who loved all children, fail to be devoted to him, even had he not been his nephew, and the godson of that good Josephine whom he never ceased to love for a single instant? At the age of seven years, when that malady, the croup, so dangerous to children, snatched him from his heart-broken family, he already gave evidence of remarkable traits of character, which were the foundation of most brilliant hopes. His proud and haughty character, while rendering him susceptible of the noblest impressions, was not incompatible with obedience and docility. The idea of injustice was revolting to him; but he readily submitted to reasonable advice and rightful authority.

First-born of the new dynasty, it was fitting he should attract as he did the deepest tenderness and solicitude of the chief. Malignity and envy, which ever seek to defame and villify the great, gave slanderous explanations of this almost paternal attachment; but wise and thoughtful men saw in this adoptive tenderness only what it plainly evinced, — the desire and hope of transmitting his immense power, and the grandest name in the universe, to an heir, indirect it is true, but of imperial blood, and who, reared under the eyes, and by the direction of the Emperor, would have been to him all that a son could be. The death of the young Napoleon appeared as a forerunner of misfortunes in the midst of his glorious career, disarranging all the plans which the monarch had conceived, and decided him to concentrate all his hopes on an heir in a direct line.

It was then that the first thoughts of divorce arose in

his mind, though it did not take place until two years later, and only began to be the subject of private conversation during the stay at Fontainebleau. The Empress readily saw the fatal results to her of the death of this godson, and from that time she dwelt upon the idea of this terrible event which ruined her life. This premature death was to her an inconsolable grief; and she shut herself up for three days, weeping bitterly, seeing no one except her women, and taking almost no nourishment. It even seemed that she feared to be distracted from her grief, as she surrounded herself with a sort of avidity with all that could recall her irreparable loss. She obtained with some difficulty from Queen Hortense some of the young prince's hair, which his heart-broken mother religiously preserved; and the Empress had this hair framed on a cushion of black velvet, and kept it always near her. I often saw it at Malmaison, and never without deep emotion.

But how can I attempt to describe the despair of Queen Hortense, of that woman who became as perfect a mother as she had been a daughter. She never left her son a moment during his illness; and when he expired in her arms, still wishing to remain near his lifeless body, she fastened her arms through those of her chair, in order that she might not be torn from this heartrending scene. At last nature succumbed to such poignant grief: the unhappy mother fainted; and the opportunity was taken to remove her to her own apartment, still in the chair which she had not left, and which her arms clasped convulsively. On awaking, the queen uttered piercing screams, and her dry and staring eyes and white lips gave reason to fear that she was near her end. Nothing could bring tears to her eyes, until at last a chamberlain conceived the idea of bringing the young prince's body, and placing it on his mother's knees; and this had such an effect on her that her tears burst forth and saved her life, while she covered with kisses the cold and adored remains. All France shared the grief of the Queen of Holland.

CHAPTER IV.

Return from the campaign of Prussia and Poland. — Restoration of the château of Rambouillet. — Portraits in the bathroom. — Surprise and disgust of the Emperor. — Stay of the count at Fontainebleau. — Unjust demands of innkeepers. — Extortion upon travelers. — Cardinal Caprara and bouillon at six hundred francs. — Fixed charges ordered by the Emperor. — Arrival at Paris of Princess Catherine of Würtemberg. — Marriage of this princess to the King of Westphalia. — Relations of King Jérôme towards his first wife. — The *valet de chambre* Rico sent to America. — Affection of the queen of Westphalia for her husband. — The queen's letter to her father. — Arrest of the queen by the Marquis de Maubreuil. — Robbery of diamonds. — Presents of the Czar to the Emperor. — Promenades of the Emperor at Fontainebleau. — Kindness shown by the Emperor and Empress to an old clergyman, and the Emperor's conversation with this old man. — The Cardinal de Belloy, Archbishop of Paris. — Touching address of a prelate, who was almost a centenarian. — The Emperor's hunt. — Costume and hunting equipages. — Gallant intrigue of the Emperor at Fontainebleau. — Mysterious commission given to Constant in the darkness. — Unsuccessful embassy. — The Emperor's gayety. — The Emperor guided by Constant in the darkness. — Jests and thanks of the Emperor. — Sudden coolness of the Emperor. — Theater at Fontainebleau. — Misadventure of Mademoiselle Mars. — Loss promptly repaired.

WE arrived at Saint-Cloud on the 27th of July; and the Emperor passed the summer partly in this residence, and partly at Fontainebleau, returning to Paris only on special occasions, and never remaining longer than twenty-four hours. During his Majesty's absence, the château of Rambouillet was restored and furnished anew, and the Emperor spent a few days there. The first time he entered the bathroom, he stopped short at the door and glanced around with every appearance of surprise and dissatisfaction; and when

I sought the cause of this, following the direction of his Majesty's eyes, I saw that they rested on various family portraits which the architect had painted on the walls of the room. They were those of madame his mother, his sisters, Queen Hortense, etc.; and the sight of such a gallery, in such a place, excited the extreme displeasure of the Emperor. "What nonsense!" he cried. "Constant, summon Marshal Duroc!" And when the grand marshal appeared, his Majesty inquired, "Who is the idiot that could have conceived such an idea? Order the painter to come and efface all that. He must have little respect for women to be guilty of such an indecency."

When the court sojourned at Fontainebleau, the inhabitants indemnified themselves amply for his Majesty's long absences by the high price at which they sold all articles of food. Their extortions became scandalous impositions, and more than one foreigner making an excursion to Fontainebleau thought himself held for ransom by a troop of Bedouins. During the stay of the court, a wretched sacking-bed in a miserable inn cost twelve francs for a single night; the smallest meal cost an incredible price, and was, notwithstanding, detestable; in fact, it amounted to a genuine pillage of travelers. Cardinal Caprara,[1] whose rigid economy was known to all Paris, went one day to Fontainebleau to pay his court to the Emperor, and at the hotel where he alighted took only a single cup of bouillon, and the six persons of his suite partook only of a very light repast, as the cardinal had arranged to return in three

---

[1] Giovanni Battista **Caprara**, born of a noble family at Bologna, **1733**; count and archbishop of Milan; cardinal, **1792**; Negotiated **the** Concordat, 1801; died 1810. — TRANS.

hours; but notwithstanding this, as he was entering his carriage, the landlord had the audacity to present him with a bill for six hundred **francs!** The prince of the church indignantly protested, flew into **a rage,** threatened, etc., but all in vain ; and the **bill was paid.**

Such an outrageous imposition could **not fail to** reach the Emperor's ears, and excited his anger **to such a degree** that he **at** once ordered **a fixed schedule of** prices, which it was forbidden the innkeepers to exceed. This put an end to **the** exactions of the bloodsuckers of Fontainebleau.

On the 21st of August, there arrived at Paris the **Princess** Catharine **of** Würtemberg, future wife of Prince Jérôme Napoleon, **King of Westphalia.** This princess was **about twenty-four years** of age, and very beautiful, with a **most** noble and gracious **bearing; and** though policy alone had **made** this **marriage, never could love or** voluntary **choice have made one that** was happier.

The courageous conduct of her Majesty **the** Queen of Westphalia in **1814,** her devotion to her dethroned husband, and her admirable letters to **her** father, who wished **to** tear her from the arms of King Jérôme, are matters of history. I have seen it stated that this prince never ceased, even after this marriage, which was so flattering to his ambition, **to** correspond with his first **wife,** Madamoiselle **Patterson,** and **that** he **often sent** to America his *valet de chambre*, **Rico, to inquire after** this lady and their child. **If this is** true, it is no less so that these attentions to his first wife, which **were** not **only very** excusable, but even, **according to my** opinion, praiseworthy in Prince Jérôme, **and of which** her Majesty the Queen **of** Westphalia **was probably well aware,** did not **necessarily prevent** her being **happy with her husband.**

No testimony more reliable than that of the queen herself can be given; and she expresses herself as follows in her second letter to his Majesty, the King of Würtemburg: —

"Forced by policy to marry the king, my husband, fate has willed that I should find myself the happiest woman in the universe. I feel towards my husband the united sentiments of love, tenderness, and esteem. In this painful moment can the best of fathers wish to destroy my domestic happiness, the only kind which now remains to me? I dare to say that you, my dear father, you and all my family, do great injustice to the king, my husband; and I trust the time will come when you will be convinced that you have done him injustice, and then you will ever find in him, as well as in myself, the most respectful and affectionate of children."

Her Majesty then spoke of a *terrible misfortune* to which she had been exposed. This event, which was indeed terrible, was nothing less than violence and robbery committed on a fugitive woman defenseless and alone, by a band at the head of which was the famous Marquis de Maubreuil,[1] who had been equerry of the King of Westphalia. I will recur in treating of the events of 1814 to this disgraceful affair, and will give some particulars, which I think are not generally known, in regard to the principal authors and participants in this daring act of brigandage.

In the following month of September, a courier from the Russian cabinet arrived from St. Petersburg, bearing a letter to his Majesty from the Emperor Alexander; and among other magnificent gifts were two very handsome fur pelisses of black fox and sable martin.

[1] A French political adventurer, born in Brittany, 1782; died 1855. — TRANS.

During their Majesties residence at Fontainebleau, the Emperor often went out in his carriage with the Empress in the streets of the city with neither escort nor guards. One day, while passing before the hospital of Mont Pierreux, her Majesty the Empress saw at a window a very aged clergyman, who saluted their Majesties. The Empress, having returned the old man's salutation with her habitual grace, pointed him out to the Emperor, who himself saluted him, and ordering his coachman to stop, sent one of the footmen with a request to the old priest to come and speak to them a moment, if it were not too great an exertion. The old man, who still walked with ease, hastened to descend; and in order to save him a few steps the Emperor had his carriage driven very close to the door of the hospital.

His Majesty conversed for some time with the good ecclesiastic, manifesting the greatest kindness and respect. He informed their Majesties that he had been, previous to the Revolution, the regular priest of one of the parishes of Fontainebleau, and had done everything possible to avoid emigrating; but that terror had at length forced him to leave his native land, although he was then more than seventy-five years old; that he had returned to France at the time of the proclamation of the Concordat, and now lived on a modest pension hardly sufficient to pay his board in the hospital. "Monsieur l'Abbé," said his Majesty after listening to the old priest attentively, "I will order your pension to be doubled; and if that is not sufficient I hope you will apply to the Empress or to me." The good ecclesiastic thanked the Emperor with tears in his eyes. "Unfortunately, Sire," said he among other things, "I am too old to long enjoy your Majesty's reign or profit by your kindness." — "You?" replied the Emperor, smiling, "why, you are a young man. Look at M. de Belloy; he is much your senior, and we hope to keep him with us for a long time yet." Their Majesties then took leave of the old man, who was much affected, leaving him in the midst of a crowd of the inhabitants who had collected before the hospital during this conversation, and who were much impressed by this interesting scene and the generous kindness of the Emperor.

M. de Belloy, cardinal and archbishop of Paris, whose name the Emperor mentioned in the conversation I have just related, was then ninety-eight years of age, though his health was excellent; and I have never seen an old man who had as venerable an air as this worthy prelate. The Emperor had the profoundest respect for him, and never failed to give evidence of it on every occasion. During this same month of September, a large number of the faithful having assembled according to custom on Mount Valerien, the archbishop likewise repaired to the spot to hear mass. As he was about to withdraw, seeing that many pious persons were awaiting his benediction, he addressed them before bestowing it in a few words which showed his kindness of heart and his evangelical simplicity: "My children, I know that I must be very old from the loss of my strength, but not of my zeal and my tenderness for you. Pray God, my children, for your old archbishop, who never fails to intercede on your behalf each day."

During his stay at Fontainebleau, the Emperor enjoyed more frequently than ever before the pleasures of the chase. The costume necessary was a French coat of green dragon

color, decorated with buttons and gold lace, white cashmere breeches, and Hessian boots without facings; this
was the costume for the grand hunt which was always a
stag hunt; that for a hunt with guns being a plain, green
French coat with no other ornament than white buttons, on
which were cut suitable inscriptions. This costume was the
same for all persons taking part in this hunt, with no distin-
guishing marks, even for his Majesty himself.

The princesses set out for the *rendezvous* in a Spanish
carriage with either or four six horses, and thus followed
the chase, their costume being an elegant riding-habit, and
a hat with white or black plumes.

One of the Emperor's sisters (I do not now recall which)
never failed to follow the hunt, accompanied by many
charming ladies who were always invited to breakfast at
the *rendezvous*, as was always the custom on similar occasions with the persons of the court. One of these ladies,
who was both beautiful and intelligent, attracted the attention of the Emperor, a short correspondence ensued, and
at last the Emperor again ordered me to carry a letter.

In the palace of Fontainebleau is a private garden called
the garden of Diana, to which their Majesties alone had
access. This garden is surrounded on four sides by buildings; on the left was the chapel with its gloomy gallery
and Gothic architecture; on the right the grand gallery (as
well as I can remember); in the middle the building which
contained their Majesties' apartments; finally, in front of
and facing the square were broad arcades, and behind them
the buildings intended for the various persons attached to
the household of the princes or the Emperor. Madame de
B ——, the lady whom the Emperor had remarked, lodged

in an appartment situated behind these arcades on the
ground floor; and his Majesty informed me that I would
find a window open, through which I must enter cautiously,
in the darkness, and give his note to a person who would
ask for it. This darkness was necessary, because this
window opened on the garden, and though behind the
arcades, would have been noticed had there been a light.
Not knowing the interior of these apartments, I entered
through the window, thinking I could then walk on a
level, but had a terrible fall over a high step which was in
the embrasure of the window. I heard some one scream
as I fell, and a door was suddenly closed. I had received
severe bruises on my knee, elbow, and head, and rising with
difficulty, at once began a search around the apartment,
groping in the dark; but hearing nothing more, and fearing
to make some fresh noise which might be heard by persons
who should not know of my presence there, I decided to
return to the Emperor, and report to him my adventures.
Finding that none of my injuries were serious, the Emperor
laughed most heartily, and then added, " Oh, oh, so there is
a step; it is well to know that. Wait till Madame B ——
is over her fright; I will go to her, and you will accompany
me." At the end of an hour, the Emperor emerged with
me from the door of his cabinet which opened on the
garden. I conducted him in silence towards the window
which was still open, and assisted him to enter, and having obtained to my cost a correct idea of the spot, directed
him how to avoid a fall.

His Majesty, having entered the chamber without accident, told me to retire. I was not without some anxiety as
I informed the Emperor; but he replied that I was a child,

and there could be no danger. It appeared that his Majesty succeeded better than I had done, as he did not return until daybreak, and then jested about my awkwardness, admitting, however, that if he had not been warned, a similar accident would have befallen him.

Although Madame de B—— was worthy of a genuine attachment, her *liaison* with the Emperor lasted only a short while, and was only a passing fancy. I think that the difficulties surrounding his nocturnal visits cooled his Majesty's ardor greatly; for the Emperor was not enough in love to be willing to brave everything in order to see his beautiful mistress. His Majesty informed me of the fright which my fall had caused her, and how anxious this amiable lady had been on my account, and how he had reassured her; this did not, however, prevent her sending next day to know how I was, by a confidential person, who told me again how interested Madame de B—— had been in my accident.

Often at Fontainebleau there was a court representation, in which the actors of the first theaters received orders to play before their Majesties scenes selected from their various répertoires. Mademoiselle Mars was to play the evening of her arrival; but at Essonne, where she was obliged to stop a moment on account of the road being filled with cattle going or returning from Fontainebleau, her trunk had been stolen, a fact of which she was not aware until she had gone some distance from the spot. Not only were her costumes missing, but she had no other clothing except what she wore; and it would be at least twelve hours before she could get from Paris what she needed. It was then two o'clock in the afternoon, and that very evening she must appear in the brilliant *rôle* of Célimène. Although much disturbed by this accident, Mademoiselle Mars did not lose her presence of mind, but visited all the shops of the town, and in a few hours had cut and made a complete costume in most excellent taste, and her loss was entirely repaired.

CHAPTER V.

The **Emperor's** journey to Italy. — Short **time for preparation.** — **Complete** services sent in various directions. — Bedroom **furniture while on the** journey. — Constant inseparable from the Emperor. — Provision wagon in the kitchen service. — The appointed order of the Emperor's meals while traveling. — The Emperor's breakfast in the open air. — The former officers of the king's kitchen in the service of the Emperor. — M. Colin and M. Pfister. — Messieurs Soupé and **Pierrugues.** — Unexpected arrival **of the Emperor at** Milan. — Improvised **illumination.** — Joy of Prince **Eugène and the** Milanese. — Affection **and** respect of the Emperor for **the vice-queen.** — Constant **complimented by the vice-king.** — The **Emperor at the theater of la Scala.** — **Passage through Brescia and Verona.** — **Appearance of Lombardy.** — **Constant's dread of official harangues.** — **Races at Vicenza.** — **The Emperor an early riser while traveling.** — **Rice-fields.** — **Picturesque landscapes.**

IN the month of November of this year I followed their Majesties to Italy. We knew a few days in advance that the Emperor would make this journey; but as happened on all other occasions, neither the day nor the hour was fixed, until we were told on the evening of the 15th that we would set out early on the morning of the 16th. I passed the night like all the household of his Majesty; for in order to carry out the incredible perfection of comfort with which the Emperor surrounded himself on his journeys, it was necessary that everybody should be on foot as soon as the hour of departure was known; consequently I passed the night arranging the service of his Majesty, while my wife packed my own baggage, and had but just finished when the Emperor asked for me, which meant that ten minutes after we would be on the road. At four o'clock in the morning his Majesty entered his carriage.

As we never knew at what hour or in what direction
the Emperor would begin his journey, the grand marshal,
the grand equerry, and the grand chamberlain sent forward
a complete service on all the different roads which they
thought his Majesty might take.   The bedroom service
comprised a *valet de chambre* and a wardrobe boy.   As for
me, I never left his Majesty's person, and my carriage always
followed immediately behind his.   The conveyance belonging to this service contained an iron bed with its accessories,
a dressing-case with linen, coats, etc.   I know little of the
service of the stables, but that of the kitchen was organized as follows: There was a conveyance almost in the
shape of the *coucou* on the Place Louis XV. at Paris, with
a deep bottom and an enormous body.   The bottom contained wines for the Emperor's table and that of the high
officers, the ordinary wine being bought at the places where
we stopped.   In the body of the wagon were the kitchen
utensils and a portable furnace, followed by a carriage
containing a steward, two cooks, and a furnace-boy.   There
was besides this, a baggage-wagon full of provisions and
wine to fill up the other as it was emptied; and all these
conveyances set out a few hours in advance of the Emperor.
It was the duty of the grand marshal to designate the
place at which breakfast should be taken.   We alighted
sometimes at the archbishop's, sometimes at the *hôtel de
ville*, sometimes at the residence of the sub-prefect, or
even at that of the mayor, in the absence of any other
dignitaries.   Having arrived at the designated house, the
steward gave orders for the provisions, the furnaces were
lighted, and spits turned; and if the Emperor alighted and
partook of the repast prepared, the provisions which had

been consumed were immediately replaced as far as possible, and the carriages filled again with poultry, pastry, etc.; before leaving all expenses were paid by the controller, presents were made to the master of the house, and everything which was not necessary for the service left for the use of their servants. It sometimes happened that the Emperor, finding that it was too soon for breakfast, or wishing to make a longer journey, gave orders to pass on, and everything was packed up again and the service continued its route. Sometimes also the Emperor, halting in the open field, alighted, took his seat under a tree, and ordered his breakfast, upon which Roustan and the footmen obtained provisions from his Majesty's carriage, which was furnished with small cooking utensils with silver covers, holding chickens, partridges, etc., while the other carriages furnished their proportion. M. Pfister served the Emperor, and every one ate a hasty morsel. Fires were lighted to heat the coffee; and in less than half an hour everything had disappeared, and the carriages rolled on in the same order as before.

The Emperor's steward and cooks had nearly all been trained in the household of the king and the princes. These were Messieurs Dunau, Léonard, Rouff, and Gérard. M. Colin was chief in command, and became steward-controller after the sad affliction of M. Pfister, who became insane during the campaign of 1809. All were capable and zealous servants; and, as is the case in the household of all sovereigns, each department of the domestic affairs had its chief. Messieurs Soupé and Pierrugues were in charge of the wines, and the sons of these gentlemen continued to hold the same office with the Emperor.

We traveled with great speed as far as Mont-Cenis, but were compelled to go more slowly after reaching this pass, as the weather had been very bad for several days, and the road was washed out by the rain, which still fell in torrents. The Emperor arrived at Milan at noon on the 22d; and, notwithstanding our delay at Mont-Cenis, the rest of the journey had been so rapid that no one was expecting the Emperor. The vice-king only learned of the arrival of his step-father when he was half a league from the town, but came in haste to meet us, escorted by only a few persons. The Emperor gave orders to halt, and, as soon as the door was opened, held out his hand to Prince Eugène, saying in the most affectionate manner: "Come, get up with us, my fine prince; we will enter together."

Notwithstanding the surprise which this unexpected arrival caused, we had hardly entered the town before all the houses were illuminated, and the beautiful palaces, Litta, Casani, Melzi, and many others, shone with a thousand lights. The magnificent cupola of the cathedral dome was covered with garlands of colored lights; and in the center of the Forum-Bonaparte, the walks of which were also illuminated, could be seen the colossal equestrian statue of the Emperor, on both sides of which transparencies had been arranged, in the shape of stars, bearing the initials S M I and R. By eight o'clock all the populace had collected around the château, where superb fireworks were discharged, while spirited and warlike music was performed. All the town authorities were admitted to the Emperor's presence.

On the morning of the next day there was held at the

château a council of ministers, over which the Emperor presided; and at noon he mounted his horse to take part in the mass celebrated by the grand chaplain of the kingdom. The square of the cathedral was covered by an immense crowd, through which the Emperor advanced on horseback, accompanied by his imperial Highness, the vice-king, and his staff. The noble countenance of Prince Eugène expressed the great joy he felt in the presence of his step-father, for whom he had always so much respect and filial affection, and in hearing the incessant acclamations of the people, which grew more vociferous every moment.

After the *Te Deum*, the Emperor held a review of the troops on the square, and immediately after set out with the viceroy for Monza, the palace at which the queen resided. For no woman did the Emperor manifest more sincere regard and respect than for Princess Amelia; but, indeed, there has never been a more beautiful or purer woman. It was impossible to speak of beauty or virtue in the Emperor's presence without his giving the vice-queen as an example. Prince Eugène was very worthy of so accomplished a wife, and justly appreciated her exalted character; and I was glad to see in the countenance of the excellent prince the reflection of the happiness he enjoyed. Amidst all the care he took to anticipate every wish of his step-father, I was much gratified that he found time to address a few words to me, expressing the great pleasure he felt at my promotion in the service and esteem of the Emperor. Nothing could have been more grateful to me than these marks of remembrance from a prince for whom I had always retained a most sincere, and, I made bold to say, most tender, attachment.

The Emperor remained a long while with the vice-queen, whose intelligence equaled her amiability and her beauty, but returned to Milan to dine; and immediately afterwards the ladies who were received at court were presented to him. In the evening, I followed his Majesty to the theater of la Scala. The Emperor did not remain throughout the play, but retired early to his apartment, and worked the greater part of the night; which did not, however, prevent our being on the road to Verona before eight o'clock in the morning.

His Majesty made no stop at Brescia and Verona. I would have been very glad to have had time on the route to examine the curiosities of Italy; but that was not an easy thing to do in the Emperor's suite, as he halted only for the purpose of reviewing troops, and preferred visiting fortifications to ruins.

At Verona his Majesty dined, or rather supped (for it was very late), with their Majesties, the King and Queen of Bavaria, who arrived at almost exactly the same time as ourselves; and very early the next day we set out for Vicenza.

Although the season was already advanced, I found great pleasure in the scene which awaits the traveler on the road from Verona to Vicenza. Imagine to yourself an immense plain, divided into innumerable fields, each bordered with different kinds of trees with slender trunks, — mostly elms and poplars, — which form avenues as far as the eye can reach. Vines twine around their trunks, climb each tree, and droop from each limb; while other branches of these vines, loosening their hold on the tree which serves as their support, droop clear to the ground, and hang in graceful festoons from tree to tree. Beyond these, lovely natural bowers could be seen far and wide, splendid fields of wheat; or, at least, this had been the case on my former journey, but at this time the harvest had been gathered for several months.

At the end of a day which I passed most delightfully amid these fertile plains, I entered Vicenza, where the authorities of the town, together with almost the entire population, awaited the Emperor under a superb arch of triumph at the entrance of the town. We were exceedingly hungry; and his Majesty himself said, that evening as he retired, that he felt very much like sitting down to the table when he entered Vicenza. I trembled, then, at the idea of those long Italian addresses, which I had found even longer than those of France, doubtless because I did not understand a single word; but, fortunately, the magistrates of Vicenza were sufficiently well-informed not to take advantage of our position, and their speeches occupied only a few moments.

That evening his Majesty went to the theater; and I was so much fatigued that I would have gladly profited by the Emperor's absence to take some repose, had not an acquaintance invited me to accompany him to the convent of the Servites, in order to witness the effect of the illumination of the town, which I did, and was repaid by the magnificent spectacle which met my eyes. The whole town seemed one blaze of light. On returning to the palace occupied by his Majesty, I learned that he had given orders that everything should be in readiness for departure two hours after midnight; consequently I had one hour to sleep, and I enjoyed it to the utmost.

At the appointed moment, the Emperor entered his carriage; and we were soon rolling along with the rapidity of lightning over the road to Stra, where we passed the night. Very early next morning we set out, following a long causeway raised through marshes. The landscape is almost the same, and yet not so beautiful, as that we passed before reaching Vicenza. We still saw groves of mulberry and olive trees, from which the finest oil is obtained, and fields of maize and hemp, interspersed with meadows. Beyond Stra the cultivation of rice commences; and, although the rice-fields must render the country unhealthy, still it has not the reputation of being more so than any other. On the right and left of the road are seen elegant houses, and cabins which, though covered with thatch, are very comfortable, and present a charming appearance. The vine is little cultivated in this part of the country, where it would hardly succeed, as the land is too low and damp; but there are, nevertheless, a few small vineyards on the slopes, and the vegetation in the whole country is incredibly rich and luxuriant. The late wars have left traces which only a long peace can efface.

CHAPTER VI.

Arrival at Fusina. — The peote and gondolas of Venice. — The appearance of Venice. — Salutes by the Emperor. — Entrance of the Imperial *cortège* on the Grand Canal. — Gardens and groves improvised by the Emperor. — A sight new to the Venetians. — Conversation of the Emperor with the vice-king and the grand marshal. — The Emperor speaking much, but not conversing. — Observation of Constant on a passage **in the** journal of the Baroness de V——. — The Emperor's opinion **of the** former government. — The lions have become old. — The Doge a French senator. — The Emperor determines to have the name of France respected. — Visit to the arsenal. — Dangerous shoals. — The tower of observation. — The workshops. — The *Bucentaure*. — Disappointment of a bargeman, an old servant of the Doge. — The marriage of the Doge to the sea interrupted by the arrival of the **French.** — Distress of the last Doge, Ludovico Manini. — The gondoliers. — **A boat-race** and tournament on **the water in the** presence of the Emperor. — A glimpse of the square of **St.** Mark during **that** night. — Industrious habits of the Emperor at Venice. — Visit to the church of St. Mark and the Doge's palace. — The dike. — The clock tower. — Mechanism of the clock. — The prisons. — Visit paid by Constant and Roustan to a Greek family. — Constant questioned by the Emperor. — Constant's curiosity disappointed. — Enthusiasm of a beautiful Greek for the Emperor. — Marital vigilance and removal. — **Decree of the** Emperor regarding the Venetians. — Departure from Venice, and return **to** France.

ON his arrival at Fusina the Emperor found the Venetian authorities **awaiting** him, embarked **on** the *peote* or gondola of **the** village, and **advanced** towards Venice, accompanied by **a** numerous floating *cortège*. We followed the Emperor **in** little **black** gondolas, which looked like floating coffins, with which **the Brenta** was covered; and nothing could **be** stranger than to hear, proceeding from these coffins of such gloomy aspect, delicious vocal concerts. The boat which carried his Majesty, **and the gondolas of** the principal persons of his suite, were handsomely ornamented.

When we arrived at the mouth of the river we were obliged to wait nearly half an hour until the locks were opened, which was done by degrees, and with every precaution; without which the waters of the Brenta, held in their canal and raised considerably above the level of the sea, would have rushed out suddenly, and in their violent descent have driven our gondolas along before them, or sunk them. Released at last from the Brenta, we found ourselves in the gulf, and saw at a distance, rising from the midst of the sea, the wonderful city of Venice. Barks, gondolas, and vessels of considerable size, filled with all the wealthy population, and all the boatmen of Venice in gala dress, appeared on every side, passing, repassing, and crossing each other, in every direction, with the most remarkable skill and speed.

The Emperor was standing at the back of the *peote*, and, as each gondola passed near his own, replied to the acclamations and cries of " *Viva Napoleone imperatore e re!* " by one of those profound bows which he made with so much grace and dignity, taking off his hat without bending his head, and carrying it along his body almost to his knees.

Escorted by this innumerable flotilla, of which the *peote* of the city seemed to be the admiral's vessel, his Majesty entered at last the Grand Canal, which flowed between magnificent palaces, hung with banners and filled with spectators. The Emperor alighted before the palace of the procurators, where he was received by a deputation of members of the Senate and the Venetian nobility. He stopped a moment in the square of St. Mark, passed through some interior streets, chose the site for a garden, the plans for which the architect of the city then presented to him, and which were carried out as if it had been in the midst of the country. It was a novel sight to the Venetians to see trees planted in the open air, while hedges and lawns appeared as if by magic. The entire absence of verdure and vegetation, and the silence which reigns in the streets of Venice, where is never heard the hoof of a horse nor the wheels of a carriage, horses and carriages being things entirely unknown in this truly marine city, must give it usually a sad and abandoned air; but this gloom entirely disappeared during his Majesty's visit.

The prince viceroy and the grand marshal were present in the evening when the Emperor retired; and, while undressing him, I heard a part of their conversation, which turned on the government of Venice before the union of this republic with the French Empire. His Majesty was almost the only spokesman, Prince Eugène and Marshal Duroc contenting themselves with throwing a few words into the conversation, as if to furnish a new text for the Emperor, and prevent his pausing, and thus ending too soon his discourse; a genuine discourse, in fact, since his Majesty took the lead, and left the others but little to say. Such was often his habit; but no one thought of complaining of this, so interesting were nearly always the Emperor's ideas, and so original and brilliantly expressed. His Majesty did not *converse*, as had been truthfully said in the journal which I have added to my memoirs, but he *spoke* with an inexpressible charm; and on this point it seems to me that the author of the "Journal of Aix-la-Chapelle" has done the Emperor injustice.

As I said just now, his Majesty spoke of the ancient State of Venice, and from what he said on this occasion I learned more than I could have done from the most interesting book. The viceroy having remarked that a few patricians regretted their former liberty, the Emperor exclaimed, " Liberty, what nonsense! liberty no longer existed in Venice, and had, indeed, never existed except for a few families of the nobility, who oppressed the rest of the population. Liberty, with a Council of Ten! Liberty, with the inquisitors of state! Liberty, with the very lions as informers, and Venetian dungeons and bullets!" Marshal Duroc remarked that towards the end these severe regulations were much modified. "Yes, no doubt," replied the Emperor. "The lion of St. Mark had gotten old; he had no longer either teeth or nails! Venice was only the shadow of her former self, and her last doge found that he rose to a higher rank in becoming a senator of the French Empire." His Majesty, seeing that this idea made the vice-king smile, added very gravely, "I am not jesting, gentlemen. A Roman senator prided himself on being more than a king; a French senator is at least the equal of a doge. I desire that foreigners shall accustom themselves to show the greatest respect towards the constituted authorities of the Empire, and to treat with great consideration even the simple title of French citizen. I will take care to insure this. Good-night, Eugène. Duroc, take care to have the reception to-morrow all that it should be. After the ceremony we will visit the arsenal. Adieu, Messieurs. Constant, come back in ten minutes to put out my light; I feel sleepy. One is cradled like an infant on these gondolas."

The next day his Majesty, after receiving the homage of the Venetian authorities, repaired to the arsenal. This is an immense building, fortified so carefully that it was practically impregnable. The appearance of the interior is singular on account of several small islands which it incloses, joined together by bridges. The magazines and numerous buildings of the fortress thus appear to be floating on the surface of the water. The entrance on the land side, by which we were introduced, is over a very handsome bridge of marble, ornamented with columns and statues. On the side next the sea, there are numerous rocks and sandbanks, the presence of which is indicated by long piles. It is said that in time of war these piles were taken up, which exposed the foreign vessels, imprudent enough to entangle themselves among these shoals, to certain destruction. The arsenal could formerly equip eighty thousand men, both infantry and cavalry, independent of complete armaments for war vessels.

The arsenal is bordered with raised towers, from which the view extends in all directions. On the tallest of these towers, which is placed in the center of the building, as well as all the others, sentinels were stationed, both day and night, to signal the arrival of vessels, which they could see at a very great distance. Nothing can be finer than the dockyards for building vessels, in which ten thousand men can work with ease. The sails are made by women, over whom other elderly women exercise an active surveillance.

The Emperor delayed only a short time to look at the *Bucentaure;* which is the title of the magnificent vessel in which the Doge of Venice was accustomed to celebrate his marriage with the sea; and a Venetian never sees without deep chagrin this old monument of the former glory of his country. I, in company with some persons of the Emperor's suite, had as our guide an old mariner, whose eyes filled with tears as he related to us in bad French that the last time he witnessed the marriage of the Doge with the Adriatic Sea was in 1796, a year before the capture of Venice. He also told us that he was at that time in the service of the last Doge of the republic, Lord Louis Manini, and that the following year (1797), the French entered Venice at the exact time when the marriage of the Doge to the sea, which took place on Ascension Day, was usually celebrated, and ever since the sea had remained a widow. Our good sailor paid a most touching tribute of praise to his old master, who he said had never succeeded in forcing himself to take the oath of allegiance to the Austrians, and had swooned away while resigning to them the keys of the city.

The gondoliers are at the same time servants, errand boys, confidants, and companions in adventures to the person who takes them into his service; and nothing can equal the courage, fidelity, and gayety of these brave seamen. They expose themselves fearlessly in their slender gondolas to tempests; and their skill is so great that they turn with incredible rapidity in the narrowest canals, cross each other, follow, and pass each other incessantly, without ever having an accident.

I found myself in a position to judge of the skill of these hardy mariners the day after our visit to the arsenal. His Majesty was conducted through the lagoons as far as the fortified gate of Mala-Mocca, and the gondoliers gave as he returned a boat-race and tournament on the water. On that day there was also a special representation at the grand theater, and the whole city was illuminated. In fact, one might think that there is a continual *fête* and general illumination in Venice; the custom being to spend the greater part of the night in business or pleasure, and the streets are as brilliant and as full of people as in Paris at four o'clock in the afternoon. The shops, especially those of the square of Saint Mark, are brilliantly lighted, and crowds fill the small decorated pavilions where coffee, ices, and refreshments of all kinds are sold.

The Emperor did not adopt the Venetian mode of life, however, and retired at the same hour as in Paris; and when he did not pass the day working with his ministers, rode in a gondola through the lagoons, or visited the principal establishments and public buildings of Venice; and I thus saw, in company with his Majesty, the church of Saint Mark, and the ancient palace of the Doge.

The church of Saint Mark has five entrances, superbly decorated with marble columns; the gates are of bronze and beautifully carved. Above the middle door were formerly the four famous bronze horses, which the Emperor carried to Paris to ornament the Arch of Triumph on the Place du Carrousel. The tower is separated from the church by a small square, from the midst of which it rises to a height of more than three hundred feet. It is ascended by an inclined platform without steps, which is very convenient; and on arriving at the summit the most magnificent panorama is spread out before you, — Venice with its innumerable islands covered with palaces, churches, and buildings, and extending at a distance into the sea;

also the immense dike, sixty feet broad, several fathoms deep, and built of great blocks of stone, which enormous work surrounds Venice and all its islands, and defends it against the rising of the sea.

The Venetians have the greatest admiration for the clock placed in the tower bearing its name, and the mechanism of which shows the progress of the sun and moon through the twelve signs of the zodiac. In a niche above the dial-plate is an image of the Virgin, which is gilded and life-size; and it is said that on certain *fête* days, each blow of the pendulum makes two angels appear, trumpet in hand, followed by the Three Wise Men, who prostrate themselves at the feet of the Virgin Mary. I saw nothing of all that, but only two large black figures striking the hour on the clock with iron clubs.

The Doge's palace is a gloomy building; and the prisons, which are separated from it only by a narrow canal, render the aspect still more depressing.

At Venice one finds merchants from every nation, Jews and Greeks being very numerous. Roustan, who understood the language of the latter, was sought after by the most distinguished among them; and the heads of a Greek family came one day to invite him to visit them at their residence on one of the islands which lie around Venice. Roustan confided to me his desire to accept this invitation, and I was delighted with his proposition that I should accompany him. On our arrival at their island, we were received by our hosts, who were very wealthy merchants, as if we had been old friends. The apartment, a kind of parlor into which we were ushered, not only evinced cultivation and refinement, but great elegance; a large divan extended around the hall, the inlaid floor of which was covered with artistically woven mats. Our hosts were six men who were associated in the same trade. I would have been somewhat embarrassed had not one of them who spoke French conversed with me, while the others talked to Roustan in their native tongue. We were offered coffee, fruits, ices, and pipes; and as I was never fond of smoking, and knew besides the disgust inspired in the Emperor by odors in general, and especially that of tobacco, I refused the pipe, and expressed a fear that my clothes might be scented by being so near the smokers. I thought I perceived that this delicacy lowered me considerably in the esteem of my hosts, notwithstanding which, as we left, they gave us most urgent invitations to repeat our visit, which it was impossible to do, as the Emperor soon after left Venice.

On my return, the Emperor asked me if I had been through the city, what I thought of it, and if I had entered any residences; in fact, what seemed to me worthy of notice. I replied as well as I could; and as his Majesty was just then in a mood for light conversation, spoke to him of our excursion, and visit to the Greek family. The Emperor asked me what these Greeks thought of him. "Sire," replied I, "the one who spoke French seemed entirely devoted to your Majesty, and expressed to me the hope which he and also his brothers entertained, that the Emperor of the French, who had successfully combated the mamelukes in Egypt, might also some day make himself the liberator of Greece."

"Ah, Monsieur Constant," said the Emperor to me, pinching me sharply, "you are meddling with politics."— "Pardon me, Sire, I only repeated what I heard, and it is not astonishing that all the oppressed count on your Majesty's aid. These poor Greeks seem to love their country passionately, and, above all, detest the Turks most cordially."—"That is good," said his Majesty; "but I must first of all attend to my own business. Constant!" continued his Majesty suddenly changing the subject of this conversation with which he had deigned to honor me, and smiling with an ironical air, "what do you think of the appearance of the beautiful Greek women? How many models have you seen worthy of Canova or of David?" I was obliged to admit to his Majesty that what had influenced me most in accepting Roustan's proposition was the hope of seeing a few of these much vaunted beauties, and that I had been cruelly disappointed in not having seen the shadow of a woman. At this frank avowal the Emperor, who had expected it in advance, laughed heartily, and took his revenge on my ears, calling me a libertine: "You do not know then, *Monsieur le drôle*, that your good friends the Greeks have adopted the customs of those Turks whom they detest so cordially, and like them seclude their wives and daughters in order that they may never appear before bad men like yourself."

Although the Greek ladies of Venice may be carefully watched by their husbands, they are neither secluded nor guarded in a seraglio like the Turkish women; for during our stay at Venice, a great person spoke to his Majesty of a young and beautiful Greek, who was an enthusiastic admirer of the Emperor of the French. This lady was very ambitious of being received by his Majesty in his private rooms, and although carefully watched by a jealous husband, had found means to send to the Emperor a letter in which she depicted the intensity of her love and admiration. This letter, written with real passion and in an exalted strain, inspired in his Majesty a desire to see and know the author, but it was necessary he should use precautions, for the Emperor was not the man to abuse his power to snatch a woman from her husband; and yet all the care that he took in keeping the affair secret did not prevent her husband from suspecting the plans of his wife, and before it was possible for her to see the Emperor, she was carried away far from Venice, and her prudent husband carefully covered her steps and concealed her flight. When her disappearance was announced to the Emperor: "He is an old fool," said his Majesty, laughing, "who thinks he is strong enough to struggle against his destiny." His Majesty formed no other *liaison* during our stay at Venice.

Before leaving this city, the Emperor rendered a decree which was received with inexpressible enthusiasm, and added much to the regret which his Majesty's departure caused the inhabitants of Venice. The department of the Adriatic, of which Venice was the chief city, was enlarged in all its maritime coasts, from the town of Aquila as far as Adria. The decree ordered, moreover, that the port should be repaired, the canals deepened and cleaned, the great wall of Palestrina of which I have spoken above, and the jetties in front of it, extended and maintained; that a canal of communication between the arsenal of Venice and the Pass of Mala-Mocco should be dug; and finally that this passage itself should be cleared and deepened sufficiently for vessels of the line of seventy-four tons burthen to pass in and out.

Other articles related to benevolent establishments, the administration of which was given to a kind of council called the *Congregation of Charities*, and the cession to the city from the royal domain of the island of Saint Christopher, to be used as a general cemetery; for until then here, as in the rest of Italy, they had the pernicious custom of interring the dead in churches. Finally the decree ordered the adoption of a new mode of lighting the beautiful square of Saint Mark, the construction of new quays, gateways, etc.

When we left Venice the Emperor was conducted to the shore by a crowd of the population fully as numerous as that which welcomed his arrival. Trevise, Undine, and Mantua rivaled each other in their eagerness to receive his Majesty in a becoming manner. King Joseph had left the Emperor to return to Naples; but Prince Murat and the vice-king accompanied his Majesty.

The Emperor stopped only two or three days at Milan, and continued his journey. On reaching the plains of Marengo, he found there the entire population of Alexandria awaiting him, and was received by the light of thousands of torches. We passed through Turin without stopping, and on the 30th of December again descended Mont Cenis, and on the evening of the 1st of January arrived at the Tuileries.

CHAPTER VII.

WE arrived in Paris on the 1st of January at nine
o'clock in the evening; and as the theater of the palace of
the Tuileries was now completed, on the Sunday following
his Majesty's return the Griselda of M. Paër was presented
in this magnificent hall. Their Majesties' boxes were situated in front of the curtain, opposite each other, and presented a charming picture, with their hangings of crimson
silk draped above, and forming a background to broad,
movable mirrors, which reflected at will the audience or the
play. The Emperor, still impressed with the recollections
of the theaters of Italy, criticised unsparingly that of the
Tuileries, saying that it was inconvenient, badly planned,
and much too large for a palace theater; but notwithstanding all these criticisms, when the day of inauguration came,
and the Emperor was convinced of the very great ingenuity
M. Fontaine had shown in distributing the boxes so as to

make the splendid toilets appear to the utmost advantage, he appeared well satisfied, and charged the Duke of Frioul to present to M. Fontaine the congratulations he so well deserved.

A week after we saw the reverse of the medal. On that day *Cinna* was presented, and a comedy, the name of which I have forgotten. It was such extremely cold weather that we were obliged to leave the theater immediately after the tragedy, in consequence of which the Emperor exhausted himself in invectives against the hall, which according to him was good for nothing but to be burnt. M. Fontaine [1] was summoned, and promised to do everything in his power to remedy the inconveniences pointed out to him; and in fact, by means of new furnaces placed under the theater, with pipes through the ceiling, and steps placed under the benches of the second tier of boxes, in a week the hall was made warm and comfortable.

For several weeks the Emperor occupied himself almost exclusively with buildings and improvements. The arch of triumph of the Place du Carrousel, from which the scaffolding had been removed in order to allow the Imperial Guard to pass beneath it on their return from Prussia, first attracted his Majesty's attention. This monument was then almost completed, with the exception of a few bas-reliefs which were still to be put in position. The Emperor took a critical view of it from one of the palace windows, and said, after knitting his brows two or three times, that this mass resembled much more a pavilion than a gate, and that he would have much preferred one constructed in the style of the porte Saint-Denis.

[1] Born at Pontoise, 1762 ; erected the arch of the Carrousel ; died 1853.

After visiting in detail the various works begun or carried on since his departure, his Majesty one morning sent for M. Fontaine, and having discoursed at length on what he thought worthy of praise or blame in all that he had seen, informed him of his intentions with regard to the plans which the architect had furnished for joining the Tuileries to the Louvre. It was agreed by the Emperor and M. Fontaine that these buildings should be united by two wings, the first of which should be finished in five years, a million to be granted each year for this purpose; and that a second wing should also be constructed on the opposite side, extending from the Louvre to the Tuileries, forming thus a perfect square, in the midst of which would be erected an opera house, isolated on all sides, and communicating with the palace by a subterranean gallery.

The gallery forming the court in front of the Louvre was to be opened to the public in winter, and decorated with statues, and also with all the shrubbery now in boxes in the garden of the Tuileries; and in this court he intended to erect an arch of triumph very similar to that of the Carrousel. Finally, all these beautiful buildings were to be used as lodgings for the grand officers of the crown, as stables, etc. The necessary expense was estimated as approximating forty-two millions.

The Emperor was occupied in succession with a palace of arts; with a new building for the Imperial library, to be placed on the spot now occupied by the Bourse; with a palace for the stock-exchange on the quay Desaix; with the restoration of the Sorbonne and the hotel Soubise; with a triumphal column at Neuilly; with a fountain on the Place Louis XV.; with tearing down the Hôtel-Dieu to enlarge

MURAT.

and beautify the Cathedral quarter; and with the construction of four hospitals at Mont-Parnasse, at Chaillot, at Montmartre, and in the Faubourg Saint-Antoine, etc. All these plans were very grand; and there is no doubt that he who had conceived them would have executed them; and it has often been said that had he lived, Paris would have had no rival in any department in the world.

At the same time his Majesty decided definitely on the form of the arch of triumph *de l'Étoile*, which had been long debated, and for which all the architects of the crown had submitted plans. It was M. Fontaine whose opinion prevailed; since among all the plans presented his was the simplest, and at the same time the most imposing.

The Emperor was also much interested in the restoration of the palace of Versailles. M. Fontaine had submitted to his Majesty a plan for the first repairs, by the terms of which, for the sum of six millions, the Emperor and Empress would have had a comfortable dwelling. His Majesty, who liked everything grand, handsome, superb, but at the same time economical, wrote at the bottom of this estimate the following note, which M. de Bausset reports thus in his *Memoirs:* —

"The plans in regard to Versailles must be carefully considered. Those which M. Fontaine submits are very reasonable, the estimate being six millions; but this includes dwellings, with the restoration of the chapel and that of the theater, only sufficiently comfortable for present use, not such as they should be one day.

"By this plan, the Emperor and Empress would have their apartments; but we must remember that this sum should also furnish lodgings for princes, grand and inferior officers.

"It is also necessary to know where will be placed the factory of arms, which will be needed at Versailles, since it puts silver in circulation.

· " It will be necessary out of these six millions to find six lodgings for princes, twelve for grand officers, and fifty for inferior officers.

" Then only can we decide to make Versailles our residence, and pass the summers there. Before adopting these plans, it will be necessary that the architect who engages to execute them should certify that they can be executed for the proposed sum."

A few days after their arrival their Majesties, the Emperor and Empress, went to visit the celebrated David [1] at his studio in the Sorbonne, in order to see the magnificent picture of the coronation, which had just been finished. Their Majesties' suite was composed of Marshal Bessières, an *aide-de-camp* of the Emperor, M. Lebrun, several ladies of the palace, and chamberlains. The Emperor and Empress contemplated with admiration for a long while this beautiful painting, which comprised every species of merit; and the painter was in his glory while hearing his Majesty name, one by one, all the different personages of the picture, for the resemblance was really miraculous. " How grand that is ! " said the Emperor; " how fine ! how the figures are brought out in relief ! how truthful ! This is not a painting; the figures live in this picture ! " First directing his attention to the grand tribune in the midst, the Emperor recognized Madame his mother, General Beaumont, M. de Cosse, M. de La Ville, Madame de Fontanges, and Madame Soult. " I see in the distance," said he, " good M. Vien." M. David replied, " Yes, Sire ; I wished to show my admiration for my illustrious master by placing him in this picture, which, on account of its subject, will be the most famous of

---

[1] Jacques Louis David, born in Paris, 1748, celebrated historical painter, member of convention, 1792, and voted for the death of the king. Died in Brussels, 1825.—TRANS.

my works." The Empress then took part in the conversation, and pointed out to the Emperor how happily M. David had seized upon and represented the interesting moment when the Emperor is on the point of being crowned. "Yes," said his Majesty, regarding it with a pleasure that he did not seek to disguise, "the moment is well chosen, and the scene perfectly represented; the two figures are very fine," and speaking thus, the Emperor looked at the Empress.

His Majesty continued the examination of the picture in all its details, and praised especially the group of the Italian clergy near the altar, which episode was invented by the painter. He seemed to wish only that the Pope had been represented in more direct action, appearing to give his blessing, and that the crown of the Empress had been borne by the cardinal legate. In regard to this group, Marshal Bessières made the Emperor laugh heartily, by relating to him the very amusing discussion which had taken place between David and Cardinal Caprara.

It is well known that the artist had a great aversion to dressed figures, especially to those clothed in the modern style. In all his paintings, there may be remarked such a pronounced love for the antique that it even shows itself in his manner of draping living persons. Now, Cardinal Caprara, one of the assistants of the Pope at the ceremony of the coronation, wore a wig; and David, in giving him a place in his picture, thought it more suitable to take off his wig, and represent him with a bald head, the likeness being otherwise perfect. The Cardinal was much grieved, and begged the artist to restore his wig, but received from David a formal refusal. "Never," said he "will I degrade my pencil so far as to paint a wig." His Eminence went away very angry, and complained to M. de Talleyrand, who was at this time Minister of Foreign Affairs, giving, among other reasons, this, which seemed to him unanswerable, that, as no Pope had ever worn a wig, they would not fail to attribute to him, Cardinal Caprara, an intention of aspiring to the pontifical chair in case of a vacancy, which intention would be clearly shown by the suppression of his wig in the picture of the coronation. The entreaties of his Eminence were all in vain; for David would not consent to restore his precious wig, saying, that "he ought to be very glad he had taken off no more than that."

After hearing this story, the particulars of which were confirmed by the principal actor in the scene, his Majesty made some observations to M. David, with all possible delicacy. They were attentively noted by this admirable artist, who, with a bow, promised the Emperor to profit by his advice. Their Majesties' visit was long, and lasted until the fading light warned the Emperor that it was time to return. M. David escorted him to the door of his studio; and there, stopping short, the Emperor took off his hat, and, by a most graceful bow, testified to the honor he felt for such distinguished talent. The Empress added to the agitation by which M. David seemed almost overcome by a few of the charming words of appreciation she so well knew how to say, and said so opportunely.

Opposite the picture of the coronation was placed that of the Sabines. The Emperor, who perceived how anxious M. David was to dispose of this, gave orders to M. Lebrun, as he left, to see if this picture could not be placed to advantage in the grand gallery at the Tuileries. But he soon changed his mind when he reflected that most of the figures were represented *in naturalibus*, which would appear incongruous in an apartment used for grand diplomatic receptions, and in which the Council of Ministers usually sat.

CHAPTER VIII.

Marriage of Mademoiselle de **Tascher to the Duke of Aremberg.** — **Marriage** of a niece of King Murat to the Prince of Hohenzollern. — Grand *fêtes* and masked balls at Paris. — The Emperor at M. de Marescalchi's ball. — The Emperor's disguise. — Constant's instructions. — The Emperor always recognized. — *Incognito* impossible. — The Emperor's amusement. — Napoleon perplexed by a masker. — The Empress at the ball of the **opera.** — **The** Emperor trying to surprise the Empress at the masked ball. — **Napoleon in a** domino. — Constant as the Emperor's companion, **and** *tutoying* him. — **Artifices of a masker,** and embarrassment of the Emperor. — **An explanation between Napoleon and Josephine.** — Who was **the masker who had mystified the Emperor ? — Parisian masquerades. —** **Doctor Gall, and heads** with wigs. — **Fancy and masked ball at the residence of the Princess Caroline.** — Constant sent to this ball **by the Emperor.** — Instructions given **to Constant by** the Emperor. — Marriage **of** the Prince of **Neuchâtel** with **a Bavarian** princess. — Present sent **the** Empress by **an** inhabitant of **the Isle** of France. — The well-reared baboon. — Civilized habits.

THE last of January, Mademoiselle de Tascher, niece of her Majesty the Empress, was married to the Duke of Aremberg. The Emperor on this occasion raised Mademoiselle de Tascher to the dignity of a princess, and deigned, in company with the Empress, to honor with his presence the marriage, which took place at the residence of her Majesty the Queen of Holland, in the Rue de Cérutti, and was celebrated with a splendor worthy of the august guests. The Empress remained some time after dinner, and opened the ball with the Duke of Aremberg.

A few days after this the Prince of Hohenzollern married the niece of the Grand Duke of Berg and Cleves, Mademoiselle Antoinette Murat.

His Majesty honored her as he had done Mademoiselle Tascher, and, in company with the Empress, also attended the ball which the Grand Duke of Berg gave on the occasion of this marriage, and at which Princess Caroline presided.

This was a brilliant winter at Paris, owing to the great number of *fêtes* and balls which were given. The Emperor, as I have already said, had an aversion to balls, and especially masked balls, which he considered the most senseless things in the world, and this was a subject on which he was often at war with the Empress; but, notwithstanding this, on one occasion he yielded to the entreaties of M. de Marescalchi,[1] the Italian ambassador, noted for his magnificent balls, which the most distinguished personages of the kingdom attended. These brilliant reunions took place in a hall which the ambassador had built for the purpose, and decorated with extraordinary luxury and splendor; and his Majesty, as I have said, consented to honor with his presence a masked ball given by this ambassador, which was to eclipse all others.

In the morning the Emperor called me, and said, "I have decided to *dance* this evening at the house of the ambassador of Italy; you will carry, during the day, ten complete costumes to the apartments he has prepared for me." I obeyed, and in the evening accompanied his Majesty to the residence of M. Marescalchi, and dressed him as best I could in a black domino, taking great pains to render him unrecognizable; and everything went well, in spite of numerous observations on the Emperor's part as to the absurdity of a disguise, the bad appearance a domino

---

[1] Ferdinand Marescalchi, born at Bologna, 1764; died 1816.—TRANS.

makes, etc. But, when it was proposed to change his shoes, he rebelled absolutely, in spite of all I could say on this point; and consequently he was recognized the moment he entered the ballroom. He went straight to a masker, *his hands behind his back*, as usual, and attempted to enter into an intrigue, and at the first question he asked was called *Sire*, in reply. Whereupon, much disappointed, he turned on his heel, and came back to me. "You are right, Constant; I am recognized. Bring me lace-boots and another costume." I put the boots on his feet, and disguised him anew, advising him to let his arms hang, if he did not wish to be recognized at once; and his Majesty promised to obey in every particular what he called my instructions. He had hardly entered the room in his new costume, however, before he was accosted by a lady, who, seeing him with his hands again crossed behind his back, said, "Sire, you are recognized!" The Emperor immediately let his arms fall; but it was too late, for already every one moved aside respectfully to make room for him. He then returned to his room, and took a third costume, promising me implicitly to pay attention to his gestures and his walk, and offering to bet that he would not be recognized. This time, in fact, he entered the hall as if it were a barrack, pushing and elbowing all around him; but, in spite of this, some one whispered in his ear, "Your Majesty is recognized." A new disappointment, new change of costume, and new advice on my part, with the same result; until at last his Majesty left the ambassador's ball, persuaded that he could not be disguised, and that the *Emperor* would be recognized whatever mask he might assume.

That evening at supper, the Prince de Neuchâtel,[1] the Duke de Trévise,[2] the Duke de Frioul,[3] and some other officers being present, the Emperor related the history of his disguises, and made many jests on his awkwardness. In speaking of the young lady who had recognized him the evening before, and who had, it appeared, puzzled him greatly, "Can you believe it, Messieurs," said he, "I never succeeded in recognizing the little wretch at all?" During the carnival the Empress expressed a wish to go once to the masked ball at the opera; and when she begged the Emperor to accompany her he refused, in spite of all the tender and enticing things the Empress could say, and all the grace with which, as is well known, she could surround a petition. She found that all was useless, as the Emperor said plainly that he would not go. "Well, I will go without you."—"As you please," and the Emperor went out.

That evening at the appointed hour the Empress went to the ball; and the Emperor, who wished to surprise her, had one of her *femmes de chambre* summoned, and obtained from her an exact description of the Empress's costume. He then told me to dress him in a domino, entered a carriage without decorations, and accompanied by the grand marshal of the palace, a superior officer, and myself, took the road to the opera. On reaching the private entrance of the Emperor's household, we encountered some difficulty, as the doorkeeper would not let us pass till I had told my name and rank. "These gentlemen are with you?"—"As you see."—"I beg your pardon, Monsieur Constant; but it is because in such times as these

---

[1] Marshal Berthier. [2] Marshal Mortier. [3] Duroc.—TRANS.

there are always persons who try to enter without paying." — "That is good!   That is good!" and the Emperor
laughed heartily at the doorkeeper's observations.   At
last we entered, and having got as far as the hall, promenaded in couples, I giving my arm to the Emperor, who
said *thou* to me, and bade me reply in the same way.
We gave each other fictitious names, the Emperor calling
himself *Auguste;* the Duke de Frioul, *François;* the superior officer, whose name escapes me, *Charles;* while I was
Joseph.   As soon as his Majesty saw a domino similar to
the one the *femme de chambre* had described, he pressed my
arm and said, "Is that she?" — "No, Si— no, *Auguste,*"
replied I, constantly correcting myself; for it was impossible
to accustom myself to calling the Emperor otherwise than
Sire or your *Majesty.*   He had, as I have said, expressly
ordered me to *tutoy* him; but he was every moment compelled to repeat this order to me, for respect tied my tongue
every time I tried to say *tu.*   At last, after having gone
in every direction, explored every corner and nook of the
saloon, the green-room, the boxes, etc., in fact, examined
everything, and looked each costume over in detail, his
Majesty, who was no more successful in recognizing her
Majesty than were we, began to feel great anxiety, which I,
however, succeeded in allaying by telling him that doubtless the Empress had gone to change her costume.   As I
was speaking, a domino arrived who seemed enamoured of
the Emperor, accosted him, mystified him, tormented him
in every way, and with so much vivacity that *Auguste* was
beside himself; and it is impossible to give even a faint idea
of the comical sight the Emperor presented in his embarrassment.   The domino, delighted at this, redoubled her

wit and raillery until, thinking it time to cease, she disappeared in the crowd.

The Emperor was completely exasperated; he had seen enough, and we left the ball.

The next morning when he saw the Empress, he remarked, " Well, you did not go to the opera ball, after all!"—" Oh, yes, indeed I did."—" Nonsense!"—" I assure you that I went. And you, my dear, what did you do all the evening?"—" I worked."—" Why, that is very singular; for I saw at the ball last night a domino who had exactly your foot and boots. I took him for you, and consequently addressed him." The Emperor laughed heartily on learning that he had been thus duped; the Empress, just as she left for the ball, had changed her costume, not thinking the first sufficiently elegant.

The carnival was extremely brilliant this year, and there were in Paris all kinds of masquerades. The most amusing were those in which the theory advocated by the famous Doctor Gall[1] was illustrated. I saw a troop passing the Place du Carrousel, composed of clowns, harlequins, fishwives, etc., all rubbing their skulls, and making expressive grimaces; while a clown bore several skulls of different sizes, painted red, blue, or green, with these inscriptions: Skull of a robber, skull of an assassin, skull of a bankrupt, etc.; and a masked figure, representing Doctor Gall, was seated on an ass, his head turned to the animal's tail, and receiving from the hands of a woman who followed him, and was also seated on an ass, heads covered with wigs made of long grass.

[1] Franz Joseph Gall, founder of the system of phrenology. Born in Baden, 1758; died in Paris, 1828.—TRANS.

Her Majesty Queen Caroline gave a masked ball, at which the Emperor and Empress were present, which was one of the most brilliant I have ever attended.

The opera of *la Vestale* was then new, and very much the fashion; it represented a quadrille of *priests* and *vestals* who entered to the sound of delicious music on the flute and harp, and in addition to this there were magicians, a Swiss marriage, Tyrolian betrothals, etc. All the costumes were wonderfully handsome and true to nature; and there had been arranged in the apartments at the palace a supply of costumes which enabled the dancers to change four or five times during the night, and which had the effect of renewing the ball as many times.

As I was dressing the Emperor for this ball, he said to me, "Constant, you must go with me in disguise. Take whatever costume you like, disguise yourself so that you cannot possibly be recognized, and I will give you instructions." I hastened to do as his Majesty ordered, donned a Swiss costume which suited me very well, and thus equipped awaited his Majesty's orders.

He had a plan for mystifying several great personages, and two or three ladies whom the Emperor designated to me with such minute details that it was impossible to mistake them, and told me some singular things in regard to them, which were not generally known, and were well calculated to embarrass them terribly. As I was starting, the Emperor called me back, saying, "Above all, Constant, take care to make no mistake, and do not confound Madame de M—— with her sister; they have almost exactly the same costume, but Madame de M—— is larger than she, so take care." On my arrival at the ball, I sought and easily found the persons whom his Majesty had designated, and the replies which they made afforded him much amusement when I narrated them as he was retiring.

There was at this time a third marriage at the court, that of the Prince de Neuchâtel and the Princess of Bavaria, which was celebrated in the chapel of the Tuileries by Cardinal Fesch.

A traveler just returned from the Isle of France presented to the Empress a female monkey of the orang-outang species; and her Majesty gave orders that the animal should be placed in the menagerie at Malmaison. This baboon was extremely gentle and docile, and its master had given it an excellent education. It was wonderful to see her, when any one approached the chair on which she was seated, take a decent position, draw over her legs and thighs the fronts of a long redingote, and, when she rose to make a bow, hold the redingote carefully in front of her, acting, in fact, exactly as would a young girl who had been well reared. She ate at the table with a knife and fork more properly than many children who are thought to be carefully trained, and liked, while eating, to cover her face with her napkin, and then uncover it with a cry of joy. Turnips were her favorite food; and, when a lady of the palace showed her one, she began to run, caper, and cut somersaults, forgetting entirely the lessons of modesty and decency her professor had taught her. The Empress was much amused at seeing the baboon lose her dignity so completely under the influence of this lady.

This poor beast had inflammation of the stomach, and, according to the directions of the traveler who brought her, was placed in bed and a night-dress put on her. She took

great care to keep the covering up to her chin, though unwilling to have anything on her head; and held her arms
out of the bed, her hands hidden in the sleeves of the
night-dress. When any one whom she knew entered the
room, she nodded to them and took their hand, pressing it
affectionately. She eagerly swallowed the medicines pre-
scribed, as they were sweet; and one day, while a draught
of manna was being prepared, which she thought too long
delayed, she showed every sign of impatience, and threw herself from side to side like a fretful child; at last, throwing
off the covering, she seized her physician by the coat with
so much obstinacy that he was compelled to yield. The
instant she obtained possession of the eagerly coveted cup
she manifested the greatest delight, and began to drink,
taking little sips, and smacking her lips with all the grati-
fication of an epicure who tastes a glass of wine which
he thinks very old and very delicious. At last the cup
was emptied, she returned it, and lay down again. It is
impossible to give an idea of the gratitude this poor animal
showed whenever anything was done for her. The Empress
was deeply attached to her.

CHAPTER IX.

AFTER remaining about a week at the château of Saint-Cloud, his Majesty set out, on the 2d of April, at 11 o'clock in the morning, to visit the departments of the South; and as this journey was to begin at Bordeaux, the Emperor requested the Empress to meet him there. This publicly announced intention was simply a pretext, in order, to mislead the curious, for we knew that we were going to the frontier of Spain.

The Emperor remained barely ten days there, and then left for Bayonne alone, leaving the Empress at Bordeaux, and reaching Bayonne on the night of the 14–15th of April, where her Majesty the Empress rejoined him two or three days afterwards.

The Prince of Neuchâtel and the grand marshal lodged at the château of Marrac, the rest of their Majesties' suite lodged at Bayonne and its suburbs, the guard camped in front of the château on a place called the Parterre, and in three days all were comfortably located.

On the morning of the 15th of April, the Emperor had hardly recovered from the fatigue of his journey, when he received the authorities of Bayonne, who came to congratulate him, and questioned them, as was his custom, most pointedly. His Majesty then set out to visit the fort and fortifications, which occupied him till the evening, when he returned to the Government palace, which he occupied temporarily while waiting till the château of Marrac should be ready to receive him.

On his return to the palace the Emperor expected to find the Infant Don Carlos, whom his brother Ferdinand, the Prince of the Asturias, had sent to Bayonne to present his compliments to the Emperor; but he was informed that the Infant was ill, and would not be able to come. The Emperor immediately gave orders to send one of his physicians to attend upon him, with a *valet de chambre* and several other persons; for the prince had come to Bayonne without attendants, and *incognito*, attended only by a military service composed of a few soldiers of the garrison.

The Emperor also ordered that this service should be replaced by one more suitable, consisting of the Guard of Honor of Bayonne, and sent two or three times each day to inquire the condition of the Infant, who it was freely admitted in the palace was very ill.

On leaving the Government palace to take up his abode at Marrac, the Emperor gave all necessary orders that it should be in readiness to receive the King and Queen of Spain, who were expected at Bayonne the last of the month; and expressly recommended that everything should be done to render to the sovereigns of Spain all the honors due their position. Just as the Emperor entered the château the sound of music was heard, and the grand marshal entered to inform his Majesty that a large company of the inhabitants in the costume of the country were assembled before the gate of the château. The Emperor immediately went to the window; and, at sight of him, seventeen persons (seven men and ten women) began with inimitable grace a dance called *la pamperruque,* in which the women kept time on tambourines, and the men with castanets, to an orchestra composed of flutes and guitars. I went out of the castle to view this scene more closely. The women wore short skirts of blue silk, and pink stockings likewise embroidered in silver; their hair was tied with ribbons, and they wore very broad black bracelets, that set off to advantage the dazzling whiteness of their bare arms. The men wore tight-fitting white breeches, with silk stockings and large epaulettes, a loose vest of very fine woolen cloth ornamented with gold, and their hair caught up in a net like the Spaniards'.

His Majesty took great pleasure in witnessing this dance, which is peculiar to the country and very ancient, which the custom of the country has consecrated as a means of rendering homage to great personages. The Emperor remained at the window until the *pamperruque* was finished, and then sent to compliment the dancers on their skill, and to express his thanks to the inhabitants assembled in crowds at the gate.

His Majesty a few days afterward received from his Royal Highness, the Prince of the Asturias, a letter, in which he announced that he intended setting out from Irun, where he then was, at an early day, in order to have the pleasure of making the acquaintance of his *brother* (it was thus Prince Ferdinand called the Emperor); a pleasure which he had long desired, and which he would at last enjoy if his *good brother* would allow him. This letter was brought to the Emperor by one of the *aides-de-camp* of the prince, who had accompanied him from Madrid, and preceded him to Bayonne by only ten days. His Majesty could hardly believe what he read and heard; and I, with several other persons, heard him exclaim, "What, he is coming here? but you must be mistaken; he must be deceiving us; that cannot be possible!" And I can certify that, in these words, the Emperor manifested no pleasure at the announcement.

It was necessary, however, to make preparations to receive the prince, since he was certainly coming; consequently the Prince of Neuchâtel, the Duke of Frioul, and a chamberlain of honor, were selected by his Majesty. And the guard of honor received orders to accompany these gentlemen, and meet the Prince of Spain just outside the town of Bayonne; the rank which the Emperor recognized in Ferdinand not rendering it proper that the escort should go as far as the frontier of the two empires. The Prince made his entrance into Bayonne at noon, on the 20th of April. Lodgings which would have been considered very inferior in Paris, but which were elegant in Bayonne, had been prepared for him and his brother, the Infant Don Carlos, who was already installed there. Prince Ferdinand made a grimace on entering, but did not dare to complain aloud; and certainly it would have been most improper for him to have done so, since it was not the Emperor's fault that Bayonne possessed only one palace, which was at this time reserved for the king, and, besides, this house, the handsomest in the town, was large and perfectly new. Don Pedro de Cevallos, who accompanied the prince, thought it horrible, and unfit for a royal personage. It was the residence of the commissariat. An hour after Ferdinand's arrival, the Emperor visited him. He was awaiting the Emperor at the door, and held out his arms on his approach; they embraced, and ascended to his apartments, where they remained about half an hour, and when they separated the prince wore a somewhat anxious air. His Majesty on his return charged the grand marshal to convey to the prince and his brother, Don Carlos, the Duke of San-Carlos, the Duke of Infantado, Don Pedro de Cevallos, and two or three other persons of the suite, an invitation to dine with him; and the Emperor's carriages were sent for these illustrious guests at the appointed hour, and they were conveyed to the château. His Majesty descended to the foot of the staircase to receive the prince; but this was the limit of his deference, for not once during dinner did he give Prince Ferdinand, who was a king at Madrid, the title of your majesty, nor even that of highness; nor did he accompany him on his departure any **farther than** the first **door of the saloon**; **and he** afterwards informed him, by a message, that **he** would **have no** other rank than that of Prince of the Asturias until **the arrival of his father,** King Charles. Orders were **given at the same time to place on** duty at the house of the **princes, the** Bayonnaise guard of honor, with the **Imperial Guard in** addition **to a** detachment of picked police.

On the 27th **of** April **the** Empress arrived **from Bordeaux at seven** o'clock in the evening, having made no **stay at** Bayonne, **where her** arrival excited little enthusiasm, **as they were** perhaps displeased that she did not **stop there.** His Majesty received her with much tenderness, **and showed** much solicitude **as to** the fatigue she **must have** experienced, **since the** roads **were so** rough, and badly **washed by the rains.** In the evening the town **and château were illuminated.**

Three days after, **on** the 30th, the King and Queen of Spain arrived at Bayonne; **and it is** impossible to describe the homage which the Emperor paid them. **The Duke** Charles de Plaisance [1] went as far **as Irun, and the** Prince **de** Neuchâtel even to the banks of the Bidassoa, in order **to pay** marked respect **to** their Catholic Majesties on the **part of their powerful friend; and** the king and queen appeared to appreciate highly **these** marks of consideration. A detachment of picked troops, superbly uniformed, awaited **them on** the frontier, and served **as** their escort; the garrison of **Bayonne was put under** arms, all the buildings of

---

[1] **Eldest son of the former third consul, Lebrun.** Born in Paris, 1775; *aide-de-camp* to **Desaix at** Marengo, *aide-de-camp* to the **Emperor** at this **time;** senator 1852; **died 1859.** — TRANS.

the port were decorated, all the bells rang, and the batteries of both the citadel and the port saluted with great salvos. The Prince of the Asturias and his brother, hearing of the arrival of the king and queen, had left Bayonne in order to meet their parents, when they encountered, a short distance from the town, two or three grenadiers who had just left Vittoria, and related to them the following occurrence :—

When their Spanish Majesties entered Vittoria, they found that a detachment of the Spanish body guards, who had accompanied the Prince of the Asturias and were stationed in this town, had taken possession of the palace which the king and queen were to occupy as they passed through, and on the arrival of their Majesties had put themselves under arms. As soon as the king perceived this, he said to them in a severe tone, " You will understand why I ask you to quit my palace. You have failed in your duty at Aranjuez. I have no need of your services, and I do not wish them. Go ! " These words, pronounced with an energy far from habitual to Charles IV., met with no reply. The detachment of the guards retired ; and the king begged General Verdier to give him a French guard, much grieved, he said, that he had not retained his brave riflemen, whose colonel he still kept near him as captain of the guards.

This news could not give the Prince of the Asturias a high opinion of the welcome his father had in store for him ; and indeed he was very coolly received, as I shall now relate.

The King and Queen of Spain, on alighting at the governmental palace, found awaiting them the grand marshal, the Duke de Frioul, who escorted them to their apartments, and presented to them General Count Reille,[1] the Emperor's *aide-de-camp*, performing the duties of governor of the palace; M. d'Audenarde, equerry, with M. Dumanoir and M. de Baral, chamberlains charged with the service of honor near their Majesties.

The grandees of Spain whom their Majesties found at Bayonne were the same who had followed the Prince of the Asturias, and the sight of them, as may well be imagined, was not pleasant to the king; and when the ceremony of the kissing of the hand took place, every one perceived the painful agitation of the unfortunate sovereigns. This ceremony, which consists of falling on your knees and kissing the hand of the king and queen, was performed in the deepest silence, as their Majesties spoke to no one but the Count of Fuentes, who by chance was at Bayonne.

The king hurried over this ceremony, which fatigued him greatly, and retired with the queen into his apartments, where the Prince of the Asturias wished to follow them; but his father stopped him at the door, and raising his arm as if to repulse him, said in a trembling tone, "Prince, do you wish still to insult my gray hairs?" These words had, it is said, the effect of a thunderbolt on the prince. He was overcome by his feelings for a moment, and withdrew without uttering a word.

Very different was the reception their Majesties gave to the Prince de la Paix[2] when he joined them at Bayonne, and he might have been taken for the nearest and dearest

---

[1] **Afterwards distinguished in** the Spanish **war, and** commanding the army of Portugal, 1812; **born** 1775; created marshal, 1847; died 1860. — TRANS.

[2] Manuel Godoï, born at Badajos, 1767. A common soldier, he became the queen's lover, and the virtual ruler of Spain; died in Paris, 1851. — TRANS.

relative of their Majesties. All three wept freely on meeting again; at least, this is what I was told by a person in the service — the same, in fact, who gave me all the preceding details.

At five o'clock his Majesty the Emperor came to visit the King and Queen of Spain; and during this interview, which was very long, the two sovereigns informed his Majesty of the insults they had received, and the dangers they had encountered during the past month. They complained greatly of the ingratitude of so many men whom they had overwhelmed with kindness, and above all of the guard which had so basely betrayed them. "Your Majesty," said the king, "does not know what it is to be forced to commiserate yourself on account of your son. May Heaven forbid that such a misfortune should ever come to you! Mine is the cause of all that we have suffered."

The Prince de la Paix had come to Bayonne accompanied by Colonel Martès, *aide-de-camp* of Prince Murat, and a *valet de chambre*, the only servant who had remained faithful to him. I had occasion to talk with this devoted servant, who spoke very good French, having been reared near Toulouse; and he told me that he had not succeeded in obtaining permission to remain with his master during his captivity, and that this unfortunate prince had suffered indescribable torments; that not a day passed without some one entering his dungeon to tell him to prepare for death, as he was to be executed that very evening or the next morning. He also told me that the prisoners were left sometimes for thirty hours without food; that he had only a bed of straw, no linen, no books, and no communication with the outside world; and that when he came out of his dungeon to be sent to Colonel Martès, he presented a horrible appearance, with his long beard, and emaciated frame, the result of mental distress and insufficient food. He had worn the same shirt for a month, as he had never been able to prevail on his captors to give him others; and his eyes had been so long unaccustomed to the light that he was obliged to close them, and felt oppressed in the open air.

On the road from Bayonne, there was handed to the prince a letter from the king and queen which was stained with tears. The prince said to his *valet de chambre* after reading it, "These are the first consoling words I have received in a month, for every one has abandoned me except my excellent masters. The body guards, who have betrayed and sold their king, will also betray and sell his son; and as for myself, I hope for nothing, except to be permitted to find an asylum in France for my children and myself." M. Martès having shown him newspapers in which it was stated that the prince possessed a fortune of five hundred million, he exclaimed vehemently that it was an atrocious calumny, and he defied his most cruel enemies to prove that.

As we have seen, their Majesties had not a numerous suite; but they were, notwithstanding, followed by baggage-wagons filled with furniture, goods, and valuable articles, and though their carriages were old-fashioned, they found them very comfortable — especially the king, who was much embarrassed the day after his arrival at Bayonne, when, having been invited to dine with the Emperor, it was necessary to enter a modern carriage with two steps. He did not dare to put his foot on the frail things, which he feared would break under his weight; and the oscillating movement of the body of the carriage made him terribly afraid that it would upset.

At the table **I had an** opportunity of observing at my leisure the king and queen. The king was of medium height, and though not strictly handsome had a pleasant face. His nose was very long, his voice high-pitched and disagreeable; and he walked with a mincing air in which there was no majesty, but this, however, I attributed to the gout. He ate heartily of everything offered him, except vegetables, which he never ate, saying that *grass was good only for cattle;* and drank only water, having it served in two carafes, one containing ice, and poured from both at the same time. The Emperor gave orders that special attention should be paid to the dinner, knowing that the king was somewhat of an epicure. He praised in high terms the French cooking, which he seemed to find much to his taste; for as each dish was served him, he would say, " Louise, take some of that, it is good;" which greatly amused the Emperor, whose abstemiousness is well known.

The queen was fat and short, dressed very badly, and had no style or grace; her complexion was very florid, and her expression harsh and severe. She held her head high, spoke very loud, in tones still more brusque and piercing than those of her husband; but it is generally conceded that she had more character and better manners than he.

Before dinner that day there was some conversation on the subject of dress; and the Empress offered the services of M. Duplan, her hairdresser, in order to give her ladies some lessons in the French toilet. Her proposition was accepted; and the queen came out soon after from the hands of M. Duplan, better dressed, no doubt, and her hair better arranged, but not beautified, however, for the talent of the hairdresser could not go as far as that.

The Prince of the Asturias, now King Ferdinand VII., made an unpleasant impression on all, with his heavy step and careworn air, and rarely ever speaking.

Their Spanish Majesties as before brought with them the Prince de la Paix, who had not been invited by the Emperor, and whom for this reason the usher on duty detained outside of the dining-hall. But as they were about to be seated, the king perceived that the prince was absent. "And Manuel," said he quickly to the Emperor, "and Manuel, Sire!" Whereupon the Emperor, smiling, gave the signal, and Don Manuel Godoï was introduced. I was told that he had been a very handsome man; but he showed no signs of this, which was perhaps owing to the bad treatment he had undergone.

After the abdication of the princes, the king and queen, the Queen of Etruria, and the Infant Don Franciso, left Bayonne for Fontainebleau, which place the Emperor had selected as their residence while waiting until the château of Compiègne should be put in a condition to make them comfortable. The Prince of the Asturias left the same day, with his brother Don Carlos and his uncle Don Antonio, for the estates of Valençay belonging to the Prince of Bénévento. They published, while passing through Bordeaux, a proclamation to the Spanish people, in which they confirmed the transmission of all their rights to the Emperor Napoleon.

Thus King Charles, freed from a throne which he had

always regarded as a heavy burden, could hereafter give himself up unreservedly in retirement to his favorite pursuits. In all the world he cared only for the Prince de la Paix, confessors, watches, and music; and the throne was nothing to him. After what had passed, the Prince de la Paix could not return to Spain; and the king would never have consented to be separated from him, even if the remembrance of the insults which he had personally received had not been powerful enough to disgust him with his kingdom. He much preferred the life of a private individual, and could not be happier than when allowed without interruption to indulge his simple and tranquil tastes. On his arrival at the château of Fontainebleau, he found there M. Rémusat, the first chamberlain; M. de Caqueray, officer of the hunt; M. de Luçay, prefect of the palace; and a household already installed. Mesdames de la Rochefoucault, Duchâtel, and de Luçay had been selected by the Emperor for the service of honor near the queen.

The King of Spain remained at Fontainebleau only until the château of Compiègne could be repaired, and as he soon found the climate of this part of France too cold for his health, went, at the end of a few months, to Marseilles with the Queen of Etruria, the Infant Don Francisco, and the Prince de la Paix. In 1811 he left France for Italy, finding his health still bad at Marseilles, and chose Rome as his residence.

I spoke above of the fondness of the King of Spain for watches. I have been told that while at Fontainebleau, he had half a dozen of his watches worn by his *valet de chambre*, and wore as many himself, giving as a reason that pocket watches lose time by not being carried. I have also heard that he kept his confessor always near him, in the antechamber, or in the room in front of that in which he worked, and that when he wished to speak to him he whistled, exactly as one would whistle for a dog. The confessor never failed to respond promptly to this royal call, and followed his penitent into the embrasure of a window, in which improvised confessional the king divulged what he had on his conscience, received absolution, and sent back the priest until he felt himself obliged to whistle for him again.

When the health of the king, enfeebled by age and gout, no longer allowed him to devote himself to the pleasures of the chase, he began playing on the violin more than ever before, in order, he said, to perfect himself in it. This was beginning rather late. As is well known, he had for his first violin teacher the celebrated Alexander Boucher,[1] with whom he greatly enjoyed playing; but he had a mania for beginning first without paying any attention to the measure; and if M. Boucher made any observation in regard to this, his Majesty would reply with the greatest coolness, "Monsieur, it seems to me that it is not my place to wait for you."

Between the departure of the royal family and the arrival of Joseph, King of Naples, the time was passed in reviews and military *fêtes*, which the Emperor frequently honored with his presence. The 7th of June, King Joseph arrived at Bayonne, where it had been known long in advance that his brother had summoned him to exchange his crown of Naples for that of Spain.

---

[1] Born in Paris, 1770, and a famous violinist; died 1861. — TRANS.

The evening of Joseph's arrival, the Emperor invited the members of the Spanish Junta, who for fifteen days had been arriving at Bayonne from all corners of the kingdom, to assemble at the château of Marrac, and congratulate the new king. The deputies accepted this somewhat sudden invitation without having time to concert together previously any course of action; and on their arrival at Marrac, the Emperor presented to them their sovereign, whom they acknowledged, with the exception of some opposition on the part of the Duke of Infantado,[1] in the name of the grandees of Spain. The deputations from the Council of Castile, from the Inquisition, and from the army, etc., submitted most readily. A few days after, the king formed his ministry, in which all were astonished to find M. de Cevallos,[2] who had accompanied the Prince of the Asturias to Bayonne, and had made such a parade of undying attachment to the person of the one whom he called his unfortunate master; while the Duke of Infantado, who had opposed to the utmost any recognition of the foreign monarch, was appointed Captain of the Guard. The king then left for Madrid, after appointing the Grand Duke of Berg lieutenant-general of the kingdom.

[1] Born 1733; defeated while commanding an army against the French, 1809; Prime minister, 1825; died 1841. — TRANS.

[2] Pedro de Cevallos, born at Santander, 1764; minister for foreign affairs under Charles IV.; died 1838. — TRANS.

CHAPTER X.

Death of M. de Belloy, **Archbishop** of Paris. — Life of **a century, and still too** short. — Anecdote concerning the Archbishop of Genoa. — The hangman's child. — The Grand Duke of Berg **returns** from **Spain**. — Departure from Marrac. — Snuff-boxes given away by the Emperor. — The room of the First Bourbon. — Souvenir of Egypt. — The pyramid and the mamelukes. — The *balladeurs*. — The Emperor's visit to the Grand Duke **of** Berg. — **Useless** preparations. — The oldest soldier in France. — **The** Centenarian. — The Emperor's deference for old age. — The soldier of Egypt. — **Arrival** at Saint-Cloud. — **The** fifteenth of August. — The **Emperor eager for praise.** — **The Emperor's ill-humor.** — **Napoleon and the god Mars.** — **The Persian ambassador.** — **Solemn audience.** — **Elegance and generosity of Asker-Khan.** — **The swords of Tamerlane and Kouli-Khan.** — **Persian gallantry.** — **Asker-Khan's love of science and the arts.** — The *long price,* **and the** *short price.* — **Calico preferred** to cashmere. — Eastern amusements. — **The arms of the sufi, and the** Emperor's **cipher.** — Asker-**Khan in** the Imperial library. — **The** Koran. — Portrait of the sufi. — The Grand Order of the Sun given to the Prince de Bénévent. — Fall **of** Asker-Khan at the Empress's concert. — M. de Barbé-Marbois a physician against his will.

At this time it was learned at Bayonne that **M. de Belloy, Archbishop** of Paris, had **just** died of **a cold,** contracted at the age of more than **ninety-eight years.** The day after this **sad news arrived,** the Emperor, who was sincerely grieved, was dilating upon **the great and** good qualities of this venerable prelate, **and said that having one day thoughtlessly** remarked **to M. de Belloy,** then already more **than ninety-six years old, that he** would **live a century, the good old archbishop had** exclaimed, smiling, **" Why, does your Majesty think that I** have no more **than four years to live ? "**

I remember that one of the persons who was present at the Emperor's *levée* related the following anecdote concerning M. de Belloy, which seemed to excite the Emperor's respect and admiration.

The wife of the hangman of Genoa gave birth to a daughter, who could not be baptized because no one would act as godfather. In vain the father begged and entreated the few persons whom he knew, in vain he even offered money; that was an impossibility. The poor child had consequently remained unbaptized four or five months, though fortunately her health gave no cause for uneasiness. At last some one mentioned this singular condition of affairs to the archbishop, who listened to the story with much interest, inquired why he had not been informed earlier, and having given orders that the child should be instantly brought to him, baptized her in his palace, and was himself her godfather.

At the beginning of July the Grand Duke of Berg returned from Spain, fatigued, ill, and out of humor. He remained there only two or three days, and held each day an interview with his Majesty, who seemed little better satisfied with the grand duke than the grand duke was with him, and left afterwards for the springs of Barèges.

Their Majesties, the Emperor and Empress, left the château of Marrac the 20th of July, at six o'clock in the evening. This journey of the Emperor was one of those which cost the largest number of snuff-boxes set in diamonds, for his Majesty was not economical with them.

Their Majesties arrived at Pau on the 22d, at ten o'clock in the morning, and alighted at the château of Gelos, situated about a quarter of a league from the birthplace of the good Henry **IV., on the bank** of the river. The day was spent in receptions and horseback excursions, on one of which **the** Emperor visited the château in which the first **king of the** house **of** Bourbon was reared, and **showed how** much this visit interested him, by prolonging it until the dinner-hour.

On the border of the department of **the** Hautes-Pyrénées, and exactly in the most desolate and miserable part, was erected an arch of triumph, which seemed a miracle fallen from heaven in the midst of those plains uncultivated and burned up by the sun. A guard of honor awaited their Majesties, ranged around this rural monument, at their head **an old** marshal of the camp, **M.** de Noé, more than eighty **years of** age. This **worthy** old soldier immediately took **his** place by the side of the **carriage, and** as cavalry escort **remained on** horseback **for a day and two** nights without **showing the** least fatigue.

As we continued our journey, **we saw,** on the plateau of a small mountain, a stone pyramid forty or fifty feet high, its four sides covered with inscriptions to the praise of their Majesties. About thirty children dressed **as** mamelukes **seemed** to guard this monument, which recalled to the Emperor glorious memories. The moment their Majesties appeared, *balladeurs*, **or** dancers, **of** the country emerged from a neighboring wood, dressed in the most picturesque **costumes, bearing** banners of different colors, and reproducing with remarkable agility and vigor the traditional **dance of** the mountaineers **of the south.**

Near the town of Tarbes was a sham mountain planted with **firs,** which opened to let the *cortège* pass through, surmounted by an imperial eagle suspended in the air, and

holding a banner on which was inscribed — "*He will open
our Pyrenees.*"

On his arrival at Tarbes, the Emperor immediately
mounted his horse to pay a visit to the Grand Duke of
Berg, who was ill in one of the suburbs. We left next
day without visiting Barèges and Bagnères, where the
most brilliant preparations had been made to receive their
Majesties.

As the Emperor passed through Agen, there was presented to him a brave fellow named Printemps, over a
hundred years old, who had served under Louis XIV., XV.,
and XVI., and who, although bending beneath the weight of
many years and burdens, finding himself in the presence of
the Emperor, gently pushed aside two of his grandsons by
whom he had been supported, and exclaimed almost angrily
that he could go very well alone. His Majesty, who was
much touched, met him half-way, and most kindly bent
over the old centenarian, who on his knees, his white head
uncovered, and his eyes full of tears, said in trembling
tones, "Ah, Sire, I was afraid I should die without seeing
you." The Emperor assisted him to rise, and conducted
him to a chair, in which he placed him with his own
hands, and seated himself beside him on another, which he
made signs to hand him. "I am glad to see you, my dear
Printemps, very glad. You have heard from me lately?"
(His Majesty had given this brave man a pension, which
his wife was to inherit after his death.) Printemps put
his hand on his heart, "Yes, I have heard from you."
The Emperor took pleasure in making him speak of his
campaigns, and bade him farewell after a long conversation,
handing him at the same time a gift of fifty napoleons.

There was also presented to his Majesty a soldier born at Agen, who had lost his sight in consequence of the campaign in Egypt. The Emperor gave him three hundred francs, and promised him a pension, which was afterwards sent him.

The day after their arrival at Saint-Cloud, the Emperor and Empress went to Paris in order to be present at the *fêtes* of the 15th of August, which it is useless to say were magnificent. As soon as he entered the Tuileries, the Emperor hastened through the château to examine the repairs and improvements which had been made during his absence, and, as was his habit, criticised more than he praised all that he saw. Looking out of the hall of the marshals, he demanded of M. de Fleurieu,[1] governor of the palace, why the top of the arch of triumph on the Carrousel was covered with a cloth; and his Majesty was told that it was because all the arrangements had not yet been made for placing his statue in the chariot to which were attached the Corinthian horses, and also because the two Victories who were to guide the four horses were not yet completed. "What!" vehemently exclaimed the Emperor; "but I will not allow that! I said nothing about it! I did not order it!" Then turning to M. Fontaine, he continued, "Monsieur Fontaine, was my statue in the design which was presented to you?" — "No, Sire, it was that of the god Mars." — "Well, why have you put me in the place of the god of war?" — "Sire, it was not I, but M. the director-general of the museum"— "The director-general was wrong," interrupted the Emperor impatiently. "I wish this statue removed; do you

---

[1] Count Charles Pierre Claret de Fleurieu, born in Lyons, 1738; minister of marine, 1790; councillor of state, 1799; senator, 1805; died 1810.—TRANS.

hear, Monsieur Fontaine? I wish it taken away; it is most unsuitable. What! shall I erect 'statues to myself! Let the chariot and the Victories be finished; but let the chariot —let the chariot remain empty." The order was executed; and the statue of the Emperor was taken down and placed in the orangery, and is perhaps still there. It was made of gilded lead, was a fine piece of work, and a most excellent likeness.

The Sunday following the Emperor's arrival, his Majesty received at the Tuileries the Persian ambassador, Asker-Khan; M. Jaubert[1] accompanied him, and acted as interpreter. This savant, learned in Oriental matters, had by the Emperor's orders received his excellency on the frontiers of France, in company with M. Outrey, vice-consul of France at Bagdad. Later his excellency had a second audience, which took place in state at the palace of Saint-Cloud.

The ambassador was a very handsome man, tall, with regular features, and a noble and attractive countenance; his manners were polished and elegant, especially towards ladies, with even something of French gallantry. His suite, composed of select personages all magnificently dressed, comprised, on his departure from Erzeroum, more than three hundred persons; but the innumerable difficulties encountered on the journey compelled his excellency to dismiss a large part of his retinue, and, though thus reduced, this suite was notwithstanding one of the most numerous ever brought by an ambassador into France. The ambassador and suite were lodged in the rue de Fréjus, in the residence formerly occupied by Mademoiselle de Conti.

[1] Pierre Amédée Jaubert, Oriental scholar, born in Provence, 1779; went to Egypt with Napoleon, 1798; peer, 1841; died 1847. — TRANS.

The presents which he brought to the Emperor in the name of his sovereign were of great value, comprising more than eighty cashmere shawls of all kinds; a great quantity of fine pearls of various sizes, a few of them very large; an Eastern bridle, the curb adorned with pearls, turquoise, emeralds, etc.; and finally the sword of Tamerlane, and that of Thamas-Kouli-Khan, the former covered with pearls and precious stones, the second very simply mounted, both having Indian blades of fabulous value with arabesques of embossed gold.

I took pleasure at the time in inquiring some particulars about this ambassador. His character was very attractive; and he showed much consideration and regard for every one who visited him, giving the ladies attar of roses, the men tobacco, perfumes, and pipes. He took much pleasure in comparing French jewels with those he had brought from his own country, and even carried his gallantry so far as to propose to the ladies certain exchanges, always greatly to their advantage; and a refusal of these proposals wounded him deeply. When a pretty woman entered his residence he smiled at first, and heard her speak in a kind of silent ecstasy; he then devoted his attention to seating her, placed under her feet cushions and carpets of cashmere (for he had only this material about him). Even his clothing and bed-coverings were of an exceedingly fine quality of cashmere. Asker-Khan did not scruple to wash his face, his beard, and hands in the presence of everybody, seating himself for this operation in front of a slave, who presented to him on his knees a porcelain ewer.

The ambassador had a decided taste for the sciences and arts, and was himself a very learned man. Messieurs

Dubois and Loyseau conducted near his residence an institution which he often visited, especially preferring to be present at the classes in experimental physics; and the questions which he propounded by means of his interpreter evinced on his part a very extensive knowledge of the phenomena of electricity. Those who traded in curiosities and objects of art liked him exceedingly, since he bought their wares without much bargaining. However, on one occasion he wished to purchase a telescope, and sent for a famous optician, who seized the opportunity to charge him an enormous price. But Asker-Khan having examined the instrument, with which he was much pleased, said to the optician, " You have given me your *long* price, now give me your *short* one."

He admired above all the printed calicoes of the manufactures of Jouy, the texture, designs, and colors of which he thought even superior to cashmere; and bought several robes to send to Persia as models.

On the day of the Emperor's *fête*, his Excellency gave in the garden of his residence an entertainment in the Eastern style, at which the Persian musicians attached to the embassy executed warlike pieces, astonishing both for vigor and originality. There were also artificial fireworks, conspicuous among which were the arms of the Sufi, on which were represented most ingeniously the cipher of Napoleon.

His Excellency visited the Imperial library, M. Jaubert serving as interpreter; and the ambassador was overcome with admiration on seeing the order in which this immense collection of books was kept. He remained half an hour in the hall of the manuscripts, which he thought very handsome, and recognized several as being copied by writers of much renown in Persia. A copy of the Koran struck him most of all; and he said, while admiring it, that *there was not a man in Persia who would not sell his children to acquire such a treasure.*

On leaving, the library, Asker-Khan presented his compliments to the librarians, and promised to enrich the collection by several precious manuscripts which he had brought from his own country.

A few days after his presentation, the ambassador went to visit the Museum, and was much impressed by a portrait of his master, the King of Persia; and could not sufficiently express his joy and gratitude when several copies of this picture were presented to him. The historical pictures, especially the battle-scenes, then engrossed his attention completely; and he remained at least a quarter of an hour in front of the one representing the surrender of the city of Vienna.

Having arrived at the end of the gallery of Apollo, Asker-Khan seated himself to rest, asked for a pipe, and indulged in a smoke; and when he had finished, rose, and seeing around him many ladies whom curiosity had attracted, paid them, through M. Jaubert, exceedingly flattering compliments. Then leaving the Museum, his Excellency went to promenade in the garden of the Tuileries, where he was soon followed by an immense crowd. On that day his Excellency bestowed on Prince de Bénévento, in the name of his sovereign, the Grand Order of the Sun, a magnificent decoration consisting of a diamond sun attached to a cordon of red cloth covered with pearls.

Asker-Khan made a greater impression at Paris than

the Turkish ambassador. He was generous and more gallant, paid his court with more address, and conformed more readily to French customs and manners. The Turk was irascible, austere, and irritable, while the Persian was fond of and well understood a joke. One day, however, he became red with anger, and it must be admitted not without good reason.

At a concert given in the apartments of the Empress Josephine, Asker-Khan, whom the music evidently did not entertain very highly, at first applauded by ecstatic gestures and rolling his eyes in admiration, until at last nature overcame politeness, and the ambassador fell sound asleep. His Excellency's position was not the best for sleeping, however, as he was standing with his back against the wall, with his feet braced against a sofa on which a lady was seated. It occurred to some of the officers of the palace that it would be a good joke to take away suddenly this point of support, which they accomplished with all ease by simply beginning a conversation with the lady on the sofa, who rising suddenly, the seat slipped over the floor; his Excellency's feet followed this movement, and the ambassador, suddenly deprived of the weight which had balanced him, extended his length on the floor. On this rude awakening, he tried to stop himself in his fall by clutching at his neighbors, the furniture, and the curtains, uttering at the same time frightful screams. The officers who had played this cruel joke upon him begged him, with the most ridiculously serious air, to place himself on a stationary chair in order to avoid the recurrence of such an accident; while the lady who had been made the accomplice in this practical joke, with much difficulty stifled her laughter, and his Excellency was consumed with an anger which he could express only in looks and gestures.

Another adventure of Asker-Khan's was long a subject of conversation, and furnished much amusement. Having felt unwell for several days, he thought that French medicine might cure him more quickly than Persian; so he sent for M. Bourdois,[1] a most skillful physician whose name he well knew, having taken care to acquaint himself with all our celebrities of every kind. The ambassador's orders were promptly executed; but by a singular mistake it was not Dr. Bourdois who was requested to visit Asker-Khan, but the president of the Court of Accounts, M. Marbois, who was much astonished at the honor the Persian ambassador did him, not being able to comprehend what connection there could be between them. Nevertheless, he repaired promptly to Asker-Khan, who could scarcely believe that the severe costume of the president of the Court of Accounts was that of a physician. No sooner had M. Marbois entered than the ambassador held out his hand and stuck out his tongue, regarding him very attentively. M. Marbois was a little surprised at this welcome; but thinking it was doubtless the Oriental manner of saluting magistrates, he bowed profoundly, and timidly pressed the hand presented to him, and he was in this respectful position when four of the servants of the ambassador brought a a vessel with unequivocal signs. M. Marbois[2] recognized the use of it with a surprise and indignation that could

---

[1] Physician to Louis XVIII. and Charles X.; born 1754; died 1830. — TRANS.

[2] Marquis Francis de Barbé-Marbois, born at Metz, 1745; in 1780 consul; general to U. S. A.; deported to Guiana by the Directory, 1797; minister of finance, 1801; president of chamber of accounts, 1808; died 1837. — TRANS.

not be expressed, and drew back angrily, inquiring what all this meant. Hearing himself called doctor, "What!" cried he, "M. le Docteur!" — "Why, yes; le Docteur Bourdois!" M. Marbois was enlightened. The similarity between the sound of his name and that of the doctor had exposed him to this disagreeable visit.

CHAPTER XI.

Removal of the colossal statue to the Place Vendôme. — The brewer's horses.
— Napoleon's **last game** of prisoner's base. — Departure for Erfurt. — The
Emperor's lodgings. — The garrison of Erfurt. — Actors and actresses of
the Théâtre Française at Erfurt. — The Emperor's dislike to Madame
Talma. — Mademoiselle Bourgoin and the Emperor Alexander. — Pater-
nal advice of the Emperor to the Czar. — Disappointment. — Entrance of
the Emperor into Erfurt. — Arrival of the Czar. — Attentions of the
Czar to the Duke of Montebello. — Meeting of the Emperor and the
Czar. — Entrance **of the** two Emperors into Erfurt. — Reciprocal deference. — The Czar dines every day with the Emperor. — Intimacy of the
Emperor and the Czar. — Dressing-case and bed given to Alexander by
Napoleon. — **The** Emperor **of Russia's present to** Constant. — The Czar
making his toilet at the Emperor's. — **Exchange of** presents. — The three
pelisses of sable fur. — **History of one of these three pelisses.** — The Princess Pauline and her *protégé*. — **The Emperor's anger.** — **Exile.**

THE day preceding the Emperor's *fête*, **or the day**
following, **the** colossal **bronze** statue which **was to** be placed
on the monument in the Place Vendôme was removed from
the studio of **M.** Launay. The brewers **of** the Faubourg
Saint-Antoine offered their handsomest horses to draw the
chariot on which the statue was carried, and twelve were
selected, one from each brewer; and as their masters requested the **privilege** of riding them, nothing could **be**
more singular than **this** *cortège*, which arrived on the
Place Vendôme **at five** o'clock in the evening, followed
by an immense **crowd,** amid **cries of** " *Vive l'Empereur.*"

A few **days before his** Majesty's departure **for** Erfurt,
the Emperor with the Empress and their households played
prisoner's base for the last time. It was in the evening; and

footmen bore lighted torches, and followed the players when they went beyond the reach of the light. The Emperor fell once while trying to catch the Empress, and was taken prisoner; but he soon broke bounds and began to run again, and when he was free, carried off Josephine in spite of the protests of the players; and thus ended the last game of prisoner's base that I ever saw the Emperor play.

It had been decided that the Emperor Alexander and the Emperor Napoleon should meet at Erfurt on the 27th of September; and most of the sovereigns forming the Confederation of the Rhine had been invited to be present at this interview, which it was intended should be both magnificent and imposing. Consequently the Duke of Frioul, grand marshal of the palace, sent M. de Canouville, marshal of lodgings of the palace, M. de Beausset, prefect of the palace, and two quartermasters to prepare at Erfurt lodgings for all these illustrious visitors, and to organize the grand marshal's service.

The government palace was chosen for the Emperor Napoleon's lodgings, as on account of its size it perfectly suited the Emperor's intention of holding his court there; for the Emperor Alexander, the residence of M. Triebel was prepared, the handsomest in the town; and for S. A. I., the Grand Duke Constantine, that of Senator Remann. Other residences were reserved for the Princes of the Confederation and the persons of their suite; and a detachment of all branches of the service of the Imperial household was established in each of these different lodgings.

There had been sent from the storehouse of the crown a large quantity of magnificent furniture, — carpets and tapestry, both Gobelin and la Savonnerie; bronzes, lusters, candelabras, girondoles, Sèvres china; in fine, everything which could contribute to the luxurious furnishing of the two Imperial palaces, and those which were to be occupied by the other sovereigns; and a crowd of workmen came from Paris. General Oudinot[1] was appointed Governor of Erfurt, and had under his orders the First regiment of hussars, the Sixth of cuirassiers, and the Seventeenth of light infantry, which the major-general had appointed to compose the garrison. Twenty select police, with a battalion chosen from the finest grenadiers of the guard, were put on duty at the Imperial palaces.

The Emperor, who sought by every means to render this interview at Erfurt as agreeable as possible to the sovereigns for whom he had conceived an affection at Tilsit, wished to have the masterpieces of the French stage played in their honor. This was the amusement most worthy of them that he could procure, so he gave orders that the theater should be embellished and repaired. M. Dazincourt was appointed director of the theater, and set out from Paris with Messieurs Talma, Lafon, Saint-Prix, Damas, Després, Varennes, Lacave; Mesdames Duchesnoir, Raucourt, Talma, Bourgoin, Rose Dupuis, Grosand, and Patrat; and everything was in order before the arrival of the sovereigns.

Napoleon disliked Madame Talma exceedingly, although she displayed most remarkable talent, and this aversion was well known, although I could never discover the cause; and no one was willing to be first to place her name on the list of those selected to go to Erfurt, but M. Talma made

---

[1] In 1809, at the battle of Wagram, created Marshal and Duke of Raggio. Born 1767; died 1847.—TRANS.

LUCIEN BONAPARTE.

so many entreaties that at last consent was given. And then occurred what everybody except M. Talma and his wife had foreseen, that the Emperor, having seen her play once, was much provoked that she had been allowed to come, and had her name struck from the list.

Mademoiselle Bourgoin, who was at that time young and extremely pretty, had at first more success; but it was necessary, in order to accomplish this, that she should conduct herself differently from Madame Talma. As soon as she appeared at the theater of Erfurt she excited the admiration, and became the object of the attentions, of all the illustrious spectators; and this marked preference gave rise to jealousies, which delighted her greatly, and which she increased to the utmost of her ability by every means in her power. When she was not playing, she took her seat in the theater magnificently dressed, whereupon all looks were bent on her, and distracted from the stage, to the very great displeasure of the actors, until the Emperor at last perceived these frequent distractions, and put an end to them by forbidding Mademoiselle Bourgoin to appear in the theater except on the stage.

This measure, which was very wisely taken by his Majesty, put him in the bad graces of Mademoiselle Bourgoin; and another incident added still more to the displeasure of the actress. The two sovereigns attended the theater together almost every evening, and the Emperor Alexander thought Mademoiselle Bourgoin charming. She was aware of this, and tried by every means to increase the monarch's devotion. One day at last the amorous Czar confided to the Emperor his feelings for Mademoiselle Bourgoin. "I do not advise you to make any advances," said the Emperor

Napoleon. "You think that she would refuse me?"—"Oh, no; but to-morrow is the day for the post, and in five days all Paris would know all about your Majesty from head to foot." These words singularly cooled the ardor of the autocrat, who thanked the Emperor for his advice, and said to him, "But from the manner in which your Majesty speaks, I should be tempted to believe that you bear this charming actress some ill-will."—"No, in truth," replied the Emperor, "I do not know anything about her." This conversation took place in his bedroom during the toilet. Alexander left his Majesty perfectly convinced, and Mademoiselle Bourgoin ceased her ogling and her assurance.

His Majesty made his entrance into Erfurt on the morning of the 27th of September, 1808. The King of Saxony, who had arrived first, followed by the Count de Marcolini, the Count de Haag, and the Count de Boze, awaited the Emperor at the foot of the stairs in the governor's palace; after them came the members of the Regency and the municipality of Erfurt, who congratulated him in the usual form. After a short rest, the Emperor mounted his horse, and left Erfurt by the gate of Weimar, making, in passing, a visit to the King of Saxony, and found outside the city the whole garrison arranged in line of battle,—the grenadiers of the guard commanded by M. d'Arquies; the First regiment of hussars by M. de Juniac; the Seventeenth infantry by M. de Cabannes-Puymisson; and the Sixth cuirassiers, the finest body of men imaginable, by Colonel d'Haugeranville. The Emperor reviewed these troops, ordered a change in some dispositions, and then continued on his way to meet the Emperor Alexander.

The latter had set out from Saint Petersburg on the

17th of September; and the King and Queen of Prussia awaited him at Koenigsberg, where he arrived on the 18th. The Duke of Montebello had the honor of receiving him at Bromberg amid a salute of twenty-one cannon. Alighting from his carriage, the Emperor Alexander mounted his horse, accompanied by the Marshals of the Empire, Soult, Duke of Dalmatia, and Lannes, Duke of Montebello, and set off at a gallop to meet the Nansouty division, which awaited him arranged in line of battle. He was welcomed by a new salute, and by oft repeated cries of "*Long live the Emperor Alexander.*" The monarch, while reviewing the different corps which formed this fine division, said to the officers, "I think it a great honor, messieurs, to be amongst such brave men and splendid soldiers."

By orders of Marshal Soult, who simply executed those given by Napoleon, relays of the post had been arranged on all the roads which the Monarch of the North would pass over, and they were forbidden to receive any compensation. At each relay were escorts of dragoons or light cavalry, who rendered military honors to the Czar as he passed.

After having dined with the generals of the Nansouty division, the Emperor of Russia re-entered his carriage, a barouche with two seats, and seated the Duke of Montebello beside him, who afterwards told me with how many marks of esteem and kind feeling the Emperor overwhelmed him during the journey, even arranging the marshal's cloak around his shoulders while he was asleep.

His Imperial Russian Majesty arrived at Weimar the evening of the 26th, and next day continued his journey to Erfurt, escorted by Marshal Soult, his staff, and the superior officers of the Nansouty division, who had not left him since he had started from Bromberg, and met Napoleon a league and a half from Erfurt, to which place the latter had come on horseback for this purpose.

The moment the Czar perceived the Emperor, he left his carriage, and advanced towards his Majesty, who had also alighted from his horse. They embraced each other with the affection of two college friends who meet again after a long absence; then both mounted their horses, as did also the Grand Duke Constantine, and passing at a gallop in front of the regiments, all of which presented arms at their approach, entered the town, while the troops, with an immense crowd collected from twenty leagues around, made the air resound with their acclamations. The Emperor of Russia wore on entering Erfurt the grand decoration of the Legion of Honor, and the Emperor of the French that of Saint Andrew of Russia; and the two sovereigns during their stay continued to show each other these marks of mutual deference, and it was also remarked that in his palace the Emperor always gave the right to Alexander. On the evening of his arrival, by his Majesty's invitation, Alexander gave the countersign to the grand marshal, and it was afterwards given alternately by the two sovereigns.

They went first to the palace of Russia, where they remained an hour; and later, when Alexander came to return the visit of the Emperor, he received him at the foot of the staircase, and accompanied him when he left as far as the entrance of the grand hall. At six o'clock the two sovereigns dined at his Majesty's residence, and it was the same each day. At nine o'clock the Emperor escorted the Emperor of Russia to his palace; and they then held a private conversation, which continued more than an hour, and in the evening the whole city was illuminated. The day after his arrival the Emperor received at his *levée* the officers of the Czar's household, and granted them the grand entry during the rest of their stay.[1]

[1] NOTE BY CONSTANT. — This is the list of the persons who comprised the suite of the two Emperors.

The grand marshal, Duke of Frioul (Duroc).

The Prince of Neuchâtel (Berthier).

General Caulaincourt, Duke of Vicenza, grand equerry, ambassador of France to St. Petersburg.

The Prince of Bénévento, grand chamberlain (Talleyrand).

The Duke of Bassano (Maret).

The Duke of Cadore, minister of foreign relations.

General Nansouty, first equerry.

M. de Rémusat, first chamberlain.

General Lauriston, the **Emperor's** *aide-de-camp*.

General Savary, Duke of Rovigo, the **Emperor's** *aide-de-camp*.

M. the Count Daru,

M. Cavaletti, equerry.

M. Eugène de Montesquieu, chamberlain.

M. de Canouville, marshal of the lodgings for the palace.

M. de Ménéval, his Majesty's private secretary.

M. Fain, another secretary.

M. de Beausset, prefect of the palace.

M. Yvan, his Majesty's surgeon.

Eight pages.

Persons composing the suite of his Majesty the Emperor of Russia.

Count Tolstoï, grand marshal of the palace.

The Prince of Galitzin, his Majesty's secretary.

Count Romanzoff, minister of foreign affairs.

General Count Tolstoï, Russian ambassador in France, come from Paris.

Count Speranki.

Prince Wolkonski.

Count Oggeroski.

Prince Trubetskoi.

Prince Gargarin.

Count Oraklscheff.

Count Schouvaloff.

General Kitroff, *aide-de-camp* to the Grand Duke Constantine.

M. Apraxin, *aide-de-camp* to the minister of war.

M. Balabin, colonel of the horse-guards.

M. Alkoukieff.

Prince Golgorouki, officer of the guards.

Count Ozanski, chamberlain attached to foreign relations.

M. Gervais, M. Creidmann, M. Sculpoff, } Councilors of state, *attachés* of the foreign relations dep't.

Count Nesselrode, M. Boubagin, } Secretaries of the embassy, arrived from Paris.

M. de Labanski, Russian consul in France, *idem*.

General Kanikoff, Russian minister to Saxony, arrived from Dresden.

M. Schoodes, secretary of the legation, *idem*.

M. Bethmann, Russian consul to Frankfort, arrived from Frankfort.

The two sovereigns gave to each other proofs of the most sincere friendship and most confidential intimacy. The Emperor Alexander almost every morning entered his Majesty's bedroom, and conversed freely with him. One day he was examining the Emperor's dressing-case in silver gilt, which cost six thousand francs, and was most conveniently arranged and beautifully carved by the goldsmith Biennais, and admired it exceedingly. As soon as he had gone, the Emperor ordered me to have a dressing-case sent to the Czar's palace exactly similar to that which had just been received from Paris.

Another time the Emperor Alexander remarked on the elegance and durability of his Majesty's iron bedstead; and the very next day by his Majesty's orders, conveyed by me, an exactly similar bed was set up in the room of the Emperor of Russia, who was delighted with these polite attentions, and two days after, as an evidence of his satisfaction, ordered M. de Rémusat to hand me two handsome diamond rings.

The Czar one day made his toilet in the Emperor's room, and I assisted. I took from the Emperor's linen a white cravat and cambric handkerchief, which I handed him, and for which he thanked me most graciously; he was an exceedingly gentle, good, amiable prince, and extremely polite.

There was an exchange of presents between these illustrious sovereigns. Alexander made the Emperor a present of three superb pelisses of martin-sable, one of which the Emperor gave to his sister Pauline, another to the Princess de Ponte-Corvo; and the third he had lined with green velvet and ornamented with gold lace, and it was this cloak which he constantly wore in Russia. The history of the one which I carried from him to the Princess Pauline is singular enough to be related here, although it may have been already told.

The Princess Pauline showed much pleasure in receiving the Emperor's present, and enjoyed displaying her cloak for the admiration of the household. One day, when she was in the midst of a circle of ladies, to whom she was dilating on the quality and excellence of this fur, M. de Canouville arrived, and the princess asked his opinion of the present she had received from the Emperor. The handsome colonel not appearing as much struck with admiration as she expected, she was somewhat piqued, and exclaimed, " What, monsieur, you do not think it exquisite ? " — " No, madame."— " In order to punish you I wish you to keep this cloak; I give it to you, and require you to wear it; I wish it, you understand." It is probable that there had been some disagreement between her Imperial highness and her *protégé*, and the princess had seized the first means of establishing peace; but however that may be, M. de Canouville needed little entreaty, and the rich fur was carried to his house. A few days after, while the Emperor was holding a review on the Place du Carrousel, M. de Canouville appeared on an unruly horse, which he had great difficulty in controlling. This caused some confusion, and attracted his Majesty's attention, who, glancing at M. de Canouville, saw the cloak which he had given his sister metamorphosed into a hussar's cape. The Emperor had great difficulty in controlling his anger. "M. de Canouville," he cried, in a voice of thunder, "your horse is young, and his blood is too warm; you will go and cool it in Russia." Three days after M. de Canouville had left Paris.

CHAPTER XII.

The Czar's consideration for French actors. — Fine parties. — Intimate friendship of the King of Westphalia and Grand Duke Constantine. — School-
boy farces. — Singular order of Prince Constantine. — Souvenirs at the
theater of Erfurt. — Deafness of the Czar, attention of the Emperor. —
Cinna, Œdipus. — An allusion acted on by the Czar. — Nocturnal alarm. —
Constant's terror. — Napoleon's nightmare. — A bear eating the Emperor's
heart. — Singular coincidence. — Hunting-party. — The smiles of the two
Emperors. — Massacre of game. — *Début* of the Czar at the chase. — Ball
opened by the Czar. — Astonishment of the Muscovite lords. — Breakfast
on Mount Napoleon. — Visit to the battle-field of Jéna. — The inhabitants of Jéna and landowners indemnified by the Emperor. — Gift of
a hundred thousand crowns made by the Emperor to the victims of the
battle of Jéna. — A lesson in strategy given by Napoleon to his allies. —
Representation of Marshal Berthier. — The Emperor's reply. — Conversation between the Emperor and the allied sovereigns. — The Emperor's
learning. — Decorations and presents distributed by the two Emperors. —
End of the interview at Erfurt. — Separation.

THE Emperor Alexander never tired of showing his
regard for actors by presents and compliments; and as for
actresses, I have told before how far he would have gone
with one of them if Napoleon had not deterred him. Each
day the Grand Duke Constantine got up parties of pleasure with Murat and other distinguished persons, at which
no expense was spared, and some of these ladies did the
honors. And what furs and diamonds they carried away
from Erfurt! The two Emperors were not ignorant of all
this, and were much amused thereby; and it was the favorite subject of conversation in the morning. Constantine
had conceived an especial affection for King Jérôme; and

the king even carried his affection so far as to *tutoy* him, and wished him to do the same. "Is it because I am a king," he said one day, "that you are afraid to say *thou* to me? Come, now, is there any need of formality between friends?" They performed all sorts of college pranks together, even running through the streets at night, knocking and ringing at every door, much delighted when they had waked up some honest *bourgeois.* As the Emperor was leaving, King Jérôme said to the grand duke: "Come, tell me what you wish me to send you from Paris." — "Nothing whatever," replied the grand duke; "your brother has presented me with a magnificent sword; I am satisfied, and desire nothing more." — "But I wish to send you something, so tell me what would give you pleasure." — "Well, send me six *demoiselles* from the Palais Royal."

The play at Erfurt usually began at seven o'clock; but the two Emperors, who always came together, never arrived till half-past seven. At their entrance, all *the pit of kings* rose to do them honor, and the first piece immediately commenced.

At the representation of *Cinna,* the Emperor feared that the Czar, who was placed by his side in a box facing the stage, and on the first tier, might not hear very well, as he was somewhat deaf; and consequently gave orders to M. de Rémusat, first chamberlain, that a platform should be raised on the floor of the orchestra, and armchairs placed there for Alexander and himself; and on the right and left four handsomely decorated chairs for the King of Saxony and the other sovereigns of the Confederation, while the princes took possession of the box abandoned by their Majesties. By this arrangement the two Emperors

found themselves in such a conspicuous position that it
was impossible for them to make a movement without being
seen by every one. On the 3d of October *Œdipus* was
presented. "All the sovereigns," as the Emperor called
them, were present at this representation; and just as the
actor pronounced these words in the first scene: —

" The friendship of a great man is a gift from the gods: "

the Czar arose, and held out his hand with much grace
to the Emperor; and immediately acclamations, which the
presence of the sovereigns could not restrain, burst forth
from every part of the hall.

On the evening of this same day I prepared the Emperor for bed as usual. All the doors which opened into
his sleeping-room were carefully closed, as well as the shut-
ters and windows; and there was consequently no means
of entering his Majesty's room except through the chamber
in which I slept with Roustan, and a sentinel was also stationed at the foot of the staircase. Every night I slept
very calmly, knowing that it was impossible any one could
reach Napoleon without waking me; but that night, about
two o'clock, while I was sleeping soundly, a strange noise
woke me with a start. I rubbed my eyes, and listened
with the greatest attention, and, hearing nothing whatever,
thought this noise the illusion of a dream, and was just
dropping to sleep again, when my ear was struck by low,
smothered screams, such as a man might utter who was
being strangled. I heard them repeated twice, and in an
instant was sitting up straight in bed, my hair on end,
and my limbs covered with a cold sweat. Suddenly it occurred to me that the Emperor was being assassinated, and

I sprang out of bed and woke Roustan; and as the cries now recommenced with added intensity, I opened the door as cautiously as my agitation allowed, and entered the sleeping-room, and with a hasty glance assured myself that no one could have entered. On advancing towards the bed, I perceived his Majesty extended across it, in a position denoting great agony, the drapery and bed-covering thrown off, and his whole body in a frightful condition of nervous contraction. From his open mouth escaped inarticulate sounds, his breathing appeared greatly oppressed, and one of his hands, tightly clinched, lay on the pit of his stomach. I was terrified at the sight, and called him. He did not reply; again, once, twice even, still no reply. At last I concluded to shake him gently; and at this the Emperor awoke with a loud cry, saying, "What is it? What is it?" then sat up and opened his eyes wide; upon which I told him that, seeing him tormented with a horrible nightmare, I had taken the liberty of waking him. "And you did well, my dear Constant," interrupted his Majesty. "Ah, my friend, I have had a frightful dream; a bear was tearing open my breast, and devouring my heart!" Thereupon the Emperor rose, and, while I put his bed in order, walked about the room. He was obliged to change his shirt, which was wet with perspiration, and at length again retired.

The next day, when he woke, he told me that it was long before he could fall to sleep again, so vivid and terrible was the impression made on him. He long retained the memory of this dream, and often spoke of it, each time trying to draw from it different conclusions, according to circumstances.

As to myself, I avow I was struck with the coincidence of the compliment of Alexander at the theater and this frightful nightmare, especially as the Emperor was not subject to disturbances of this kind. I do not know whether his Majesty related his dream to the Emperor of Russia.

On the 6th of October their Majesties attended a hunting-party which the Grand Duke of Weimar prepared for them in the forest of Ettersbourg. The Emperor set out from Erfurt at noon, with the Emperor of Russia in the same coach. They arrived in the forest at one o'clock, and found prepared for them a hunting-pavilion, which had been erected expressly for this occasion, and was very handsomely decorated. This pavilion was divided into three parts, separated by open columns; that in the middle, raised higher than the others, formed a pretty room, arranged and furnished for the two Emperors. Around the pavilion were placed numerous orchestras, which played inspiriting airs, with which were mingled the acclamations of an immense crowd, who had been attracted by a desire to see the Emperor.

The two sovereigns were received on their descent from their carriage by the Grand Duke of Weimar and his son, the hereditary prince, Charles Frederic; while the King of Bavaria, King of Saxony, King of Würtemberg, Prince William of Prussia, the Princes of Mecklenburg, the Prince Primate, and the Duke of Oldenburg awaited them at the entrance to the saloon.

The Emperor had in his suite the Prince of Neuchâtel; the Prince of Bénévento; the grand marshal of the palace, Duke de Frioul; General Caulaincourt, Duke of Vicenza;

the Duke of Rovigo; General Lauriston, his Majesty's *aide-de-camp;* General Nansouty, first equerry; the chamberlain, Eugène de Montesquiou; the Count de Beausset, prefect of the palace; and M. Cavaletti.

The Emperor of Russia was accompanied by the Grand Duke Constantine; the Count Tolstoï, grand marshal; and Count Oggeroski, *aide-de-camp* to his Majesty.

The hunt lasted nearly two hours, during which time about sixty stags and roebucks were killed. The space in which these poor animals had to run was inclosed by netting, in order that the monarchs might shoot them at pleasure, without disturbing themselves while seated in the windows of the pavilion. I have never seen anything more absurd than hunts of this sort, which, nevertheless, give those who engage in them a reputation as fine shots. What skill is there in killing an animal which the gamekeepers, so to speak, take by the ears and place in front of your gun.

The Emperor of Russia was near-sighted, and this infirmity had deterred him from an amusement which he would have enjoyed very much; but that day, however, he wished to make the attempt, and, having expressed this wish, the Duke of Montebello handed him a gun, and M. de Beauterne had the honor of giving the Emperor his first lesson. A stag was driven so as to pass within about eight steps of Alexander, who brought him down at the first shot.

After the hunt their Majesties repaired to the palace of Weimar; and the reigning duchess received them, as they alighted from their carriages, accompanied by her whole court. The Emperor saluted the duchess affectionately, remembering that he had seen her two years before under very different circumstances, which I mentioned in its place.

The Duke of Weimar had requested from the grand marshal French cooks to prepare the Emperor's dinner, but the Emperor preferred being served in the German style.

Their Majesties invited to dine with them the Duke and Duchess of Weimar, the Queen of Westphalia, the King of Würtemberg, the King of Saxony, the Grand Duke Constantine, Prince William of Prussia, the Prince Primate, the Prince of Neuchâtel, Prince Talleyrand, the Duke of Oldenburg, the hereditary Prince of Weimar, and the Prince of Mecklenburg-Schwerin.

After this dinner there was a play, followed by a ball, the play being at the town theater, where the ordinary comedians of his Majesty presented the death of Cæsar; and the ball, at the ducal palace. The Emperor Alexander opened the ball with the Queen of Westphalia, to the great astonishment of every one; for it was well known that this monarch had never danced since his accession to the throne, conduct which the older men of the court thought very praiseworthy, holding the opinion that a sovereign occupies too high a place to share in the tastes and take pleasure in amusements common to the rest of mankind. Except this, however, there was nothing in the ball of Weimar to scandalize them, as they did not dance, but promenaded in couples, whilst the orchestra played marches.

The morning of the next day their Majesties entered carriages to visit Mount Napoleon, near Jéna, where a splendid breakfast was prepared for them under a tent which the Duke of Weimar had erected on the identical spot where the Emperor's bivouac stood on the day of the battle of Jéna. After breakfast the two Emperors ascended a temporary pavilion which had been erected on Mount

Napoleon; this pavilion, which was very large, had been decorated with plans of the battle. A deputation from the town and university of Jéna arrived, and were received by their Majesties; and the Emperor inquired of the deputies the most minute particulars relating to their town, its re sources, and the manners and character of its inhabitants; questioned them on the approximate damages which the military hospital, which had been so long left with them, had caused the inhabitants of Jéna; inquired the names of those who had suffered most from fire and war, and gave orders that a gratuity should be distributed among them, and the small proprietors entirely indemnified. His Majesty informed himself with much interest of the condition of the Catholic worship, and promised to endow the vicarage in perpetuity, granting three hundred thousand francs for immediate necessities, and promising to give still more.

After having visited, on horseback, the positions which the two armies had held the evening before, and on the day of, the battle of Jéna, as well as the plain of Aspolda, on which the duke had prepared a hunt with guns, the two Emperors returned to Erfurt, which they reached at five o'clock in the evening, almost at the very moment the grand hereditary duke of Baden and the Princess Stéphanie arrived.

During the entire visit of the sovereigns to the battle-field, the Emperor most graciously made explanations to the young Czar, to which he listened with the greatest interest. His Majesty seemed to take pleasure in explaining at length, —first, the plan which he had formed and carried out at Jéna, and afterwards the various plans of his other campaigns, the maneuvers which he had executed, his usual tactics, and, in fine, his whole ideas on the art of war. The Emperor thus, for several hours, carried on the whole conversation alone; and his royal audience paid him as much attention as scholars, eager to learn, pay to the instructions of their teacher.

When his Majesty returned to his apartment, I heard Marshal Berthier say to him, "Sire, are you not afraid that the sovereigns may some day use to advantage against you all that you have just taught them? Your Majesty just now seemed to forget what you formerly told us, that it is necessary to act with our allies as if they were afterwards to be our enemies." — "Berthier," replied the Emperor, smiling, "that is a good observation on your part, and I thank you for it; I really believe I have made you think I was an idiot. You think, then," continued his Majesty, pinching sharply one of the Prince de Neuchâtel's ears, "that I committed the indiscretion of giving them whips with which to return and flog us? Calm yourself, I did not tell them all."

The Emperor's table at Erfurt was in the form of a half-moon; and at the upper end, and consequently at the rounded part, of this table their Majesties were seated, and on the right and left the sovereigns of the Confederation according to their rank. The side facing their Majesties was always empty; and there stood M. de Beausset, the prefect of the palace, who relates in his *Memoirs* that one day he overheard the following conversation: —

"On that day the subject of conversation was the Golden Bull, which, until the establishment of the Confederation of the Rhine, had served as a constitution, and had regulated the law for the election of emperors, the number and rank of the electors, etc. The Prince Primate entered into some details regarding this Golden Bull, which he said was made in 1409; whereupon the Emperor Napoleon pointed out to him that the date which was assigned to the Golden Bull was not correct, and that it was proclaimed in 1336, during the reign of the Emperor Charles IV. 'That is true, Sire,' replied the Prince Primate, 'I was mistaken; but how does it happen that your Majesty is so well acquainted with these matters?' — '*When I was a mere sub-lieutenant in the artillery,*' said Napoleon, — at this beginning, there was on the part of the guests a marked movement of interest, and he continued, smiling, — 'when I had the honor to be simply sub-lieutenant in the artillery I remained three years in the garrison at Valence, and, as I cared little for society, led a very retired life. By fortunate chance I had lodgings with a kind and intelligent bookseller. I read and re-read his library during the three years I remained in the garrison, and have forgotten nothing, even matters which have had no connection with my position. Nature, besides, has given me a good memory for figures, and it often happens with my ministers that I can give them details and the sum total of accounts they presented long since.'"

A few days before his departure from Erfurt, the Emperor bestowed the cross of the Legion of Honor on M. de Bigi, commandant of arms at this place; M. Vegel, burgomaster of Jéna; Messrs. Weiland and Goethe; M. Starlk, senior physician at Jéna. He gave to General Count Tolstoï, ambassador from Russia, who had been recalled from this post by his sovereign to take a command in the army, the grand decoration of the Legion of Honor; to M. the dean Meimung, who had said mass twice at the palace, a ring of brilliants, with the cipher N surmounted by a crown; and a hundred napoleons to the two priests who had assisted him; finally, to the grand marshal of the palace, Count Tolstoï, the beautiful Gobelin tapestry, Savonnerie carpets, and Sèvres porcelain, which had been brought from Paris to furnish the palace of Erfurt. The minister's grand officers, and officers of Alexander's suite, received from his Majesty magnificent presents; and the Emperor Alexander did likewise in regard to the persons attached to his Majesty. He gave the Duke of Vicenza the grand cordon of Saint Andrew, and a badge of the same order set in diamonds to the Princes of Bénévento and Neuchâtel.

Charmed by the talent of the French comedians, especially that of Talma, the Emperor Alexander sent very handsome presents to her as well as all her companions; he sent compliments to the actresses, and to the director, M. Dazincourt, whom he did not forget in his distribution of gifts.

This interview at Erfurt, which was so brilliant with illuminations, splendor, and luxury, ended on the 14th of October; and all the great personages whom it had attracted left between the 8th and the 14th of October.[1]

[1] This is the list of the principal persons.

The King of Bavaria.
The King of Würtemberg.
The King of Saxony.
The King and Queen of Westphalia.
The Prince Primate.
The Grand Duke and the Grand Duchess of Hesse-Darmstadt.
The Grand Duke and the Grand Duchess of Baden.
The Duke and the Duchess of Weimar.
The hereditary Prince of Weimar.
Prince Leopold of Saxe-Coburg.
The Duke of Saxe-Gotha.
The Duke of Oldenburg.
Prince William of Prussia.
The Prince of Mecklenburg-Schwerin.
The Prince of Mecklenburg-Strelitz.
The Prince of Anhalt-Dessau.
The Prince of Waldeck.
The Prince of Laleyen.
The Prince of Reuss.
The Prince of Ebersdorff.
The Prince of Gera.
The Prince of Schleitz.

The Princess de la Tour and Taxis.
The Prince of Salm-Dyck, *aide-de-camp* of the King of Würtemberg.
The Prince of Hohenlohe-Kirkberg, *idem*.
The Prince of Salm-Salm.
The Prince of Schaumburg.
The Prince of Bernburg.
The Prince of Isemburg.
The Prince of Rudolstadt.
The Prince of Hohenzollern-Sigmaringen.
Duke William of Bavaria.
The Duchess of Hildburghausen.
The Countess of Truxès.
The Count and Countess of Bochols.
The Count of Mongellaz.
The Count of Würtemberg.
The Count of Reuss.
The Baron Vincent.
The Duke of Mondragone.
The Duke of Birkenfeld.
The Count of Goerliz, grand equerry of the King of Würtemberg.
The Count of Taube, prime minister, *idem*.
The Count de Dille, *aide-de-camp*, *idem*, etc.

The day of his departure the Emperor gave an audience, after his toilet, to Baron Vincent, envoy extraordinary of Austria, and sent by him a letter to his sovereign. At eleven o'clock the Emperor of Russia came to his Majesty, who received him, and reconducted him to his residence with great ceremony; and soon after his Majesty repaired to the Russian palace, followed by his whole suite. After mutual compliments they entered the carriage together, and did not part till they reached the spot on the road from Weimar where they had met on their arrival. There they embraced each other affectionately and separated; and the 18th of October, at half-past nine in the evening, the Emperor was at Saint-Cloud, having made the whole trip *incognito*.

CHAPTER XIII.

His Majesty remained only ten days at Saint-Cloud, passed two or three of these in Paris at the opening of the session of the Corps Législatif, and at noon on the 29th set out a second time for Bayonne.

The Empress, who to her great chagrin could not accompany the Emperor, sent for me on the morning of his departure, and renewed in most touching accents the same recommendations which she made on all his journeys, for the character of the Spaniards made her timid and fearful as to his safety.

Their parting was sad and painful; for the Empress was

exceedingly anxious to accompany him, and the Emperor
had the greatest difficulty in satisfying her, and making
her understand that this was impossible.   Just as he was
setting out he returned to his dressing-room a moment,
and told me to unbutton his coat and vest; and I saw the
Emperor pass around his neck between his vest and shirt a
black silk ribbon on which was hung a kind of little bag
about the size of a large hazel-nut, covered with black silk.
Though I did not then know what this bag contained, when
he returned to Paris he gave it to me to keep; and I found
that this bag had a pleasant feeling, as under the silk covering was another of skin.   I shall hereafter tell for what
purpose the Emperor wore this bag.

I set out with a sad heart.   The recommendations of
her Majesty the Empress, and fears which I could not throw
off, added to the fatigue of these repeated journeys, all
conspired to produce feelings of intense sadness, which
was reflected on almost all the countenances of the Imperial
household; while the officers said among themselves that
the combats in the North were trifling compared with those
which awaited us in Spain.

We arrived on the 3d of November at the château of
Marrac, and four days after were at Vittoria in the midst of
the French army, where the Emperor found his brother and
a few grandees of Spain who had not yet deserted his cause.

The arrival of his Majesty electrified the troops; and a
part of the enthusiasm manifested, a very small part it is
true, penetrated into the heart of the king, and somewhat
renewed his courage.   They set out almost immediately, in
order to at once establish themselves temporarily at Burgos, which had been seized by main force and pillaged in a

few hours, since the inhabitants had abandoned it, and left to the garrison the task of stopping the French as long as possible.

The Emperor occupied the archiepiscopal palace, a magnificent building situated in a large square on which the grenadiers of the Imperial Guard bivouacked. This bivouac presented a singular scene. Immense kettles, which had been found in the convents, hung, full of mutton, poultry, rabbits, etc., above a fire which was replenished from time to time with furniture, guitars, or mandolins, and around which grenadiers, with pipes in their mouths, were gravely seated in gilded chairs covered with crimson damask, while they intently watched the kettles as they simmered, and communicated to each other their conjectures on the campaign which had just opened.

The Emperor remained ten or twelve days at Burgos, and then gave orders to march on Madrid, which place could have been reached by way of Valladolid, and the road was indeed safer and better; but the Emperor wished to seize the Pass of Somo-Sierra, an imposing position with natural fortifications which had always been regarded as impregnable. This pass, between two mountain peaks, defended the capital, and was guarded by twelve thousand insurgents, and twelve pieces of cannon placed so advantageously that they could do as much injury as thirty or forty elsewhere, and were, in fact, a sufficient obstacle to delay even the most formidable army; but who could then oppose any hindrance to the march of the Emperor?

On the evening of the 29th of November we arrived within three leagues of this formidable defile, at a village called Basaguillas; and though the weather was very cold, the Emperor did not lie down, but passed the night in his tent, writing, wrapped in the pelisse which the Emperor Alexander had given him. About three o'clock in the morning he came to warm himself by the bivouac fire where I had seated myself, as I could no longer endure the cold and dampness of a cellar which had been assigned as my lodging, and where my bed was only a few handfuls of straw, filled with manure.

At eight o'clock in the morning the position was attacked and carried, and the next day we arrived before Madrid.

The Emperor established his headquarters at the château of Champ-Martin, a pleasure house situated a quarter of a league from the town, and belonging to the mother of the Duke of Infantado; and the army camped around this house. The day after our arrival, the owner came in tears to entreat of his Majesty a revocation of the fatal decree which put her son outside the protection of the law; the Emperor did all he could to reassure her, but he could promise her nothing, as the order was general.

We had some trouble in capturing this town; in the first place, because his Majesty recommended the greatest moderation in making the attack, not wishing, as he said, to present to his brother a burned-up city; in the second place, because the Grand Duke of Berg during his stay at Madrid had fortified the palace of Retiro, and the Spanish insurgents had intrenched themselves there, and defended it most courageously. The town had no other defense, and was surrounded only by an old wall, almost exactly similar to that of Paris, consequently at the end of three days it was taken; but the Emperor preferred not to enter, and still resided at Champ-Martin, with the exception of one day when he came *incognito* and in disguise, to visit the queen's palace and the principal districts.

One striking peculiarity of the Spaniards is the respect they have always shown for everything relating to royalty, whether they regard it as legitimate or not. When King Joseph left Madrid the palace was closed, and the government established itself in a passably good building which had been used as the post-office. From this time no one entered the palace except the servants, who had orders to clean it from time to time; not a piece of furniture even, not a book, was moved. The portrait of Napoleon on Mont St. Bernard, David's masterpiece, remained hanging in the grand reception hall, and the queen's portrait opposite, exactly as the king had placed them; and even the cellars were religiously respected. The apartments of King Charles had also remained untouched, and not one of the watches in his immense collection had been removed.

The act of clemency which his Majesty showed toward the Marquis of Saint-Simon, a grandee of Spain, marked in an especial manner the entrance of the French troops into Madrid. The Marquis of Saint-Simon, a French emigrant, had been in the service of Spain since the emigration, and had the command of a part of the capital. The post which he defended was exactly in front of that which the Emperor commanded at the gates of Madrid, and he had held out long after all the other leaders had surrendered.

The Emperor, impatient at being so long withstood at this point, gave orders to make a still more vigorous charge; and in this the marquis was taken prisoner. In his extreme anger the Emperor sent him to be tried before a military commission, who ordered him to be shot; and this order was on the point of being executed, when Mademoiselle de Saint-Simon, a charming young person, threw herself at his Majesty's feet, and her father's pardon was quickly granted.

The king immediately re-entered his capital; and with him returned the noble families of Madrid, who had withdrawn from the stirring scenes enacted at the center of the insurrection; and soon balls, *fêtes*, festivities, and plays were resumed as of yore.

The Emperor left Champ-Martin on the 22d of December, and directed his march towards Astorga, with the intention of meeting the English, who had just landed at Corunna; but dispatches sent to Astorga by a courier from Paris decided him to return to France, and he consequently gave orders to set out for Valladolid.

We found the road from Benavente to Astorga covered with corpses, slain horses, artillery carriages, and broken wagons, and at every step met detachments of soldiers with torn clothing, without shoes, and, indeed, in a most deplorable condition. These unfortunates were all fleeing towards Astorga, which they regarded as a port of safety, but which soon could not contain them all. It was terrible weather, the snow falling so fast that it was almost blinding; and, added to this, I was ill, and suffered greatly during this painful journey.

The Emperor while at Tordesillas had established his headquarters in the buildings outside the convent of Saint-Claire, and the abbess of this convent was presented to his Majesty. She was then more than sixty-five years old, and from the age of ten years had never left this place. Her intelligent and refined conversation made a most agreeable impression on the Emperor, who inquired what were her wishes, and granted each one.

We arrived at Valladolid the 6th of January, 1809, and found it in a state of great disorder. Two or three days after our arrival, a cavalry officer was assassinated by Dominican monks; and as Hubert, one of our comrades, was passing in the evening through a secluded street, three men threw themselves on him and wounded him severely; and he would doubtless have been killed if the grenadiers of the guard had not hastened to his assistance, and delivered him from their hands. It was the monks again. At length the Emperor, much incensed, gave orders that the convent of the Dominicans should be searched; and in a well was found the corpse of the aforesaid officer, in the midst of a considerable mass of bones, and the convent was immediately suppressed by his Majesty's orders; he even thought at one time of issuing the same rigorous orders against all the convents of the city. He took time for reflection, however, and contented himself by appointing an audience, at which all the monks of Valladolid were to appear before him. On the appointed day they came; not all, however, but deputations from each convent, who prostrated themselves at the Emperor's feet, while he showered reproaches upon them, called them assassins and brigands, and said they all deserved to be hung. These poor men listened in silence and humility to the terrible language of the irritated conqueror whom their patience alone could appease; and finally, the Emperor's anger having exhausted itself, he grew calmer, and at last, struck by the reflection that it was hardly just to heap abuse on men thus prostrate on their knees and uttering not a word in their own defense, he left the group of officers who surrounded him, and advanced into the midst of the monks, making them a sign to rise from their supplicating posture; and as these good men obeyed him, they kissed the skirts of his coat, and pressed around him with an eagerness most alarming to the persons of his Majesty's suite; for had there been among these devotees any Dominican, nothing surely could have been easier than an assassination.

During the Emperor's stay at Valladolid, I had with the grand marshal a disagreement of which I retain most vivid recollections, as also of the Emperor's intervention wherein he displayed both justice and good-will towards me. These are the facts of the case: one morning the Duke de Frioul, encountering me in his Majesty's apartments, inquired in a very brusque tone (he was very much excited) if I had ordered the carriage to be ready, to which I replied in a most respectful manner that *they were always ready.* Three times the duke repeated the same question, raising his voice still more each time; and three times I made him the same reply, always in the same respectful manner. "Oh, you fool!" said he at last, "you do not understand, then." — "That arises evidently, Monseigneur, from your Excellency's imperfect explanations!" Upon which he explained that he was speaking of a new carriage which had come from Paris that very day, a fact of which I was entirely ignorant. I was on the point of explaining this to his Excellency; but without deigning to listen, the grand marshal rushed out of the room exclaiming, swearing, and addressing me in terms to which I was totally unaccustomed. I followed him as far as his own room in order to make an explanation; but when he reached his door he entered, and slammed it in my face.

In spite of all this I entered a few moments later; but his Excellency had forbidden his *valet de chambre* to introduce me, saying that he had nothing to say to me, nor to hear from me, all of which was repeated to me in a very harsh and contemptuous manner.

Little accustomed to such experiences, and entirely unnerved, I went to the Emperor's room; and when his Majesty entered I was still so agitated that my face was wet with tears. His Majesty wished to know what had happened, and I related to him the attack which had just been made upon me by the grand marshal. "You are very foolish to cry," said the Emperor; "calm yourself, and say to the grand marshal that I wish to speak to him."

His Excellency came at once in response to the Emperor's invitation, and I announced him. "See," said he, pointing to me, "see into what a state you have thrown this fellow! What has he done to be thus treated?" The grand marshal bowed without replying, but with a very dissatisfied air; and the Emperor went on to say that he should have given me his orders more clearly, and that any one was excusable for not executing an order not plainly given. Then turning toward me, his Majesty said, "Monsieur Constant, you may be certain this will not occur again."

This simple affair furnishes a reply to many false accusations against the Emperor. There was an immense distance between the grand marshal of the palace and the simple *valet de chambre* of his Majesty, and yet the marshal was reprimanded for a wrong done to the *valet de chambre.*

The Emperor showed the utmost impartiality in meting out justice in his domestic affairs; and never was the interior of a palace better governed than his, owing to the fact that in his household he alone was master.

The grand marshal felt unkindly toward me for sometime after; but, as I have already said, he was an excellent man, his bad humor soon passed away, and so completely, that on my return to Paris he requested me to stand for him at the baptism of the child of my father-in-law, who had begged him to be its godfather; the godmother was Josephine, who was kind enough to choose my wife to represent her. M. le Duke de Frioul did things with as much nobility and magnanimity as grace; and afterwards I am glad to be able to state in justice to his memory, he eagerly seized every occasion to be useful to me, and to make me forget the discomfort his temporary excitement had caused me.

I fell ill at Valladolid with a violent fever a few days before his Majesty's departure. On the day appointed for leaving, my illness was at its height; and as the Emperor feared that the journey might increase, or at any rate prolong, my illness, he forbade my going, and set out without me, recommending to the persons whom he left at Valladolid to take care of my health. When I had gotten somewhat better I was told that his Majesty had left, whereupon I could no longer be controlled, and against my physician's orders, and in spite of my feebleness, in spite of everything, in fact, had myself placed in a carriage and set out. This was wise; for hardly had I put Valladolid two leagues behind me, than I felt better, and the fever left me. I arrived at Paris five or

six days after the Emperor, just after his Majesty had
appointed the Count Montesquiou grand chamberlain in
place of Prince Talleyrand, whom I met that very day,
and who seemed in no wise affected by this disgrace, —
perhaps he was consoled by the dignity of vice-grand elector which was bestowed on him in exchange.

CHAPTER XIV.

Arrival at Paris. — The Palace of Madrid and the Louvre. — The château of Chambord intended for the Prince de Neuchâtel. — Constant employment of the Emperor. — The Emperor as a musical critic. — The Emperor's falsetto voice and habit of humming. — The Marseillaise the signal for departure. — The Emperor's gayety as he sets out on the Russian campaign. — Crescentini and Madame Grassini. — Play of Crescentini. — Satisfaction and generosity of the Emperor. — Illness and death of Dazincourt. — Ingratitude of the public. — A word about Dazincourt. — The Emperor's stay at the Élysée. — Marriage of the Duke of Castiglione. — The Grand Duchess of Tuscany. — The chase at Rambouillet. — The Emperor's skill. — Talma. — Their Majesties' departure from Strasbourg. — The Emperor passes the Rhine. — The Battle of Ratisbonne. — The Emperor wounded. — Much alarm in the army. — The Emperor's endurance. — The papers advised to be silent. — Orders of the Emperor before each battle. — A Bavarian family saved by Constant. — The Emperor's vexation. — M. Pfister becomes insane. — The Emperor's anxiety. — Conspiracy against the Emperor. — A million in diamonds. — Insult to the bearer of a flag of truce. — The Emperor's moderation. — Letter of the Prince de Neuchâtel to the Archduke Maximilian. — Bombardment of Vienna. — The life of Marie Louise protected by the Emperor. — Flight of the Archduke Maximilian, and the taking of Vienna. — Stupidity of the Austrians.

THE Emperor arrived at Paris on the 23d of January, and. passed the remainder of the winter there, with the exception of a few days spent at Rambouillet and Saint-Cloud.

On the very day of his arrival in Paris, although he must have been much fatigued by an almost uninterrupted ride from·Valladolid, the Emperor visited the buildings of the Louvre and the rue de Rivoli.

His mind was full of what he had seen at Madrid, and

repeated suggestions to M. Fontaine and the other architects showed plainly his desire to make the Louvre the finest palace in the world. His Majesty then had a report made him as to the château of Chambord, which he wished to present to the Prince of Neuchâtel. M. Fontaine found that repairs sufficient to make this place a comfortable residence would amount to 1,700,000 francs, as the buildings were in a state of decay, and it had hardly been touched since the death of Marshal Saxe.

His Majesty passed the two months and a half of his stay working in his cabinet, which he rarely left, and always unwillingly; his amusements being, as always, the theater and concerts. He loved music passionately, especially Italian music, and like all great amateurs was hard to please. He would have much liked to sing had he been able, but he had no voice, though this did not prevent his humming now and then pieces which struck his fancy; and as these little reminiscences usually recurred to him in the mornings, he regaled me with them while he was being dressed. The air that I have heard him thus mutilate most frequently was that of *The Marseillaise.* The Emperor also whistled sometimes, but very rarely; and the air, *Malbrook s'en va-t-en guerre,*[1] whistled by his Majesty was an unerring announcement to me of his approaching departure for the army. I remember that he never whistled so much, and was never so gay, as just before he set out for the Russian campaign.

His Majesty's favorite singers were Crescentini [2] and Ma-

---

[1] The Emperor is said to have hummed this air as he crossed the Niemen. — TRANS.

[2] Girolamo Crescentini, born at Urbania, 1769; died 1846. In 1809 Napoleon appointed him first singer at his court. — TRANS.

dame Grassini. I saw Crescentini's *début* at Paris in the *rôle* of Romeo, in *Romeo and Juliet*. He came preceded by a reputation as the first singer of Italy; and this reputation was found to be well deserved, notwithstanding all the prejudices he had to overcome, for I remember well the disparaging statements made concerning him before his *début* at the court theater. According to these self-appointed connoisseurs, he was a bawler without taste, without method, a maker of absurd trills, an unimpassioned actor of little intelligence, and many other things besides. He knew, when he appeared on the stage, how little disposed in his favor his audience were, yet he showed not the slightest embarrassment; this, and his noble, dignified mien, agreeably surprised those who expected from what they had been told to behold an awkward man with an ungainly figure. A murmur of approbation ran through the hall on his appearance; and electrified by this welcome, he gained all hearts from the first act. His movements were full of grace and dignity; he had a perfect knowledge of the scene, modest gestures perfectly in harmony with the dialogue, and a countenance on which all shades of passion were depicted with the most astonishing accuracy; and all these rare and precious qualities combined to give to the enchanting accents of this artist a charm of which it is impossible to give an idea.

At each scene the interest he inspired became more marked, until in the third act the emotion and delight of the spectators were carried almost to frenzy. In this act, played almost solely by Crescentini, this admirable singer communicated to the hearts of his audience all that is touching and pathetic in a love expressed by means of delicious melody, and by all that grief and despair can find sublime in song.

The Emperor was enraptured, and sent Crescentini a considerable compensation, accompanied by most flattering testimonials of the pleasure he had felt in hearing him.

On this day, as always when they played together afterwards, Crescentini was admirably supported by Madame Grassini, a woman of superior talent, and who possessed the most astonishing voice ever heard in the theater. She and Madame Barilli then divided the admiration of the public.

The very evening or the day after the *début* of Crescentini, the French stage suffered an irreparable loss in the death of Dazincourt, only sixty years of age. The illness of which he died had begun on his return from Erfurt, and was long and painful; and yet the public, to whom this great comedian had so long given such pleasure, took no notice of him after it was found his sickness was incurable and his death certain. Formerly when a highly esteemed actor was kept from his place for some time by illness (and who deserved more esteem than Dazincourt?), the pit was accustomed to testify its regret by inquiring every day as to the condition of the afflicted one, and at the end of each representation the actor whose duty it was to announce the play for the next day gave the audience news of his comrade. This was not done for Dazincourt, and the pit thus showed ingratitude to him.

I liked and esteemed sincerely Dazincourt, whose acquaintance I had made several years before his death; and few men better deserved or so well knew how to gain esteem and affection. I will not speak of his genius, which

SOULT.

rendered him a worthy successor of Préville,[1] whose pupil
and friend he was, for all his contemporaries remember
Figaro as played by Dazincourt; but I will speak of the
nobility of his character, of his generosity, and his well-
tested honor. It would seem that his birth and education
should have kept him from the theater, where circumstances alone placed him; but he was able to protect himself against the seductions of his situation, and in the green-
room, and in the midst of domestic intrigues, remained a
man of good character and pure manners. He was welcomed in the best society, where he soon became a favorite
by his piquant sallies, as much as by his good manners and
urbanity, for he amused without reminding that he was a
comedian.

At the end of February his Majesty went to stay
for some time at the palace of the Élysée; and there I
think was signed the marriage contract of one of his best
lieutenants, Marshal Augereau, recently made Duke of
Castiglione, with Mademoiselle Bourlon de Chavanges, the
daughter of an old superior officer; and there also was
rendered the imperial decree which gave to the Princess
Eliza the grand duchy of Tuscany, with the title of grand
duchess.

About the middle of March, the Emperor passed several
days at Rambouillet; there were held some exciting hunts,
in one of which his Majesty himself brought to bay and
killed a stag near the pool of Saint-Hubert. There was also
a ball and concert, in which appeared Crescentini, Mesdames
Grassini, Barelli, and several celebrated virtuosos, and lastly
Talma recited.

---

[1] Pierre Louis Préville, a popular French comic actor, born in Paris, 1721;
died 1799. — TRANS.

On the 13th of April, at four o'clock in the morning, the Emperor having received news of another invasion of Bavaria by the Austrians, set out for Strasburg with the Empress, whom he left in that city; and on the 15th, at eleven o'clock in the morning, he passed the Rhine at the head of his army. The Empress did not long remain alone, as the Queen of Holland and her sons, the Grand Duchess of Baden and her husband, soon joined her.

The splendid campaign of 1809 at once began. It is known how glorious it was, and that one of its least glorious victories was the capture of Vienna.

At Ratisbon, on the 23d of April, the Emperor received in his right foot a spent ball, which gave him quite a severe bruise. I was with the service when several grenadiers hastened to tell me that his Majesty was wounded, upon which I hastened to him, and arrived while M. Yvan was dressing the contusion. The Emperor's boot was cut open, and laced up, and he remounted his horse immediately; and, though several of the generals insisted on his resting, he only replied: "My friends, do you not know that it is necessary for me to see everything?" The enthusiasm of the soldiers cannot be expressed when they learned that their chief had been wounded, though his wound was not dangerous. "The Emperor is exposed like us," they said; "he is not a coward, not he." The papers did not mention this occurrence.

Before entering a battle, the Emperor always ordered that, in case he was wounded, every possible measure should be taken to conceal it from his troops. "Who knows," said he, "what terrible confusion might be produced by such news? To my life is attached the destiny of a great Empire. Remember this, gentlemen; and if I am wounded, let no one know it, if possible. If I am slain, try to win the battle without me; there will be time enough to tell it afterwards."

Two weeks after the capture of Ratisbon, I was in advance of his Majesty on the road to Vienna, alone in a carriage with an officer of the household, when we suddenly heard frightful screams in a house on the edge of the road. I gave orders to stop at once, and we alighted; and, on entering the house, found several soldiers, or rather stragglers, as there are in all armies, who, paying no attention to the alliance between France and Bavaria, were treating most cruelly a family which lived in this house, and consisted of an old grandmother, a young man, three children, and a young girl.

Our embroidered coats had a happy effect on these madmen, whom we threatened with the Emperor's anger; and we succeeded in driving them out of the house, and soon after took our departure, overwhelmed with thanks. In the evening I spoke to the Emperor of what I had done; and he approved highly, saying, "It cannot be helped. There are always some cowardly fellows in the army; and they are the ones who do the mischief. A brave and good soldier would blush to do such things!"

I had occasion, in the beginning of these Memoirs, to speak of the steward, M. Pfister, one of his Majesty's most faithful servants, and also one of those to whom his Majesty was most attached. M. Pfister had followed him to Egypt, and had faced countless dangers in his service. The day of the battle of Landshut, which either preceded or followed very closely the taking of Ratisbon this poor man became insane, rushed **out of** his tent, and concealed himself in a wood near the **field** of battle, after taking off all his clothing.   **At the** end **of a few hours** his Majesty asked for M. Pfister.   **He was** sought for, and **every** one was questioned; **but no** one **could tell** what had **become of** him. The Emperor, fearing **that he might have** been taken prisoner, sent an orderly officer **to the** Austrians to recover his steward, and propose **an** exchange; but the officer returned, saying that the Austrians had not seen M. Pfister. **The** Emperor, **much** disquieted, ordered **a search to be made in the** neighborhood; **and by** this means the poor fellow **was discovered entirely naked, as I have** said, cowering **behind a tree, in a frightful** condition, his body torn **by thorns.   He was brought back, and** having become perfectly **quiet, was thought to be well, and** resumed his duties; but **a** short time after **our return to** Paris he had **a new attack.** The **character of his** malady was exceedingly obscene; and he **presented himself before** the Empress Josephine **in such a state of disorder, and** with such indecent gestures, that it was necessary **to take** precautions **in** regard to him.   He was confided **to the care of** the wise Doctor Esquirol, **who, in** spite of his great **skill, could not** effect a cure.   I **went to see him often.   He had no more** violent attacks; **but his** brain was **diseased, and** though he heard and understood perfectly, his replies **were** those of a real madman.   **He** never lost his **devotion to the** Emperor, spoke of him incessantly, **and** imagined himself **on** duty **near him.   One day he told me with a most** mysterious air that he wished to confide **to me** a terrible secret, the **plot of a** conspiracy against his **Majesty's life,** handing me at the **same time a** note **for his** Majesty, with a package of about twenty scraps of paper, which he had scribbled off himself, and thought were the details of the plot. Another time he handed me, for the Emperor, a handful of little stones, which he called diamonds of great value. "There is more than a million in what I hand you," said he. The Emperor, whom I told of my visits, was exceedingly touched by the continued monomania of this poor unfortunate, whose every thought, every act, related to his old master, and who died without regaining his reason.

On the 10th of May, at nine o'clock in the morning, the first line of defense of the Austrian capital was attacked and taken by Marshal Oudinot:[1] the faubourgs surrendering at discretion. The Duke of Montebello then advanced on the esplanade at the head of his division; but the gates having been closed, the garrison poured a frightful discharge from the top of the ramparts, which fortunately however killed only a very small number. The Duke of Montebello summoned the garrison to surrender the town, but the response of the Archduke Maximilian was that he would defend Vienna with his last breath; which reply was conveyed to the Emperor.

After taking counsel with his generals, his Majesty charged Colonel Lagrange to bear a new demand to the archduke; but the poor colonel had hardly entered the town than he was attacked by the infuriated populace. General O'Reilly saved his life by having him carried away by his soldiers: but the Archduke Maximilian, in order to defy the Emperor still further, paraded in triumph in the

---

[1] Oudinot was not made a marshal till the battle of Wagram, a few weeks after. — TRANS.

midst of the national guard the individual who had struck the first blow at the bearer of the French summons. This attempt, which had excited the indignation of many of the Viennese themselves, did not change his Majesty's intentions, as he wished to carry his moderation and kindness as far as possible; and he wrote to the archduke by the Prince of Neuchâtel the following letter, a copy of which accidentally fell into my hands: —

"The Prince de Neuchâtel to his Highness the Archduke Maximilian,[1] commanding the town of Vienna, —

"His Majesty the Emperor and King desires to spare this large and worthy population the calamities with which it is threatened, and charges me to represent to your Highness, that if he continues the attempt to defend this place, it will cause the destruction of one of the finest cities of Europe. In every country where he has waged war, my sovereign has manifested his anxiety to avoid the disasters which armies bring on the population. Your Highness must be persuaded that his Majesty is much grieved to see this town, which he has the glory of having already saved, on the point of being destroyed. Nevertheless, contrary to the established usage of fortresses, your Highness has fired your cannon from the city walls, and these cannon may kill, not an enemy of your sovereign, but the wives or children of his most devoted servants. If your Highness prolongs the attempt to defend the place, his Majesty will be compelled to begin his preparations for attack; and the ruin of this immense capital will be consummated in thirty-six hours, by the shells and bombs from our batteries, as the outskirts of the town will be destroyed by the effect of yours. His Majesty does not doubt that these considerations will influence your Highness to renounce a determination which will only delay for a short while the capture of the place. If, however, your Highness has decided not to pursue a course which will save the town from destruction, its population plunged by your fault into such terrible misfortunes will become, instead of faithful subjects, the enemies of your house."

[1] Brother of the Emperor of Austria. — TRANS.

This letter did not deter the grand duke from persisting in his defense; and this obstinacy exasperated the Emperor to such a degree that he at last gave orders to place two batteries in position, and within an hour cannon-balls and shells rained upon the town. The inhabitants, with true German indifference, assembled on the hillsides to watch the effect of the fires of attack and defense, and appeared much interested in the sight. A few cannon-balls had already fallen in the court of the Imperial palace when a flag of truce came out of the town to announce that the Archduchess Marie Louise had been unable to accompany her father, and was ill in the palace, and consequently exposed to danger from the artillery; and the Emperor immediately gave orders to change the direction of the firing so that the bombs and balls would pass over the palace. The archduke did not long hold out against such a sharp and energetic attack, but fled, abandoning Vienna to the conquerors.

On the 12th of May the Emperor made his entrance into Vienna, one month after the occupation of Munich by the Austrians. This circumstance made a deep impression, and did much to foster the superstitious ideas which many of the troops held in regard to the person of their chief. "See," said one, "he needed only the time necessary for the journey. That man must be a god." — "He is a devil rather," said the Austrians, whose stupefaction was indescribable. They had reached a point when many allowed the arms to be taken out of their hands without making the least resistance, or without even attempting to fly, so deep was their conviction that the Emperor and his guard were not men, and that sooner or later they must fall into the power of these supernatural enemies.

CHAPTER XV.

The Emperor at Schoenbrunn. — Description of **this residence.** — **Tho Em**-
peror's **apartments.** — Inconvenience of the **stoves.** — **The** winged chariot
of Maria Theresa. — The parks of Versailles, Malmaison, and Schoen-
brunn. — **The** *Gloriette.* — The ruins. — The menagerie **and kiosk of**
Maria Theresa. — Reviews held by the Emperor. — Manner in which **tho**
Emperor made promotions. — Gratuities paid by the Emperor. — **An act**
of heroism. — Kindness of the Emperor. — A visit with **bags, account**
books, and arms. — Unexpected orders. — **A young officer's self-possession.**
— **Wagons** inspected by the Emperor.

THE Emperor did not remain in Vienna, but established
his headquarters at the château of Schoenbrunn, an imperial
residence situated about half a league from the town; and
the ground in front of the château was arranged for the
encampment of the guard. The château of Schoenbrunn,
erected by the Empress Maria Theresa in 1754, and situated in a commanding position, is built in a very irregular,
and defective, but at the same time majestic, style of architecture. In order to reach it, there has been thrown over
the little river, *la Vienne*, a broad and well-constructed
bridge, ornamented with four stone sphinxes; and in front
of the bridge is a large iron gate, opening on an immense
court, in which seven or eight thousand men could be
drilled. This court is square, surrounded by covered gal-
leries, and ornamented with two large basins with marble
statues; and on each side of the gateway are two large
obelisks in rose-colored stone, surmounted by eagles of
gilded lead.

Schoenbrunn, in German, signifies *beautiful fountain ;*[1] and this name comes from a clear and limpid spring, which rises in a grove in the park, on a slight elevation, around which has been built a little pavilion, carved on the inside to imitate stalactites. In this pavilion lies a sleeping Naiad, holding in her hand a shell, from which the water gushes and falls into a marble basin. This is a delicious retreat in summer.

We can speak only in terms of admiration regarding the interior of the palace, the furniture of which was handsome and of an original and elegant style. The Emperor's sleeping-room, the only part of the building in which there was a fireplace, was ornamented with wainscoting in Chinese lacquer work, then very old, though the painting and gilding were still fresh, and the cabinet was decorated like the bedroom; and all the apartments, except this, were warmed in winter by immense stoves, which greatly injured the effect of the interior architecture. Between the study and the Emperor's room was a very curious machine, called *the flying chariot*, a kind of mechanical contrivance, which had been made for the Empress Maria Theresa, and was used in conveying her from one story to the other, so that she might not be obliged to ascend and descend staircases like the rest of the world. This machine was operated by means of cords, pulleys, and weights, like those at the theater.[2]

The beautiful grove which serves as park and garden to the palace of Schoenbrunn is much too small to belong

[1] It is the equivalent of the French Fontainebleau; i.e., Fontaine-belleeau. — TRANS.

[2] This novelty of that day is simply the elevator now seen in every hotel. — TRANS.

to an imperial residence ; **but,** on the other hand, it would **be hard to find one** more beautiful **or** better arranged. The park of Versailles **is** grander and more imposing ; but it has not the picturesque irregularity, the fantastic and unexpected beauties, of the **park** of Schoenbrunn, and more closely resembles the park at **Malmaison.** In front of the interior façade of the palace **was a** magnificent lawn, sloping down to a broad lake, decorated with **a** group of statuary representing the triumph of Neptune. This group is **very** fine ; but French amateurs (every Frenchman, as **you are** aware, desires to be considered a connoisseur) insisted that **the** women were more Austrian than Grecian, **and** that they did not possess **the slender** grace belonging **to** antique forms ; **and, for my part, I** must confess that these statues **did not appear to** me very remarkable.

At the end of the grand avenue, and bounding **the horizon, rose a** hill, which overlooked the park, and was **crowned by** a handsome building, which bore the name of *la Gloriette.* This building was a circular gallery, inclosed with glass, supported **by a** charming colonnade, between the arches of which hung various trophies. On entering the avenue from the direction of Vienna, *la Gloriette* rose at the farther end, seeming almost **to form a part of the** palace ; and the effect **was** very fine.

What the Austrians especially admired **in** the palace of Schoenbrunn **was a grove,** containing what they called the *Ruins,* and a lake with a fountain springing from the midst, and several small cascades flowing from it ; by this **lake were the ruins of an** aqueduct **and a** temple, fallen vases, tombs, broken bas-reliefs, statues without heads, arms, **or limbs,** while limbs, **arms, and heads** lay thickly scattered

around; columns mutilated and half-buried, others standing and supporting the remains of pediments and entabla-
tures; all combining to form a scene of beautiful disorder,
and representing a genuine ancient ruin when viewed from
a short distance. Viewed more closely, it is quite another
thing: the hand of the modern sculptor is seen; it is evident that all these fragments are made from the same kind
of stone; and the weeds which grow in the hollows of these
columns appear what they really are, that is to say, made
of stone, and painted to imitate verdure.

But if the productions of art scattered through the
park of Schoenbrunn were not all irreproachable, those of
nature fully made up the deficiency. What magnificent
trees! What thick·hedges! What dense and refreshing
shade! The avenues were remarkably high and broad,
and bordered with trees, which formed a vault impene-
trable to the sun, while the eye lost itself in their many
windings; from these other smaller walks diverged, where
fresh surprises were in store at every step. At the end of
the broadest of these was placed the menagerie, which was
one of the most extensive and varied in Europe, and its
construction, which was very ingenious, might well serve
as a model; it was shaped like a star, and in the round
center of this star had been erected a small but very elegant kiosk, placed there by the Empress Maria Theresa
as a resting-place for herself, and from which the whole
menagerie could be viewed at leisure.

Each point of this star formed a separate garden, where
there could be seen elephants, buffaloes, camels, drome-
daries, stags, and kangaroos grazing; handsome and sub-
stantial cages held tigers, bears, leopards, lions, hyenas,

etc.; and swans and rare aquatic birds and amphibious animals sported in basins surrounded by iron gratings. In this menagerie I specially remarked a very extraordinary animal, which his Majesty had ordered brought to France, but which had died the day before it was to have started. This animal was from Poland, and was called a *curus;* it was a kind of ox, though much larger than an ordinary ox, with a mane like a lion, horns rather short and somewhat curved, and enormously large at the base.

Every morning, at six o'clock, the drums beat, and two or three hours after the troops were ordered to parade in the court of honor; and at precisely ten o'clock his Majesty descended, and put himself at the head of his generals.

It is impossible to give an idea of these parades, which in no particular resembled reviews in Paris. The Emperor, during these reviews, investigated the smallest details, and examined the soldiers one by one, so to speak, looked into the eyes of each to see whether there was pleasure or work in his head, questioned the officers, sometimes also the soldiers themselves; and it was usually on these occasions that the Emperor made his promotions. During one of these reviews, if he asked a colonel who was the bravest officer in his regiment, there was no hesitation in his answer; and it was always prompt, for he knew that the Emperor was already well informed on this point. After the colonel had replied, he addressed himself to all the other officers, saying, "Who is the bravest among you?"—"Sire, it is such an one;" and the two answers were almost always the same. "Then," said the Emperor, "I make him a baron; and I reward in him, not only his own personal bravery, but that of the corps of which he forms a part. He does

not owe this favor to me alone, but also to the esteem of
his comrades." It was the same case with the soldiers; and
those most distinguished for courage or good conduct were
promoted or received rewards, and sometimes pensions, the
Emperor giving one of twelve hundred francs to a soldier,
who, on his first campaign, had passed through the enemy's
squadron, bearing on his shoulders his wounded general,
protecting him as he would his own father.

On these reviews the Emperor could be seen personally
inspecting the haversacks of the soldiers, examining their
certificates, or taking a gun from the shoulders of a young
man who was weak, pale, and suffering, and saying to him,
in a sympathetic tone, "That is too heavy for you." He
often drilled them himself; and when he did not, the drill-
ing was directed by Generals Dorsenne, Curial, or Mouton.[1]
Sometimes he was seized with a sudden whim; for example, one morning, after reviewing a regiment of the
Confederation, he turned to the ordnance officers, and addressing Prince Salm, who was among them, remarked:
" M. de Salm, the soldiers ought to get acquainted with
you; approach, and order them to make a charge in twelve
movements." The young prince turned crimson, without
being disconcerted, however, bowed, and drawing his sword
most gracefully, executed the orders of the Emperor with
an ease and precision which charmed him.

Another day, as the engineer corps passed with about
forty wagons, the Emperor cried, "Halt!" and pointing out
a wagon to General Bertrand, ordered him to summon one

[1] George Mouton, Count de Lobau, born at Pfalzburg, 1770; entered the
army, 1792; aide-de-camp to Joubert 1798, and to Napoleon 1805; general of
division, 1807; created Count de Lobau, 1809. Taken prisoner at Waterloo,
where he commanded an army corps. Marshal, 1831, died 1838. — TRANS.

of the officers. " **What does that** wagon contain? " — " Sire, bolts, **bags of** nails, ropes, hatchets, and **saws.**" — "How **much of each?**" The officer gave the exact account. His **Majesty, to** verify this report, had **the wagon** emptied, **counted the pieces, and found the number correct;** and in order to assure himself that nothing was left in the wagon, climbed **up into it by** means **of** the **wheel,** holding on to **the spokes.** There was a murmur of approbation and cries **of joy all along the line.** " Bravo ! " **they said ;** " well and **good! that is the** way to **make** sure of not being deceived." All **these** things **conspired to make the** soldiers adore the **Emperor.**

CHAPTER XVI.

Attempt against the life of Napoleon. — Happy sagacity of General Rapp. — Arrest of Frédéric Stabs. — The fanatical student. — Incredible perseverance. — The Duke of Rovigo at the residence of the Emperor. — Stabs questioned by the Emperor. — The Emperor's pity. — Immobility of Stabs. — Stabs and M. Corvisart. — Pardon twice offered and refused. — Emotion of his Majesty. — Condemnation of Stabs. — Fasting four days. — Last words of Stabs.

AT one of the reviews which I have just described, and which usually attracted a crowd of curious people from Vienna and its suburbs, the Emperor came near being assassinated. It was on the 13th of October, his Majesty had just alighted from his horse, and was crossing the court on foot with the Prince de Neuchâtel and General Rapp beside him, when a young man with a passably good countenance pushed his way rudely through the crowd, and asked in bad French if he could speak to the Emperor. His Majesty received him kindly, but not understanding his language, asked General Rapp to see what the young man wanted, and the general asked him a few questions; and not satisfied apparently with his answers, ordered the police-officer on duty to remove him. A sub-officer conducted the young man out of the circle formed by the staff, and drove him back into the crowd. This circumstance had been forgotten, when suddenly the Emperor, on turning, found again near him the pretended suppliant, who had returned holding his right hand in his breast, as if to draw a petition from the pocket of his coat. General Rapp seized the man by the arm, and said to him, "Monsieur, you have already been ordered away; what do you want?" As he was about to retire a second time the general, thinking his appearance suspicious, gave orders to the police-officer to arrest him, and he accordingly made a sign to his subalterns. One of them seizing him by the collar shook him slightly, when his coat became partly unbuttoned, and something fell out resembling a package of papers; on examination it was found to be a large carving-knife, with several folds of gray paper wrapped around it as a sheath; thereupon he was conducted to General Savary.

This young man was a student, and the son of a Protestant minister of Naumbourg; he was called Frédéric Stabs, and was about eighteen or nineteen years old, with a pallid face and effeminate features. He did not deny for an instant that it was his intention to kill the Emperor; but on the contrary boasted of it, and expressed his intense regret that circumstances had prevented the accomplishment of his design.

He had left his father's house on a horse which the want of money had compelled him to sell on the way, and none of his relatives or friends had any knowledge of his plan. The day after his departure he had written to his father that he need not be anxious about him nor the horse; that he had long since promised some one to visit Vienna, and his family would soon hear of him with pride. He had arrived at Vienna only two days before, and had occupied himself first in obtaining information as to the Emperor's habits, and finding that he held a review every morning in the court of the château, had been there once

in order to acquaint himself with the locality. The next
day he had undertaken to make the attack, and had been
arrested.

The Duke of Rovigo, after questioning Stabs, sought
the Emperor, who had returned to his apartments, and
acquainted him with the danger he had just escaped.
The Emperor at first shrugged his shoulders, but having
been shown the knife which had been taken from Stabs,
said, " Ah, ha! send for the young man; I should like very
much to talk with him." The duke went out, and returned
in a few moments with Stabs. When the latter entered,
the Emperor made a gesture of pity, and said to the Prince
de Neuchâtel, " Why, really, he is nothing more than a
child!" An interpreter was summoned and the interroga-
tion begun.

His Majesty first asked the assassin if he had seen him
anywhere before this. " Yes; I saw you," replied Stabbs,
"at Erfurt last year." — "It seems that a crime is nothing
in your eyes. Why did you wish to kill me?"—"To kill
you is not a crime; on the contrary, it is the duty of every
good German. I wished to kill you because you are the
oppressor of Germany."—"It is not I who commenced the
war; it is your nation. Whose picture is this?" (the Emperor held in his hands the picture of a woman that had
been found on Stabs). "It is that of my best friend, my
father's adopted daughter."—"What! and you are an
assassin! and have no fear of afflicting and destroying
beings who are so dear to you?"—"I wished to do my
duty, and nothing could have deterred me from it."—"But
how would you have succeeded in striking me?"—"I
would first have asked you if we were soon to have

peace ; and if you had answered no, I should have stabbed you."—"He is mad!" said the Emperor; "he is evidently mad! And how could you have hoped to escape, after you had struck me thus in the midst of my soldiers?" —"I knew well to what I was exposing myself, and am astonished to be still alive." This boldness made such a deep impression on the Emperor that he remained silent for several moments, intently regarding Stabs, who remained entirely unmoved under this scrutiny. Then the Emperor continued, "The one you love will be much distressed." —"Oh, she will no doubt be distressed because I did not succeed, for she hates you at least as much as I hate you myself."—"Suppose I pardoned you?"—"You would be wrong, for I would again try to kill you." The Emperor summoned *M. Corvisart and said to him*, "This young man is either sick or insane, it cannot be otherwise."—"I am neither the one nor the other," replied the assassin quickly. M. Corvisart felt Stabs's pulse. "This gentleman is well," he said. "I have already told you so," replied Stabs with a triumphant air. "Well, doctor," said his Majesty, "this young man who is in such good health has traveled a hundred miles to assassinate me."

Notwithstanding this declaration of the physician and the avowal of Stabs, the Emperor, touched by the coolness and assurance of the unfortunate fellow, again offered him his pardon, upon the sole condition of expressing some repentance for his crime; but as Stabs again asserted that his only regret was that he had not succeeded in his undertaking, the Emperor reluctantly gave him up to punishment.

After he was conducted to prison, as he still persisted

in his assertions, he was immediately brought before a military commission, which condemned him to death. He did not undergo his punishment till the 17th; and after the 13th, the day on which he was arrested, took no food, saying that he would have strength enough to go to his death. The Emperor had ordered that the execution should be delayed as long as possible, in the hope that sooner or later Stabs would repent; but he remained unshaken. As he was being conducted to the place where he was to be shot, some one having told him that peace had just been concluded, he cried in a loud voice, " Long live liberty! Long live Germany!" These were his last words.

CHAPTER XVII.

During his stay at Schoenbrunn the Emperor was constantly engaged in gallant adventures. He was one day
promenading on the *Prater* in Vienna, with a very numerous suite (the *Prater* is a handsome promenade situated in
the Faubourg Léopold), when a young German, widow of
a rich merchant, saw him, and exclaimed involuntarily to
the ladies promenading with her, "It is he!" This exclamation was overheard by his Majesty, who stopped short,
and bowed to the ladies with a smile, while the one who
had spoken blushed crimson; the Emperor comprehended
this unequivocal sign, looked at her steadfastly, and then
continued his walk.

For sovereigns there are neither long attacks nor great
difficulties, and this new conquest of his Majesty was not
less rapid than the others. In order not to be separated
from her illustrious lover, Madame B —— followed the
army to Bavaria, and afterwards came to him at Paris,
where she died in 1812.

His Majesty's attention was attracted by a charming

young person one morning in the suburbs of Schoenbrunn; and some one was ordered to see this young lady, and arrange for a *rendezvous* at the château the following evening. Fortune favored his Majesty on this occasion. The *éclat* of so illustrious a name, and the renown of his victories, had produced a deep impression on the mind of the young girl, and had disposed her to listen favorably to the propositions made to her. She therefore eagerly consented to meet him at the château; and at the appointed hour the person of whom I have spoken came for her, and I received her on her arrival, and introduced her to his Majesty. She did not speak French, but she knew Italian well, and it was consequently easy for the Emperor to converse with her; and he soon learned with astonishment that this charming young lady belonged to a very honorable family of Vienna, and that in coming to him that evening she was inspired alone by a desire to express to him her sincere admiration. The Emperor respected the innocence of the young girl, had her reconducted to her parents' residence, and gave orders that a marriage should be arranged for her, and that it should be rendered more advantageous by means of a considerable dowry.

At Schoenbrunn, as at Paris, his Majesty dined habitually at six o'clock; but since he worked sometimes very far into the night, care was taken to prepare every evening a light supper, which was placed in a little locked basket covered with oil-cloth. There were two keys to this basket, one of which the steward kept, and I the other. The care of this basket belonged to me alone; and as his Majesty was extremely busy, he hardly ever asked for supper. One evening Roustan, who had been busily occupied all day in his master's service, was in a little room next to the Emperor's, and meeting me just after I had assisted in putting his Majesty to bed, said to me in his bad French, looking at the basket with an envious eye, " I could eat a chicken wing myself; I am very hungry." I refused at first; but finally, as I knew that the Emperor had gone to bed, and had no idea he would take a fancy to ask me for supper that evening, I let Roustan have it. He, much delighted, began with a leg, and next took a wing; and I do not know if any of the chicken would have been left had I not suddenly heard the bell ring sharply. I entered the room, and was shocked to hear the Emperor say to me, " Constant, my chicken." My embarrassment may be imagined. I had no other chicken; and by what means, at such an hour, could I procure one! At last I decided what to do. It was best to cut up the fowl, as thus I would be able to conceal the absence of the two limbs Roustan had eaten; so I entered proudly with the chicken replaced on the dish, Roustan following me, for I was very willing, if there were any reproaches, to share them with him. I picked up the remaining wing, and presented it to the Emperor; but he refused it, saying to me, " Give me the chicken; I will choose for myself." This time there was no means of saving ourselves, for the dismembered chicken must pass under his Majesty's eyes. " See here," said he, " since when did chickens begin to have only one wing and one leg? That is fine; it seems that I must eat what others leave. Who, then, eats half of my supper?" I looked at Roustan, who in confusion replied, " I was very hungry, Sire, and I ate a wing and leg." — " What, you idiot! so it was you, was it?

Ah, I will punish you for it."   And without another word the Emperor ate the remaining leg and wing.

The next day at his toilet he summoned the grand marshal for some purpose, and during the conversation said, "I leave you to guess what I ate last night for my supper.   The scraps which M. Roustan left.   Yes, the wretch took a notion to eat half of my chicken."   Roustan entered at that moment.   "Come here, you idiot," continued the Emperor; "and the next time this happens, be sure you will pay for it."   Saying this, he seized him by the ears and laughed heartily.

CHAPTER XVIII.

The battle of Essling. — Controversy between two friends of the Emperor. — Aversion of the Duke of Montebello to the Duke of ——. — Rudeness of the Duke of Montebello. — His bitterness on the occasion of the plague at Jaffa. — Presentiments of Marshal Lannes. — A fatal mischance. — Marshal Lannes struck by a cannon-ball. — The Emperor's grief. — The Emperor on his knees before the marshal. — Heroic courage of Marshal Lannes. — His death caused, perhaps, by a fast of twenty-four hours. — The Emperor's affliction. — Tears of the old grenadiers. — Last words of the marshal. — The corpse embalmed. — A horrible spectacle. — Courage of physicians in the army. — Grief of the Duchess of Montebello. — Thoughtlessness of the Emperor. — The Duchess of Montebello wishes to quit the service of the Empress.

On the 22d of May, ten days after the triumphant entry of the Emperor into the Austrian capital, the battle of Essling took place, a bloody combat lasting from four in the morning till six in the evening. This battle was sadly memorable to all the old soldiers of the Empire, since it cost the life of perhaps the bravest of them all, — the Duke of Montebello, the devoted friend of the Emperor, the only one who shared with Marshal Augereau the right to speak to him frankly face to face.

The evening before the battle the marshal entered his Majesty's residence, and found him surrounded by several persons. The Duke of —— always undertook to place himself between the Emperor and persons who wished to speak with him. The Duke of Montebello, seeing him play his usual game, took him by the lappel of his coat, and, wheeling him around, said to him : "Take yourself away from here! The Emperor does not need you to stand guard. It is singular that on the field of battle you are always so far from us that we cannot see you, while here we can say nothing to the Emperor without your being in the way." The duke was furious. He looked first at the marshal, then at the Emperor, who simply said, "Gently Lannes."

That evening in the domestic apartments they were discussing this apostrophe of the marshal's. An officer of the army of Egypt said that he was not surprised, since the Duke of Montebello had never forgiven the Duke of —— for the three hundred sick persons poisoned at Jaffa.

Dr. Lannefranque, one of those who attended the unfortunate Duke of Montebello, said that as he was mounting his horse on starting to the island of Lobau, the duke was possessed by gloomy presentiments. He paused a moment, took M. Lannefranque's hand, and pressed it, saying to him with a sad smile, "*Au revoir;* you will soon see us again, perhaps. There will be work for you and for those gentlemen to-day," pointing to several surgeons and doctors standing near. "M. le Duc," replied Lannefranque, "this day will add yet more to your glory." — "My glory," interrupted the marshal eagerly; "do you wish me to speak frankly? I do not approve very highly of this affair; and, moreover, whatever may be the issue, this will be my last battle." The doctor wished to ask the marshal his reasons for this conviction; but he set off at a gallop, and was soon out of sight.

On the morning of the battle, about six or seven o'clock, the Austrians had already advanced, when an *aide-de-camp* came to announce to his Majesty that a sudden rise in the

Danube had washed down a great number of large trees which had been cut down when Vienna was taken, and that these trees had driven against and broken the bridges which served as communication between Essling and the island of Lobau; and in consequence of this the reserve corps, part of the heavy cavalry, and Marshal Davoust's entire corps, found themselves forced to remain inactive on the other side. This misfortune arrested the movement which the Emperor was preparing to make, and the enemy took courage.

The Duke of Montebello received orders to hold the field of battle, and took his position, resting on the village of Essling, instead of continuing the pursuit of the Austrians which he had already begun, and held this position from nine o'clock in the morning till the evening; and at seven o'clock in the evening the battle was gained. At six o'clock the unfortunate marshal, while standing on an elevation to obtain a better view of the movements, was struck by a cannon-ball, which broke his right thigh and his left knee.

He thought at first that he had only a few moments to live, and had himself carried on a litter to the Emperor, saying that he wished to embrace him before he died. The Emperor, seeing him thus weltering in his blood, had the litter placed on the ground, and, throwing himself on his knees, took the marshal in his arms, and said to him, weeping, "Lannes, do you know me?"— "Yes, Sire; you are losing your best friend." — "No! no! you will live. Can you not answer for his life, M. Larrey?" The wounded soldiers hearing his Majesty speak thus, tried to rise on their elbows, and cried, " *Vive l'Empereur!*"

The surgeons carried the marshal to a little village called Ebersdorf, on the bank of the river, and near the field of battle. At the house of a brewer they found a room over a stable where the heat was stifling, and was rendered still more unendurable from the odor of the corpses by which the house was surrounded.

But as no other place could be found, it was necessary to make the best of it. The marshal bore the amputation of his limb with heroic courage; but the fever which came on immediately was so violent that, fearing he would die under the operation, the surgeons postponed cutting off his other leg. This fever was caused partly by exhaustion, for at the time he was wounded the marshal had eaten nothing for twenty-four hours. Finally Messieurs Larrey,[1] Yvan, Paulet, and Lannefranque decided on the second amputation; and after this had been performed the quiet condition of the wounded man made them hopeful of saving his life. But it was not to be. The fever increased, and became of a most alarming character; and in spite of the attentions of these skillful surgeons, and of Doctor Frank, then the most celebrated physician in Europe, the marshal breathed his last on the 31st of May, at five o'clock in the morning, barely forty years of age.

During his week of agony (for his sufferings may be called by that name) the Emperor came often to see him, and always left in deep distress. I also went to see the marshal each day for the Emperor, and admired the patience with which he endured these sufferings, although

[1] Baron Dominique Jean Larrey, eminent surgeon, born at Bagnères-de-Bigorre, 1766. Accompanied Napoleon to Egypt. Surgeon-in-chief of the grand army, 1812. Wounded and taken prisoner at Waterloo. In his will the Emperor styles him the best man he had ever known. Died 1842. — TRANS.

he had no hope; for he knew well that he was dying, and saw these sad tidings reflected in every face. It was touching and terrible to see around his house, his door, in his chamber even, these old grenadiers of the guard, always stolid and unmoved till now, weeping and sobbing like children. What an atrocious thing war seems at such moments!

The evening before his death the marshal said to me, "I see well, my dear Constant, that I must die. I wish that your master could have ever near him men as devoted as I. Tell the Emperor I would like to see him." As I was going out the Emperor entered, a deep silence ensued, and every one retired; but the door of the room being half open we could hear a part of the conversation, which was long and painful. The marshal recalled his services to the Emperor, and ended with these words, pronounced in tones still strong and firm: "I do not say this to interest you in my family; I do not need to recommend to you my wife and children. Since I die for you, your glory will bid you protect them; and I do not fear in addressing you these last words, dictated by sincere affection, to change your plans towards them. You have just made a great mistake, and although it deprives you of your best friend you will not correct it. Your ambition is insatiable, and will destroy you. You sacrifice unsparingly and unnecessarily those men who serve you best; and when they fall you do not regret them. You have around you only flatterers; I see no friend who dares to tell you the truth. You will be betrayed and abandoned. Hasten to end this war; it is the general wish. You will never be more powerful, but you may be more beloved. Pardon these truths in a dying man — who, dying, loves you."

The marshal, as he finished, held out his hand to the Emperor, who embraced him, weeping, and in silence.

The day of the marshal's death his body was given to M. Larrey and M. Cadet de Gassicourt,[1] ordinary chemist to the Emperor, with orders to preserve it, as that of Colonel Morland had been, who was killed at the battle of Austerlitz. For this purpose the corpse was carried to Schoenbrunn, and placed in the left wing of the château, far from the inhabited rooms. In a few hours putrefaction became complete, and they were obliged to plunge the mutilated body into a bath filled with corrosive sublimate. This extremely dangerous operation was long and painful; and M. Cadet de Gassicourt deserves much commendation for the courage he displayed under these circumstances; for notwithstanding every precaution, and in spite of the strong disinfectants burned in the room, the odor of this corpse was so fetid, and the vapor from the sublimate so strong, that the distinguished chemist was seriously indisposed.

Like several other persons, I had a sad curiosity to see the marshal's body in this condition. It was frightful. The trunk, which had been covered by the solution, was greatly swollen; while on the contrary, the head, which had been left outside the bath, had shrunk remarkably, and the muscles of the face had contracted in the most hideous manner, the wide-open eyes starting out of their sockets. After the body had remained eight days in the corrosive sublimate, which it was necessary to renew, since the emanations from the interior of the corpse had decom-

---

[1] Charles Louis Cadet de Gassicourt, born in Paris, 1769, pharmacist, lawyer, and author. Died 1821. — TRANS.

posed the solution, it was put into a cask made for the purpose, and filled with the same liquid; and it was in this cask that it was carried from Schoenbrunn to Strasburg. In this last place it was taken out of the strange coffin, dried in a net, and wrapped in the Egyptian style; that is, surrounded with bandages, with the face uncovered. M. Larrey and M. de Gassicourt confided this honorable task to M. Fortin, a young chemist major, who in 1807 had by his indefatigable courage and perseverance saved from certain death nine hundred sick, abandoned, without physicians or surgeons, in a hospital near Dantzic, and nearly all suffering from an infectious malady. In the month of March, 1810 (what follows is an extract from the letter of M. Fortin to his master and friend M. Cadet de Gassicourt), the Duchess of Montebello, in passing through Strasburg, wished to see again the husband she loved so tenderly.

"Thanks to you and M. Larrey (it is M. Fortin who speaks), the embalming of the marshal has succeeded perfectly. When I drew the body from the cask I found it in a state of perfect preservation. I arranged a net in a lower hall of the mayor's residence, in which I dried it by means of a stove, the heat being carefully regulated. I then had a very handsome coffin made of hard wood well oiled; and the marshal wrapped in bandages, his face uncovered, was placed in an open coffin near that of General Saint-Hilaire in a subterranean vault, of which I have the key. A sentinel watches there day and night. M. Wangen de Gueroldseck, mayor of Strasburg, has given me every assistance in my work.

"This was the state of affairs when, an hour after her Majesty the Empress's arrival, Madame, the Duchess of

Montebello, who accompanied her as lady of honor, sent M. Crétu, her cousin at whose house she was to visit, to seek me. I came in answer to her orders; and the duchess questioned and complimented me on the honorable mission with which I was charged, and then expressed to me, with much agitation, her desire to see for the last time the body of her husband. I hesitated a few moments before answering her, and foreseeing the effect which would be produced on her by the sad spectacle, told her that the orders which I had received would prevent my doing what she wished; but she insisted in such a pressing manner that I yielded. We agreed (in order not to compromise me, and that she might not be recognized) that I would go for her at midnight, and that she would be accompanied by one of her relatives.

"I went to the duchess at the appointed hour; and as soon as I arrived, she rose and said that she was ready to accompany me. I waited a few moments, begging her to consider the matter well. I warned her of the condition in which she would find the marshal, and begged her to reflect on the impression she would receive in the sad place she was about to visit. She replied that she was well prepared for this, and felt that she had the necessary courage, and she hoped to find in this last visit some amelioration of the bitter sorrow she endured. While speaking thus, her sad and beautiful countenance was calm and pensive. We then started, M. Crétu giving his arm to his cousin. The duchess's carriage followed at a distance, empty; and two servants followed us.

"The city was illuminated; and the good inhabitants were all taking holiday, and in many houses gay music was inspiriting them to the celebration of this memorable day. What a contrast between this gayety and the quest in which we were engaged! I saw that the steps of the duchess dragged now and then, while she sighed and shuddered; and my own heart seemed oppressed, my ideas confused.

"At last we arrived at the mayor's residence, where Madame de Montebello gave her servants orders to await her, and descended slowly, accompanied by her cousin and myself, to the door of the lower hall. A lantern lighted our way, and the duchess trembled while she affected a sort of bravery; but when she entered a sort of cavern, the silence of the dead which reigned in this subterranean vault, the mournful light which filled it, the sight of the corpse extended in its coffin, produced a terrible effect on her; she gave a piercing scream, and fainted. I had foreseen this, and had watched her attentively; and as soon as I saw her strength failing, supported her in my arms and seated her, having in readiness everything necessary to restore her. I used these remedies, and she revived at the end of a few moments; and we then begged her to withdraw, but she refused; then rose, approached the coffin, and walked around it slowly in silence; then stopping and letting her folded hands fall by her side, she remained for some time immovable, regarding the inanimate figure of her husband, and watering it with her tears. At last she in a measure regained her self-control, and exclaimed in stifled tones through her sobs, 'Mon Dieu, mon Dieu! how he is changed!' I made a sign to M. Crétu that it was time to retire; but we could drag the duchess away only by promising her to bring her back next day,—a promise which could not be kept. I closed the door quickly, and gave my arm to the duchess, which she gratefully accepted. When we left the mayoralty I took leave of her; but she insisted on my entering her carriage, and gave orders to carry me to my residence. In this short ride she shed a torrent of tears; and when the carriage stopped, said to me with inexpressible kindness, 'I shall never forget, Monsieur, the important service you have just rendered me.' "

Long after this the Emperor and Empress Marie Louise visited together the manufacture of Sèvres porcelain, and the Duchess of Montebello accompanied the Empress as lady of honor. The Emperor, seeing a fine bust of the marshal, in bisque, exquisitely made, paused, and, not noticing the pallor which overspread the countenance of the duchess, asked her what she thought of this bust, and if it was a good likeness. The widow felt as if her old wound was reopened; she could not reply, and retired, bathed in tears, and it was several days before she reappeared at court. Apart from the fact that this unexpected question renewed her grief, the inconceivable thoughtlessness the Emperor had shown wounded her so deeply that her friends had much difficulty in persuading her to resume her duties near the Empress.

CHAPTER XIX.

Disasters of the battle of Essling. — Murmurs of **the soldiers.** — Addresses to the generals. — Courageous patience. — Bravery **of Marshal** Masséna. — Continued happiness. — Zeal of **the** army **surgeons.** — **A** word **from** the Emperor. — M. Larrey. — Horse-soup. — Soup made in **their helmets.** — Fortitude of the wounded. — Suicide of a cannoneer. — **The old German** doorkeeper. — Princess Lichtenstein. — Good fare and **dry** linen. — **Insulting letter to** the Princess Lichtenstein. — The Emperor furious. — The **Emperor's filial piety.** — **Kindness of** Princess **Lichtenstein.** — Pardon **granted by the Emperor.** — M. Larrey's remonstrances. — Two anecdotes **about this celebrated surgeon.**

THE battle of Essling was disastrous in every respect. Twelve thousand Frenchmen were slain; and the source of all this trouble was the destruction of the bridges, which could have been prevented, it seems to me, for the same accident had occurred two or three days before the battle. The soldiers complained loudly, and several corps of the infantry cried out to the generals to dismount and fight in their midst; but this ill humor in no wise affected their courage or patience, for regiments remained five hours under arms, exposed to the most terrible fire. Three times during the evening the Emperor sent to inquire of General Masséna if he could hold his position; and the brave captain, who that day saw his son on the field of battle for the first time, and his friends and his bravest officers falling by dozens around him, held it till night closed in. "I will not fall back," said he, "while there is light. Those rascally Austrians would

be too glad." The constancy of the marshal saved the
day; but, as he himself said, he was always blessed with
good luck. In the beginning of the battle, seeing that
one of his stirrups was too long, he called a soldier to
shorten it, and during this operation placed his leg on his
horse's neck; a cannon-ball whizzed by, killed the soldier,
and cut off the stirrup, without touching the marshal or
his horse. "There," said he, "now I shall have to get
down and change my saddle;" which observation the
marshal made in a jesting tone.

The surgeon and his assistants conducted themselves
admirably on this terrible day, and displayed a zeal equal
to every emergency, combined with an activity which delighted the Emperor so much, that several times, in passing near them, he called them "my brave surgeons." M.
Larrey above all was sublime. After having attended to
all the wounded of the guard, who were crowded together
on the Island of Lobau, he asked if there was any broth to
give them. "No," replied the assistants. "Have some
made," said he, "have some made of that group," pointing
to several horses near him; but these horses belonged to
a general, and when it was attempted to carry out M.
Larrey's orders, the owner indignantly refused to allow
them to be taken. "Well, take mine then," said the
brave soldier, "and have them killed, in order that my
comrades may have broth." This was done; and as no pots
could be found on the island it was boiled in helmets,
and salted with cannon powder in place of salt. Marshal
Masséna tasted this soup, and thought it very good. One
hardly knows which to admire most,—the zeal of the surgeons, the courage with which they confronted danger in

caring for the wounded on the field of battle, and even in the midst of the conflict; or the stoical constancy of the soldiers, who, lying on the ground, some without an arm, some without a leg, talked over their campaigns with each other while waiting to be operated on, some even going so far as to show excessive politeness. " M. Docteur, begin with my neighbor; he is suffering more than I. I can wait."

A cannoneer had both legs carried away by a ball; two of his comrades picked him up and made a litter with branches of trees, on which they placed him in order to convey him to the island. The poor mutilated fellow did not utter a single groan, but murmured, "I am very thirsty," from time to time, to those who bore him. As they passed one of the bridges, he begged them to stop and seek a little wine or brandy to restore his strength. They believed him, and did as he requested, but had not gone twenty steps when the cannoneer called to them, " Don't go so fast, my comrades; I have no legs, and I will reach the end of my journey sooner than you. *Vive la France;* " and, with a supreme effort, he rolled off into the Danube.

The conduct of a surgeon-major of the guard, some time after, came near compromising the entire corps in his Majesty's opinion. This surgeon, M. M——, lodged with General Dorsenne and some superior officers in a pretty country seat, belonging to the Princess of Lichtenstein, the *concierge* of the house being an old German who was blunt and peculiar, and served them with the greatest repugnance, making them as uncomfortable as possible. In vain, for instance, they requested of him linen for the beds and table; he always pretended not to hear.

General Dorsenne wrote to the princess, complaining of this condition of affairs; and in consequence she no doubt gave orders, but the general's letter remained unanswered, and several days passed with no change of affairs. They had had no change of napkins for a month, when the general took a fancy to give a grand supper, at which Rhenish and Hungarian wine were freely indulged in, followed by punch. The host was highly complimented; but with these praises were mingled energetic reproaches on the doubtful whiteness of the napery, General Dorsenne excusing himself on the score of the ill-humor and sordid economy of the *concierge*, who was a fit exponent of the scant courtesy shown by the princess. "That is unendurable!" cried the joyous guests in chorus. "This hostess who so completely ignores us must be called to order. Come, M——, take pen and paper and write her some strong epigrams; we must teach this princess of Germany how to live. French officers and conquerors sleeping in rumpled sheets, and using soiled napkins! What an outrage!" M. M—— was only too faithful an interpreter of the unanimous sentiments of these gentlemen; and under the excitement of the fumes of these Hungarian wines wrote the Princess of Lichtenstein a letter such as during the Carnival itself one would not dare to write even to public women. How can I express what must have been Madame Lichtenstein's horror on reading this production, — an incomprehensible collection of all the low expressions that army slang could furnish! The evidence of a third person was necessary to convince her that the signature, M——, *Surgeon-major of the Imperial French Guard*, was not the forgery of some miserable drunkard. In her profound indignation the princess hastened to General Andreossy,[1] his Majesty's Governor of Vienna, showed him this letter, and demanded vengeance. Whereupon the general, even more incensed than she, entered his carriage, and, proceeding to Schoenbrunn, laid the wonderful production before the Emperor. The Emperor read it, recoiled three paces, his cheeks reddened with anger, his whole countenance was disturbed, and in a terrible tone ordered the grand marshal to summon M. M——, while every one waited in trembling suspense.

"Did you write this disgusting letter?"—"Sire."—"Reply, I order you; was it you?"—"Yes, Sire, in a moment of forgetfulness, after a supper."—"Wretch!" cried his Majesty, in such a manner as to terrify all who heard him. "You deserve to be instantly shot! Insult a woman so basely! And an old woman too. Have you no mother? I respect and honor every old woman because she reminds me of my mother!"—"Sire, I am guilty, I admit, but my repentance is great. Deign to remember my services. I have followed you through eighteen campaigns; I am the father of a family." These last words only increased the anger of his Majesty. "Let him be arrested! Tear off his decorations; he is unworthy to wear them. Let him be tried in twenty-four hours." Then turning to the generals, who stood stupefied and immovable around him, he exclaimed, "Look, gentlemen! read

---

[1] **Count Antoine François Andreossy, born in Languedoc, 1761. Served under Napoleon in Italy and Egypt, and was his Chief of Staff on 18th Brumaire. Ambassador to London, Vienna, and Turkey. Died 1828. —TRANS.**

this ! See how this blackguard addresses a princess, and at
the very moment when her husband is negotiating a peace
with me." [1]

The parade was very short that day; and as soon as it
was ended, Generals Dorsenne and Larrey hastened to Madame Lichtenstein, and, describing to her the scene which
had just taken place, made her most humble apologies, in
the name of the Imperial Guard, and at the same time
entreated her to intercede for the unfortunate fellow, who
deserved blame, no doubt, but who was not himself when
he wrote the offensive epistle. "He repents bitterly, Madame," said good M. Larrey; "he weeps over his fault,
and bravely awaits his punishment, esteeming it a just
reparation of the insult to you. But he is one of the best
officers of the army; he is beloved and esteemed; he has
saved the life of thousands, and his distinguished talents
are the only fortune his family possesses. What will
become of them if he is shot?" — "Shot!" exclaimed the
princess; "shot! *Bon Dieu!* would the matter be carried
as far as that?" Then General Dorsenne described to her
the Emperor's resentment as incomparably deeper than her
own; and the princess, much moved, immediately wrote
the Emperor a letter, in which she expressed herself as
grateful, and fully satisfied with the reparation which
had already been made, and entreated him to pardon
M. M——.

His Majesty read the letter, but made no reply. The
princess was again visited; and she had by this time become
so much alarmed that she regretted exceedingly having

---

[1] Prince John Joseph Lichtenstein, born in Vienna, 1760. General and
diplomat. Died 1836. — TRANS.

shown the letter of M. M—— to the general; and, having decided at any cost to obtain the surgeon's pardon, she addressed a petition to the Emperor, which closed with this sentence, expressing angelic forgiveness : " Sire, I am going to fall on my knees in my oratory, and will not rise until I have obtained from Heaven your Majesty's pardon." The Emperor could no longer hold out; he granted the pardon, and M. M—— was released after a month of close confinement. M. Larrey was charged by his Majesty to reprove him most severely, with a caution to guard more carefully the honor of the corps to which he belonged; and the remonstrances of this excellent man were made in so paternal a manner that they doubled in M. M——'s eyes the value of the inestimable service M. Larrey had rendered him.

M. le Baron Larrey was always most disinterested in his kind services, a fact which was well known and often abused. General d'A——, the son of a rich senator, had his shoulder broken by a shell at Wagram; and an exceedingly delicate operation was found necessary, requiring a skilled hand, and which M. Larrey alone could perform. This operation was a complete success; but the wounded man had a delicate constitution, which had been much impaired, and consequently required the most incessant care and attention. M. Larrey hardly ever left his bedside, and was assisted by two medical students, who watched by turns, and assisted him in dressing the wound. The treatment was long and painful, but a complete cure was the result; and when almost entirely recovered, the general took leave of the Emperor to return to France. A pension and decorations canceled the debt of the head of

BERNADOTTE.

the state to him, but the manner in which he acquitted his own towards the man who had saved his life is worthy of consideration.

As he entered his carriage he handed to one of his friends a letter and a little box, saying to this general, "I cannot leave Vienna without thanking M. Larrey; do me the favor of handing to him for me this mark of my gratitude. Good Larrey, I will never forget the services he has rendered me." Next day the friend performed his commission; and a soldier was sent with the letter and the present, and, as he reached Schoenbrünn during the parade, sought M. Larrey in the line. "Here is a letter and a box which I bring from General A——." M. Larrey put both in his pocket, but after the parade examined them, and showed the package to Cadet de Gassicourt, saying, "Look at it, and tell me what you think of it." The letter was very prettily written; as for the box, it contained a diamond worth about sixty francs.

This pitiful recompense recalls one both glorious and well-earned which M. Larrey received from the Emperor during the campaign in Egypt. At the battle of Aboukir, General Fugières was operated on by M. Larrey under the enemies' fire for a dangerous wound on the shoulder; and thinking himself about to die, offered his sword to General Bonaparte, saying to him, "General, perhaps one day you may envy my fate." The general-in-chief presented this sword to M. Larrey, after having engraved on it the name of M. Larrey and that of the battle. However, General Fugières did not die; his life was saved by the skillful operation he had undergone, and for seventeen years he commanded the Invalids at Avignon.

CHAPTER XX.

Some reflections on the manners of the officers in the army. — **Military style.**
— The Prince de Neuchâtel. — Generals Bertrand, Bacler **d'Albe, etc.** —
Prince Eugène, Marshals Oudinot, Davoust, Bessières, **Generals Rapp,**
Lebrun, Lauriston, etc. — Affability and dignity. — Foppishness of **the**
jay-birds of the army. — Cartridge-box used as a dressing-case. — Officers
by courtesy. — Officers of the line. — Bravery and modesty. — Real courage
averse to duelling. — Disinterestedness. — Attachment of the officers to
their soldiers. — Breakfast of the grenadiers the day before the battle of
Wagram. — The Emperor's **orders** disregarded. — The Emperor indig-
nant. — The culprit shot. — The dog of the regiment. — Death of General
Oudet at Wagram. — Confidence reposed in Constant by an officer, one of
his friends. — The Philadelphi. — Republican conspiracy against Napoleon. — Oudet chief of **the** conspiracy. — Bravery of this general. — His
mysterious death. — Suicides. — Military breakfast the day after **the bat-**
tle of Wagram. — A bold robbery. — Heroic courage of a Saxon surgeon.

It is not in the presence of the enemy that differences
in the manner and bearing of soldiers can be remarked,
for the requirements of the service completely engross both
the ideas and time of officers, whatever their grade, and
uniformity of occupation produces also a kind of uniformity of habit and character; but, in the monotonous
life of the camp, differences due to nature and education reassert themselves. I noted this many times after
the truces and treaties of peace which crowned the most
glorious campaigns of the Emperor, and had occasion to
renew my observations on this point during the long so-
journ which we made at Schoenbrunn with the army.
Military tone in the army is a most difficult thing to define,
and differs according to rank, time of service, and kind

of service; and there are no genuine soldiers except those who form part of the line, or who command it. In the soldiers' opinion, the Prince de Neuchâtel and his brilliant staff, the grand marshal, Generals Bertrand, Bacler d'Albe,[1] etc., were only men of the cabinet council, whose experience might be of some use in such deliberations, but to whom bravery was not indispensable.

The chief generals, such as Prince Eugène, Marshals Oudinot, Davoust, Bessières, and his Majesty's *aides-de-camp*, Rapp, Lebrun, Lauriston, Mouton, etc., were exceedingly affable, and every one was most politely received by them; their dignity never became haughtiness, nor their ease an excessive familiarity, though their manners were at all times slightly tinged by the austerity inseparable from the character of a warrior. This was not the idea held in the army in regard to a few of the ordnance and staff officers (*aides-de-camp*); for, while according them all the consideration due both to their education and their courage, they called them the *jay-birds of the army;* receiving favors which others deserved; obtaining cordons and promotions for carrying a few letters into camp, often without having even seen the enemy; insulting by their luxury the modest temperance of the braver officers; and more foppish in the midst of their battalions than in the boudoirs of their mistresses. The silver-gilt box of one of these gentlemen was a complete portable dressing-case, and contained, instead of cartridges, essence bottles, brushes, a mirror, a tongue-scraper, a shell-comb,

---

[1] Louis Albert Bacler d'Albe, general of brigade and chief of topographical engineers, also a painter, born at St. Pol, 1762; distinguished himself at Arcola; died 1824. — TRANS.

and—I do not know that it lacked even a pot of rouge. It could not be said that they were not brave, for they would allow themselves to be killed for a glance; but they were very rarely exposed to danger. Foreigners would be right in maintaining the assertion that the French soldier is frivolous, presumptuous, impertinent, and immoral, if they formed their judgment alone from these officers by courtesy, who, in place of study and faithful service, had often no other title to their rank than the merit of having emigrated.

The officers of the line, who had served in several campaigns and had gained their epaulettes on the field of battle, held a very different position in the army. Always grave, polite, and considerate, there was a kind of fraternity among them; and having known suffering and misery themselves, they were always ready to help others; and their conversation, though not distinguished by brilliant information, was often full of interest. In nearly every case boasting quitted them with their youth, and the bravest were always the most modest. Influenced by no imaginary points of honor, they estimated themselves at their real worth; and all fear of being suspected of cowardice was beneath them. With these brave soldiers, who often united to the greatest kindness of heart a mettle no less great, a flat contradiction or even a little hasty abuse from one of their brothers in arms was not obliged to be washed out in blood; and examples of the moderation which true courage alone has a right to show were not rare in the army. Those who cared least for money, and were most generous, were most exposed,— the artillerymen and the hussars, for instance. At Wagram I saw a lieutenant pay a louis for a bottle of brandy, and immediately divide it among the soldiers of his company; and brave officers often formed such an attachment to their regiment, especially if it had distinguished itself, that they sometimes refused promotion rather than be separated from their children, as they called them. In them we behold the true model of the French soldier; and it is this kindness, mingled with the austerity of a warrior, this attachment of the chief to the soldier, which the latter is so capable of appreciating, and an impregnable honor, which serve to distinguish our soldiers from all others, and not, as foreigners think, presumption, braggadocio, and libertinage, which latter are ever the characteristics of the parasites of glory alone.

In the camp of Lobau on the evening before the battle of Wagram, the Emperor, as he was walking outside his tent, stopped a moment watching the grenadiers of his guard who were breakfasting. "Well, my children, what do you think of the wine?"—"It will not make us tipsy, Sire; there is our cellar," said a soldier pointing to the Danube. The Emperor, who had ordered a bottle of good wine to be distributed to each soldier, was surprised to see that they were so abstemious the evening before a battle. He inquired of the Prince de Neuchâtel the cause of this; and upon investigation, it was learned that two storekeepers and an employee in the commissary department had sold forty thousand bottles of the wine which the Emperor had ordered to be distributed, and had replaced it with some of inferior quality. This wine had been seized by the Imperial Guard in a rich abbey, and was valued at thirty thousand florins. The culprits were arrested, tried, and condemned to death.

There was in the camp at Lobau a dog which I think all the army knew by the name of *corps-de-garde*. He was old, emaciated, and ugly; but his moral qualities caused his exterior defects to be quickly lost sight of. He was sometimes called the brave dog of the Empire; since he had received a bayonet stroke at Marengo, and had a paw broken by a gun at Austerlitz, being at that time attached to a regiment of dragoons. He had no master. He was in the habit of attaching himself to a corps, and continuing faithful so long as they fed him well and did not beat him. A kick or a blow with the flat of a sword would cause him to desert this regiment, and pass on to another. He was unusually intelligent; and whatever might be the position of the corps in which he was serving, he did not abandon it, or confound it with any other, and in the thickest of the fight was always near the banner he had chosen; and if in the camp he met a soldier from the regiment he had deserted, he would droop his ears, drop his tail between his legs, and scamper off quickly to rejoin his new brothers in arms. When his regiment was on the march he circled as a scout all around it, and gave warning by a bark if he found anything unusual, thus on more than one occasion saving his comrades from ambush.

Among the officers who perished at the battle of Wagram, or rather in a small engagement which took place after the battle had ended, one of those most regretted by the soldiers was General Oudet.[1] He was one of the bravest generals of the army; but what brings his name especially to mind, among all those whom the army lost on that mem-

---

[1] Jacques Joseph Oudet, born at Meynal, 1773, a zealous republican. Killed at Wagram. — TRANS.

orable day, is a note which I have preserved of a conversation I held several years after this battle with an excellent officer who was one of my sincerest friends.

In a conversation with Lieutenant-colonel B—— in 1812, he remarked, "I must tell you, my dear Constant, of a strange adventure which happened to me at Wagram. I did not tell you at the time, because I had promised to be silent; but since at the present time no one can be compromised by my indiscretion, and since those who then had most to fear if their singular ideas (for I can call them by no other name) had been revealed, would now be first to laugh at them, I can well inform you of the mysterious discovery I made at that period.

"You well know that I was much attached to poor F—— whom we so much regretted; and he was one of our most popular and attractive officers, his good qualities winning the hearts of all, especially of those who like himself had an unfailing fund of frankness and good humor. All at once I noticed a great change in his manner, as well as in that of his habitual companions; they appeared gloomy, and met together no more for gay conversation, but on the contrary spoke in low tones and with an air of mystery. More than once this sudden change had struck me; and if by chance I met them in retired places, instead of receiving me cordially as had always been their custom, they seemed as if trying to avoid me. At last, weary of this inexplicable mystery, I took F—— aside, and asked him what this strange conduct meant. 'You have forestalled me, my dear friend,' said he. 'I was on the point of making an important disclosure; I trust you will not accuse me of want of confidence, but swear to me before I confide in you that

you will tell no living soul what I am now going to reveal.
When I had taken this oath, which he demanded of me in
a tone of gravity which surprised me inexpressibly, he
continued, 'If I have not already told you of the *Philadelphi*, it is only because I knew that reasons which I respect would prevent your ever joining them; but since
you have asked this secret, it would be a want of confidence
in you, and at the same time perhaps an imprudence, not to
reveal it. Some patriots have united themselves under the
title of Philadelphi, in order to save our country from the
dangers to which it is exposed. The Emperor Napolèon
has tarnished the glory of the First Consul Bonaparte; he
had saved our liberty, but he has since destroyed it by the
re-establishment of the nobility and by the Concordat. The
society of the Philadelphi has as yet no well-defined plans
for preventing the evils with which ambition will continue
to overwhelm France; but when peace is restored we shall
see if it is impossible to force Bonaparte to restore republican institutions, and meanwhile we are overcome by grief
and despair. The brave chief of the Philadelphi, the pure
Oudet, has been assassinated, and who is worthy to take
his place? Poor Oudet! never was one braver or more
eloquent than he! With a noble haughtiness and an immovable firmness of character, he possessed an excellent
heart. His first battle showed his intrepid spirit. When
cut down at Saint Bartholomew by a ball, his comrades
wished to bear him away, "No, no," cried he; "don't waste
time over me. The Spaniards! the Spaniards!" — "Shall
we leave you to the enemy?" said one of those who had
advanced towards him. "Well, drive them back if you do
not wish me to be left with them." At the beginning of

the campaign of Wagram, he was colonel of the Ninth regiment of the line, and was made general of brigade on the evening before the battle, his corps forming part·of the left wing commanded by Masséna. Our line was broken on this side for a moment, and Oudet made heroic efforts to reform it; and after he had been wounded by three bayonet strokes, with the loss of much blood, and dragged away by those of us who were forced to fall back, still had himself fastened on his horse in order that he might not be forced to leave the battlefield.

"'After the battle, he received orders to advance to the front, and to place himself with his regiment in an advantageous position for observation, and then return immediately to headquarters, with a certain number of his officers, to receive new orders. He executed these orders, and was returning in the night, when a discharge of musketry was suddenly heard, and he fell into an ambush; he fought furiously in the darkness, knowing neither the number nor character of his adversaries, and at break of day was found, covered with wounds, in the midst of twenty officers who had been slain around him. He was still breathing, and lived three days; but the only words he pronounced were those of commiseration for the fate of his country. When his body was taken from the hospital to prepare it for burial, several of the wounded in their despair tore the bandages from their wounds, a sergeant-major threw himself on his sword near the grave, and a lieutenant there blew out his brains. Behold,' said F——, 'a death that plunges us into the deepest despair!' I tried to prove to him that he was mistaken, and that the plans of the Philadelphi were mad, but succeeded very imperfectly; and though he listened to my advice, he again earnestly recommended secrecy."

The day after the battle of Wagram, I think, a large number of officers were breakfasting near the Emperor's tent, the generals seated on the grass, and the officers standing around them. They discussed the battle at length, and related numerous remarkable anecdotes, some of which remain engraven on my memory. A staff-officer of his Majesty said, "I thought I had lost my finest horse. As I had ridden him on the 5th and wished him to rest, I gave him to my servant to hold by the bridle; and when he left him one moment to attend to his own, the horse was stolen in a flash by a dragoon, who instantly sold him to a dismounted captain, telling him he was a captured horse. I recognized him in the ranks, and claimed him, proving by my saddle-bags and their contents that he was not a horse taken from the Austrians, and had to repay the captain the five louis which he had paid to the dragoon for this horse which had cost me sixty."

The best anecdote, perhaps, of the day was this: M. Salsdorf, a Saxon, and surgeon in Prince Christian's regiment, in the beginning of the battle had his leg fractured by a shell. Lying on the ground, he saw, fifteen paces from him, M. Amédée de Kerbourg, who was wounded by a bullet, and vomiting blood. He saw that this officer would die of apoplexy if something was not done for him, and collecting all his strength, dragged himself along in the dust, bled him, and saved his life.

M. de Kerbourg had no opportunity to embrace the one who had saved his life; for M. de Salsdorf was carried to Vienna, and only survived the amputation four days.

CHAPTER XXI.

At Schoenbrunn, as elsewhere, his Majesty marked his presence by his benefactions. I still retain vivid recollections of an occurrence which long continued to be the subject of conversation at this period, and the singular details of which render it worthy of narration.

A little girl nine years old, belonging to a very wealthy and highly esteemed family of Constantinople, was carried away by bandits as she was promenading one day with her attendant outside the city. The bandits carried their two captives to Anatolia, and there sold them. The little girl, who gave promise of great beauty, fell to the lot of a rich merchant of Broussa, the harshest, most severe, and intractable man of the town ; but the artless grace of this child touched even his ferocious heart. He conceived a great affection for her, and distinguished her from his other slaves by giving her only light employment, such as the care of flowers, etc. A European gentleman who lived with this merchant offered to take charge of her education ; to which the man consented, all the more willingly since she had gained his heart, and he wished to make her his wife as soon as she reached a marriageable age. But the European had the same idea ; and as he was young, with an agreeable and intelligent countenance, and very rich, he succeeded in winning the young slave's affection ; and she escaped one day from her master, and, like another Héloïse, followed her Abélard to Kutahié, where they remained concealed for six months.

She was then ten years old. Her preceptor, who became more devoted to her each day, carried her to Constantinople, and confided her to the care of a Greek bishop, charging him to make her a good Christian, and then returned to Vienna, with the intention of obtaining the consent of his family and the permission of his government to marry a slave.

Two years then passed, and the poor girl heard nothing from her future husband. Meanwhile the bishop had died, and his heirs had abandoned Marie (this was the baptismal name of the convert) ; and she, with no means and no protector, ran the risk of being at any moment discovered by some relation or friend of her family — and it is well known that the Turks never forgive a change of religion.

Tormented by a thousand fears, weary of her retreat and the deep obscurity in which she was buried, she took the bold resolution of rejoining her benefactor, and not deterred by dangers of the road set out from Constantinople alone on foot. On her arrival in the capital of Austria, she learned that her intended husband had been dead for more than a year.

The despair into which the poor girl was plunged by this sad news can be better imagined than described. What was to be done? What would become of her? She decided to return to her family, and for this purpose repaired to Trieste, which town she found in a state of great commotion. It had just received a French garrison; but the disturbances inseparable from war were not yet ended, and young Marie consequently entered a Greek convent to await a suitable opportunity of returning to Constantinople. There a sub-lieutenant of infantry, named Dartois, saw her, became madly in love, won her heart, and married her at the end of a year.

The happiness which Madame Dartois now enjoyed did not cause her to renounce her plan of visiting her own family; and, as she now had become a Frenchwoman, she thought this title would accelerate her return to her parents' favor. Her husband's regiment received orders to leave Trieste; and this gave Madame Dartois the opportunity to renew her entreaties to be allowed to visit Constantinople, to which her husband gave his consent, not without explaining to her, however, all she had to fear, and all the dangers to which this journey would again expose her. At last she started, and a few days after her arrival was on the point of making herself known to her family,

when she recognized on the street through her veil, the
Broussan merchant, her former master, who was seeking
her throughout Constantinople, and had sworn to kill her
on sight.

This terrible *rencontre* threw her into such a fright,
that for three days she lived in constant terror, scarcely
daring to venture out, even on the most urgent business,
and always fearing lest she should see again the ferocious
Anatolian. From time to time she received letters from
her husband, who still marched with the French army; and,
as it was now advancing, he conjured her in his last letters to
return to France, hoping to be able soon to rejoin her there.

Deprived of all hope of a reconciliation with her family,
Madame Dartois determined to comply with her husband's
request; and, although the war between Russia and Turkey
rendered the roads very unsafe, she left Constantinople in
the month of July, 1809.

After passing through Hungary and the midst of the
Austrian camp, Madame Dartois bent her steps towards
Vienna, where she had the sorrow to learn that her husband had been mortally wounded at the battle of Wagram,
and was now in that town; she hastened to him, and he
expired in her arms.

She mourned her husband deeply, but was soon compelled to think of the future, as the small amount of
money remaining to her when she left Constantinople had
been barely sufficient for the expenses of her journey, and
M. Dartois had left no property. Some one having advised
the poor woman to go to Schoenbrunn and ask his Majesty's
assistance, a superior officer gave her a letter of recommen-
dation to M. Jaubert, interpreting secretary of the Emperor.

Madame Dartois arrived as his Majesty was preparing to leave Schoenbrunn, and made application to M. Jaubert, the Duke of Bassano, General Lebrun,[1] and many other persons who became deeply interested in her misfortunes.

The Emperor, when informed by the Duke of Bassano of the deplorable condition of this woman, at once made a special order granting Madame Dartois an annual pension of sixteen hundred francs, the first year of which was paid in advance. When the Duke of Bassano announced to the widow his Majesty's decision, and handed her the first year's pension, she fell at his feet and bathed them with her tears.

The Emperor's *fête* was celebrated at Vienna with much brilliancy; and as all the inhabitants felt themselves obliged to illumine their windows, the effect was extraordinarily brilliant. They had no set illuminations; but almost all the windows had double sashes, and between these sashes were placed lamps, candles, etc., ingeniously arranged, the effect of which was charming. The Austrians appeared as gay as our soldiers; they had not *fêted* their own Emperor with so much ardor, and, though deep down in their hearts they must have experienced a feeling of constraint at such unaccustomed joy, appearances gave no sign of this.

On the evening of the *fête*, during the parade, a terrible explosion was heard at Schoenbrunn, the noise of which seemed to come from the town; and a few moments afterwards a gendarme appeared, his horse in a gallop. "Oh, oh!" said Colonel Mechnem, "there must be a fire at

---

[1] Anne Charles Lebrun, son of the third consul, born in Paris, 1775; *aide-de-camp* of Desaix at Marengo and of Napoleon at Eylau and Wagram; general of division, 1812; became, on the death of his father, Duke of Plaisance, 1824; died 1859. — TRANS.

Vienna, if a gendarme is galloping." In fact, he brought tidings of a very deplorable event. While an artillery company had been preparing, in the arsenal of the town, numerous fireworks to celebrate his Majesty's *fête*, one of them, in preparing a rocket, accidentally set the fuse on fire, and becoming frightened threw it away from him. It fell on the powder which the shop contained, and eighteen cannoneers were killed by the explosion, and seven wounded.

During his Majesty's *fête*, as I entered his cabinet one morning, I found with him M. Charles Sulmetter, commissary general of the police of Vienna, whom I had seen often before. He had begun as head spy for the Emperor; and this had proved such a profitable business that he had amassed an income of forty thousand pounds.

He had been born at Strasburg; and in his early life had been chief of a band of smugglers, to which vocation he was as wonderfully adapted by nature as to that which he afterwards pursued. He admitted this in relating his adventures, and maintained that smuggling and police service had many points of similarity, since the great art of smuggling was to know how to evade, while that of a spy was to know how to seek.

He inspired such terror in the Viennese that he was equal to a whole army-corps in keeping them in subjection. His quick and penetrating glance, his air of resolution and severity, the abruptness of his step and gestures, his terrible voice, and his appearance of great strength, fully justified his reputation; and his adventures furnish ample materials for a romance. During the first campaigns of Germany, being charged with a message from the French government to one of the most prominent persons in the Austrian army, he passed among the enemy disguised as a German peddler, furnished with regular passports, and provided with a complete stock of diamonds and jewelry. He was betrayed, arrested, and searched; and the letter concealed in the double bottom of a gold box was found, and very foolishly read before him. He was tried and condemned to death, and delivered to the soldiers by whom he was to be executed; but as night had arrived by this time, they postponed his execution till morning. He recognized among his guards a French deserter, talked with him, and promised him a large sum of money: he had wine brought, drank with the soldiers, intoxicated them, and disguised in one of their coats, escaped with the Frenchman. Before re-entering the camp, however, he found means to inform the person for whom the letter was intended, of its contents, and of what had happened.

Countersigns difficult to remember were often given in the army in order to attract the soldiers' attention more closely. One day the word was *Périclès, Persépolis;* and a captain of the guard who had a better knowledge of how to command a charge than of Greek history and geography, not hearing it distinctly, gave as the countersign, *perce l'église,* which mistake furnished much amusement. The old captain was not at all angry, and said that after all he was not very far wrong.

The secretary of General Andréossy, Governor of Vienna, had an unfortunate passion for gambling; and finding that he did not gain enough to pay his debts, sold himself to the enemy. His correspondence was seized; he admitted his treachery, and was condemned to death, and in confronting death evinced astonishing self-possession. "Come nearer," said he to the soldiers who were to shoot, "so that you may see me better, and I will have less to suffer."

In one of his excursions in the environs of Vienna, the Emperor met a very young conscript who was rejoining his corps. He stopped him, asked his name, his age, regiment, and country. "Monsieur," said the soldier, who did not know him, "my name is Martin; I am séventeen years old, and from the Upper Pyrenees." — "You are a Frenchman, then?" — "Yes, Monsieur." — "Ah, you are a miserable Frenchman. Disarm this man, and hang him!" — "Yes, you fool, I am French," repeated the conscript; "and *vive l'Empereur!*" His Majesty was much amused; the conscript was undeceived, congratulated, and hastened to rejoin his comrades, with the promise of a reward, — a promise which the Emperor was not slow to perform.

Two or three days before his departure from Schoenbrunn, the Emperor again came near being assassinated. This time the attack was to have been made by a woman.

The Countess —— at this time was well known, both on account of her astonishing beauty and the scandal of her *liaisons* with Lord Paget,[1] the English ambassador.

It would be hard to find words which would truthfully describe the grace and charms of this lady, whom the best society of Vienna admitted only with the greatest repugnance, but who consoled herself for their scorn by receiving at her own house the most brilliant part of the French army.

---

[1] Henry William Paget, afterward Lord **Anglesey**, British statesman and general, born 1768, served in Holland and Spain, lost his leg at Waterloo, died 1854. — Trans.

An army contractor conceived the idea of procuring this lady for the Emperor, and, without informing his Majesty, made propositions to the countess through one of his friends, a cavalry officer attached to the military police of the town of Vienna.

The cavalry officer thought he was representing his Majesty, and in good faith said to the countess that his Majesty was exceedingly anxious to see her at Schoenbrunn. One morning, accordingly, he made propositions for that evening, which, appearing somewhat abrupt to the countess, she did not decide at once, but demanded a day for reflection, adding that she must have good proof that the Emperor was really sincere in this matter. The officer protested his sincerity, promised, moreover, to give every proof she required, and made an appointment for that evening. Having given the contractor an account of his negotiation, the latter gave orders that a carriage, escorted by the cavalry officer, should be ready for the countess on the evening indicated. At the appointed hour the officer returned to the countess, expecting her to accompany him, but she begged him to return next day, saying that she had not yet decided, and needed the night for longer reflection. At the officer's solicitations she decided, however, and appointed the next day, giving her word of honor to be ready at the appointed hour.

The carriage was then sent away, and ordered for the next evening at the same hour. This time the contractor's envoy found the countess well disposed; she received him gayly, eagerly even, and told him that she had given orders in regard to her affairs as if she were going on a journey; then, regarding him fixedly, said, *tutoying* him, " You may

return in an hour and I will be ready; I will go to him,
you may rely upon it. Yesterday I had business to finish,
but to-day I am free. If you are a good Austrian, you will
prove it to me; you know how much harm he has done
our country! This evening our country will be avenged!
Come for me; do not fail!"

The cavalry officer, frightened at such a confidence
as this, was unwilling to accept the responsibility, and repeated everything at the château; in return for which the
Emperor rewarded him generously, urged him for his own
sake not to see the countess again, and expressly forbade
his having anything more to do with the matter. All
these dangers in no wise depressed the Emperor; and he
had a habit of saying, "What have I to fear? I cannot
be assassinated; I can die only on the field of battle."
But even on the field of battle he took no care of himself, and at Essling, for example, exposed himself like a
chief of battalion who wants to be a colonel; bullets slew
those in front, behind, beside him, but he did not budge.
It was then that a terrified general cried, "Sire, if your
Majesty does not retire, it will be necessary for me to have
you carried off by my grenadiers." This anecdote proves
whether the Emperor took any precautions in regard to
himself. The signs of exasperation manifested by the inhabitants of Vienna made him very watchful, however, for
the safety of his troops, and he expressly forbade their
leaving their cantonments in the evening. His Majesty
was afraid for them.

The château of Schoenbrunn was the *rendezvous* of all
the illustrious savants of Germany; and no new work, no
curious invention, appeared, but the Emperor immediately

gave orders to have the author presented to him. It was thus that M. Maelzel, the famous inventor of metronomy, was allowed the honor of exhibiting before his Majesty several of his own inventions. The Emperor admired the artificial limbs intended to replace more comfortably and satisfactorily than wooden ones those carried off by balls, and gave him orders to have a wagon constructed to convey the wounded from the field of battle. This wagon was to be of such a kind that it could be folded up and easily carried behind men on horseback, who accompanied the army, such as surgeons, aides, servants, etc. M. Maelzel had also built an automaton known throughout Europe under the name of *the chess-player*, which he brought to Schoenbrunn to show to his Majesty, and set it up in the apartments of the Prince de Neuchâtel. The Emperor visited the Prince; and I, in company with several other persons, accompanied him, and found this automaton seated before a table on which the chessmen were arranged. His Majesty took a chair, and seating himself in front of the automaton, said, with a laugh, "Come, my comrade, we are ready." The automaton bowed and made a sign with his hand to the Emperor, as if to tell him to begin, upon which the game commenced. The Emperor made two or three moves, and intentionally made a wrong one. The automaton bowed, took the piece, and put it in its proper place. His Majesty cheated a second time; the automaton bowed again, and took the piece. "That is right," said the Emperor; and when he cheated a third time, the automaton, passing his hand over the chess-board, spoiled the game.

The Emperor complimented the inventor highly. As

we left the room, accompanied by the Prince de Neuchâtel'
we found in the antechamber **two** young girls, who **pre-**
sented to the prince, in the name of their mother, a basket
of beautiful fruit. As the prince welcomed them with **an**
air of familiarity, the Emperor, curious to find out who they
were, drew near and questioned them; **but they** did not
understand French. Some one then told his Majesty that
these two pretty girls were daughters of a good woman,
whose life Marshal Berthier had saved in **1805.** On this
occasion he was alone on horseback, **the cold** was terrible,
and the ground covered with snow, when he perceived,
lying at the foot of a tree, a woman who appeared to **be**
dying, and had been seized with a stupor. The marshal
took her in his arms, and placed her on his horse with **his**
cloak wrapped around her, and thus conveyed her to her
home, where her daughters were mourning her absence. He
left without making himself **known;** but they recognized
him at the capture **of Vienna, and** every week the two
sisters came to see their benefactor, bringing him flowers
or fruit as a token of their gratitude.

CHAPTER XXII.

Excursion to Raab. — The bishop and Soliman. — M. Jardin's mistake. — Sympathy of the Emperor. — A painful duty. — Chouans of Normandy. — The female brigand. — Heart-rending scene. — Conjugal tenderness. — Despair and madness. — Appointment for a hunt with the Archduke Charles. — Departure from Schoenbrunn. — Arrival at Passau. — The widow of a German physician. — Terror of the inhabitants of Augsburg. — Kindness of General Lecourbe. — A grenadier's act of humanity. — Maternal despair and joy. — The Emperor's rapid journey. — Arrival at Fontainebleau. — The Emperor's ill-humor. — The Emperor's partiality for the manufactures of Lyons. — A forced walk of his Majesty. — The Emperor's harsh welcome to the Empress. — Josephine's tears. — The Emperor's reparation.

TOWARDS the end of September the Emperor made a journey to Raab; and, as he was mounting his horse to return to his residence at Schoenbrunn, he saw the bishop a few steps from him. "Is not that the bishop?" said he to M. Jardin, who was holding his horse's head. "No, Sire, it is Soliman." — "I asked you if that was not the bishop," repeated his Majesty, pointing to the prelate. M. Jardin, intent on business, and thinking only of the Emperor's horse which bore the name of Bishop, again replied, "Sire, you forget that you rode him on the last relay." The Emperor now perceived the mistake, and broke into a laugh. I was witness at Wagram of an act which furnished a fine illustration of the Emperor's kindness of heart and consideration for others, of which I have already given several instances; for, although in the one I shall now relate, he was forced to refuse an act of clemency, his very refusal challenges admiration as an exhibition of the generosity and greatness of his soul.

A very rich woman, named Madame de Combray, who lived near Caen, allowed her château to be occupied by a band of royalists, who seemed to think they upheld their cause worthily by robbing diligences on the highway. She constituted herself treasurer of this band of partisans, and consigned the funds thus obtained to a pretended treasurer of Louis XVIII. Her daughter, Madame Aquet, joined this troop, and, dressed in men's clothing, showed most conspicuous bravery. Their exploits, however, were not of long duration; and pursued and overcome by superior forces, they were brought to trial, and Madame Aquet was condemned to death with her accomplices. By means of a pretended illness she obtained a reprieve, of which she availed herself to employ every means in her power to obtain a pardon, and finally, after eight months of useless supplications, decided to send her children to Germany to intercede with the Emperor. Her physician, accompanied by her sister and two daughters, reached Schoenbrunn just as the Emperor had gone to visit the field of Wagram, and for an entire day awaited the Emperor's return on the steps of the palace; and these children, one ten, the other twelve, years old, excited much interest. Notwithstanding this, their mother's crime was a terrible one; for although in political matters opinions may not be criminal, yet under every form of government opinions are punished, if thereby one becomes a robber and an assassin. The children, clothed in black, threw themselves at the Emperor's feet, crying, "Pardon, pardon, restore to us our mother." The Emperor raised them tenderly, took the petition from the hands of the aunt, read every word attentively, then questioned the physician with much interest, looked at the children, hesitated — but just as I, with all who witnessed this touching scene, thought he was going to pronounce her pardon, he recoiled several steps, exclaiming, "I cannot do it!" His changing color, eyes suffused with tears, and choking voice, gave evidence of the struggle through which he was passing; and witnessing this, his refusal appeared to me an act of sublime courage.

Following upon the remembrance of these violent crimes, so much the more worthy of condemnation since they were the work of a woman, who, in order to abandon herself to them, was forced to begin by trampling under foot all the gentle and modest virtues of her sex, I find recorded in my notes an act of fidelity and conjugal tenderness which well deserved a better result. The wife of an infantry colonel, unwilling to be parted from her husband, followed the march of his regiment in a coach, and on the days of battle mounted a horse and kept herself as near as possible to the line. At Friedland she saw the colonel fall, pierced by a ball, hastened to him with her servant, carried him from the ranks, and bore him away in an ambulance, though too late, for he was already dead. Her grief was silent, and no one saw her shed a tear. She offered her purse to a surgeon, and begged him to embalm her husband's corpse, which was done as well as possible under the circumstances; and she then had the corpse wrapped in bandages, placed in a box with a lid, and put in a carriage, and seating herself beside it, the heart-broken widow set out on her return to France. A grief thus repressed soon affected her mind; and at each halt she made on the journey, she shut herself up with her precious burden, drew the corpse from its box, placed it on a bed, uncovered its face, and lavished on it the most tender caresses, talking to it as if it was living, and slept beside it. In the morning she replaced her husband in the box, and, resuming her gloomy silence, continued her route. For several days her secret remained unknown, and was discovered only a few days before she reached Paris.

The body had not been embalmed in such a manner as to preserve it long from decay; and this soon reached such a point, that, when she arrived at an inn, the horrible odor from the box aroused suspicion, and the unhappy wife's room was entered that evening, and she was found clasping in her arms the already sadly disfigured corpse of her husband. "Silence," she cried to the frightened innkeeper. "My husband is asleep, why do you come to disturb his glorious rest?" With much difficulty the corpse was removed from the arms of the insane woman who had guarded it with such jealous care, and she was conveyed to Paris, where she afterward died, without recovering her reason for an instant.

There was much astonishment at the château of Schoenbrunn because the Archduke Charles never appeared there; for he was known to be much esteemed by the Emperor, who never spoke of him except with the highest consideration. I am entirely ignorant what motives prevented the prince from coming to Schoenbrunn, or the Emperor from visiting him; but, nevertheless, it is a fact, that, two or three days before his departure from Munich, his Majesty one morning attended a hunting-party, composed of several officers and myself; and that we stopped at a hunting-box

called la Vénerie on the road between Vienna and Bukus-
dorf, and on our arrival we found the Archduke Charles
awaiting his Majesty, attended by a suite of only two persons. The Emperor and the archduke remained for a long
while alone in the pavilion; and we did not return to Schoenbrunn until late in the evening.

On the 16th of October at noon the Emperor left this
residence with his suite, composed of the grand marshal,
the Duke of Frioul; Generals Rapp, Mouton, Savary, Nansouty, Durosnel[1] and Lebrun; of three chamberlains; of
M. Labbé, chief of the topographical bureau; of M. de
Menéval, his Majesty's secretary, and M. Yvan; and accompanied by the Duke of Bassano, and the Duke of Cadore,
then minister of foreign relations.

We arrived at Passau on the morning of the 18th;
and the Emperor passed the entire day in visiting Forts
Maximilian and Napoleon, and also seven or eight redoubts
whose names recalled the principal battles of the campaign.
More than twelve thousand men were working on these
important fortifications, to whom his Majesty's visit was a
fête. That evening we resumed our journey, and two days
after we were at Munich.

At Augsburg, on leaving the palace of the Elector of
Trèves, the Emperor found in his path a woman kneeling
in the dust, surrounded by four children; he raised her up
and inquired kindly what she desired. The poor woman,
without replying, handed his Majesty a petition written in
German, which General Rapp translated. She was the
widow of a German physician named Buiting, who had

---

[1] Antoine Jean Auguste Henri Durosnel, born in Paris, 1771; in 1809
general of division and *aide-de-camp* to Napoleon; peer, 1837; died 1849.

died a short time since, and was **well known in** the army from his faithfulness in ministering to **the** wounded French soldiers when **by** chance any fell into his hands. The Elector of Trèves, and many persons of the Emperor's suite, supported earnestly this petition of Madame Buiting, whom her husband's death had reduced almost to poverty, and in which she besought the **Emperor's** aid **for** the children of this German physician, whose attentions had saved the lives of so many of his brave soldiers. His Majesty gave orders to pay the petitioner the first year's salary of **a pension** which he at once allowed her; and when General Rapp had informed the widow of the Emperor's action, the poor woman fainted with **a** cry of joy.

I witnessed another scene which was equally as touch**ing. When** the Emperor **was** on the march **to Vienna, the** inhabitants of Augsburg, who had been guilty of some acts of cruelty towards the Bavarians, trembled lest his Majesty should take a terrible revenge on them; and this terror was at its height when **it was** learned that a part of the French army was to pass through the town.

A young woman of remarkable beauty, only a few months **a widow, had** retired to this place with her child in the hope of being **more** quiet than anywhere else, but, frightened by the approach of the troops, fled with her child in her arms. But, instead **of** avoiding our soldiers as she intended, she left Augsburg by the wrong gate, and fell **into the** midst **of** the advance **posts** of the French army. Fortunately, she encountered General Lecourbe, and trembling, and almost beside herself with terror, conjured him **on** her knees to **save her** honor, even at the expense of her life, and immediately swooned away. Moved even to tears, the general showed her every attention, ordered a safe-conduct given her, and an escort to accompany her to a neighboring town, where she had stated that several of her relatives lived. The order to march was given at the same instant; and, in the midst of the general commotion which ensued, the child was forgotten by those who escorted the mother, and left in the outposts. A brave grenadier took charge of it, and, ascertaining where the poor mother had been taken, pledged himself to restore it to her at the earliest possible moment, unless a ball should carry him off before the return of the army. He made a leather pocket, in which he carried his young *protégé*, arranged so that it was sheltered from the weather. Each time he went into battle the good grenadier dug a hole in the ground, in which he placed the little one, and returned for it when the battle was over; and though his comrades ridiculed him the first day, they could not but fail to admire the nobility of his conduct. The child escaped all danger, thanks to the incessant care of its adopted father; and, when the march to Munich was again begun, the grenadier, who was singularly attached to the little waif, almost regretted to see the moment draw near when he must restore it to its mother.

It may easily be understood what this poor woman suffered after losing her child. She besought and entreated the soldiers who escorted her to return; but they had their orders, which nothing could cause them to infringe. Immediately on her arrival she set out again on her return to Augsburg, making inquiries in all directions, but could obtain no information of her son, and at last being convinced that he was dead, wept bitterly for him. She had

mourned thus for nearly six months, when the army re-
passed Augsburg; and, while at work alone in her room
one day, she was told that a soldier wished to see her, and
had something precious to commit to her care; but he was
unable to leave his corps, and must beg her to meet him on
the public square. Little suspecting the happiness in store
for her, she sought the grenadier, and the latter leaving the
ranks, pulled the " little good man " out of his pocket, and
placed him in the arms of the poor mother, who could not
believe the evidence of her own eyes. Thinking that this
lady was probably not rich, this excellent man had collected
a sum of money, which he had placed in one of the pockets
of the little one's coat.

The Emperor remained only a short time at Munich;
and the day of his arrival a courier was sent in haste by
the grand marshal to M. de Luçay to inform him that his
Majesty would be at Fontainebleau on the 27th of October,
in the evening probably, and that the household of the
Emperor, as well as that of the Empress, should be at this
residence to receive his Majesty. But, instead of arriving
on the evening of the 27th, the Emperor had traveled
with such speed, that, on the 26th at ten o'clock in the
morning, he was at the gates of the palace of Fontainebleau;
and consequently, with the exception of the grand marshal,
a courier, and the gate-keeper of Fontainebleau, he found
no one to receive him on his descent from the carriage.
This mischance, which was very natural, since it had been
impossible to foresee an advance of more than a day in the
time appointed, nevertheless incensed the Emperor greatly.
He was regarding every one around him as if searching for
some one to scold, when, finding that the courier was pre-

paring to alight from his horse, on which he was more stuck than seated, he said to him: "You can rest to-morrow; hasten to Saint-Cloud and announce my arrival," and the poor courier recommenced his furious gallop.

This accident, which vexed his Majesty so greatly, could not be considered the fault of any one; for by the orders of the grand marshal, received from the Emperor, M. de Luçay had commanded their Majesties' service to be ready on the morning of the next day. Consequently, that evening was the earliest hour at which the service could possibly be expected to arrive; and he was compelled to wait until then.

During this time of waiting, the Emperor employed himself in visiting the new apartments that had been added to the château. The building in the court of the *Cheval-Blanc*, which had been formerly used as a military school, had been restored, enlarged, and decorated with extraordinary magnificence, and had been turned entirely into apartments of honor, in order, as his Majesty said, to give employment to the manufacturers of Lyons, whom the war deprived of any outside market. After repeated promenades in all directions, the Emperor seated himself with every mark of extreme impatience, asking every moment what time it was, or looking at his watch; and at last ordered me to prepare writing materials, and took his seat all alone at a little table, doubtless swearing internally at his secretaries, who had not arrived.

At five o'clock a carriage came from Saint-Cloud; and as the Emperor heard it roll into the court he descended the stairs rapidly, and while a footman was opening the door and lowering the steps, he said to the persons inside:

"Where is the Empress?" The answer was given that her Majesty the Empress would arrive in a quarter of an hour at most. "That is well," said the Emperor; and turning his back, quickly remounted the stairs and entered a little study, where he prepared himself for work.

At last the Empress arrived, exactly at six o'clock. It was now dark. The Emperor this time did not go down; but listening until he learned that it was her Majesty, continued to write, without interrupting himself to go and meet her. It was the first time he had acted in this manner. The Empress found him seated in the cabinet. "Ah!" said his Majesty, "have you arrived, Madame? It is well, for I was about to set out for Saint-Cloud." And the Emperor, who had simply lifted his eyes from his work to glance at her Majesty, lowered them again, and resumed his writing. This harsh greeting distressed Josephine exceedingly, and she attempted to excuse herself; but his Majesty replied in such a manner as to bring tears to her eyes, though he afterwards repented of this, and begged pardon of the Empress, acknowledging that he had been wrong.

CHAPTER XXIII.

Erroneous opinions as to the divorce. — The Emperor's motives. — Tender attentions. — Painful sacrifice. — Courage and resignation of the Empress. — A disappointed guest. — The Emperor's gayety. — The King of Saxony at Fontainebleau. — Friendship of the two monarchs. — Excursion on foot to the bridge of Jena. — The eye of the master. — Compliment of the King of Saxony to his Majesty. — Preoccupation of the Emperor. — Embarrassment of the Emperor and Empress. — Mutual constraint. — Sadness of the stay at Fontainebleau. — The Emperor's dejection. — The 30th of November. — A mournful repast. — A terrible scene. — The Empress faints. — Words uttered by the Emperor. — *Fêtes* given by the city of Paris. — The pitiable condition of the Empress. — Inexpressible enthusiasm. — The Emperor's agitation. — Description of a grand imperial hunt. — Arrival of Prince Eugène. — His despair. — Interview between the Emperor and the vice-king. — Touching words of the Emperor. — Nocturnal visit of Josephine. — Josephine's departure for Malmaison.

IT is not, as has been stated in some Memoirs, because and as a result of the slight disagreement which I have related above, that the first idea of a divorce came to his Majesty. The Emperor thought it necessary for the welfare of France that he should have an heir of his own line; and as it was now certain that the Empress would never bear him one, he was compelled to think of a divorce. But it was by most gentle means, and with every mark of tender consideration, that he strove to bring the Empress to this painful sacrifice. He had no recourse, as has been said, to either threats or menaces, for it was to his wife's reason that he appealed; and her consent was entirely voluntary. I repeat that there was no violence on the part of the

Emperor; but there was courage, resignation, and submission on that of the Empress. Her devotion to the Emperor would have made her submit to any sacrifice, she would have given her life for him; and although this separation might break her own heart, she still found consolation in the thought that by this means she would save the one she loved more than all beside from even one cause of distress or anxiety. And when she learned that the King of Rome was born, she lost sight of her own disappointment in sympathizing with the happiness of her friend; for they had always treated each other with all the attention and respect of the most perfect friendship.

The Emperor had taken, during the whole day of the 26th, only a cup of chocolate and a little soup; and I had heard him complain of hunger several times before the Empress arrived. Peace being restored, the husband and wife embraced each other tenderly, and the Empress passed on into her apartments in order to make her toilet. During this time the Emperor received Messieurs **Decrès** and De Montalivet,[1] whom he had summoned in the morning by a mounted messenger; and about half-past seven the Empress reappeared, dressed in perfect taste. In spite of the cold, she had had her hair dressed with silver wheat and blue flowers, and wore a white satin polonaise, edged with swan's down, which costume was exceedingly becoming. The Emperor interrupted his work to regard her. "I did not take long at my toilet, did I?" said she, smiling; whereupon his Majesty, without replying, showed her the clock,

---

[1] Count Jean Pierre Bachasson de Montalivet, born near Sarreguemines, 1766; counselor of state, 1805; minister of interior, 1809; peer, 1819; died 1823. — TRANS.

then rose, gave her his hand, and was about to enter the dining-room, saying to Messieurs De Montalivet and Decrès, "I will be with you in five minutes." — "But," said the Empress, "these gentlemen have perhaps not yet dined, as they have come from Paris." — "Ah, that is so!" and the ministers entered the dining-room with their Majesties. But hardly had the Emperor taken his seat, than he rose, threw aside his napkin, and re-entered his cabinet, where these gentlemen were compelled to follow him, though much against their inclinations.

The day ended better than it had begun. In the evening there was a reception, not large, but most agreeable, at which the Emperor was very gay, and in excellent humor, and acted as if anxious to efface the memory of the little scene with the Empress. Their Majesties remained at Fontainebleau till the 14th of November. The King of Saxony had arrived the evening before at Paris; and the Emperor, who rode on horseback nearly all the way from Fontainebleau to Paris, repaired on his arrival to the Palace de l'Élysée. The two monarchs appeared very agreeably impressed with each other, and went in public together almost every day, and one morning early left the Tuileries on foot, each accompanied by a single escort. I was with the Emperor. They directed their steps, following the course of the stream, towards the bridge of Jéna, the work on which was being rapidly carried to completion, and reached the Place de la Révolution, where fifty or sixty persons collected with the intention of accompanying the two sovereigns; but as this seemed to annoy the Emperor, agents of the police caused them to disperse. When he had reached the bridge, his Majesty examined the work attentively; and finding some defects in the construction, had the architect called, who admitted the correctness of his observations, although, in order to convince him, the Emperor had to talk for some time, and often repeated the same explanations. His Majesty, turning then towards the King of Saxony, said to him, "You see, my cousin, that the master's eye is necessary everywhere." — "Yes," replied the King of Saxony; "especially an eye so well trained as your Majesty's."

We had not been long at Fontainebleau, when I noticed that the Emperor in the presence of his august spouse was preoccupied and ill at ease. The same uneasiness was visible on the countenance of the Empress; and this state of constraint and mutual embarrassment soon became sufficiently evident to be remarked by all, and rendered the stay at Fontainebleau extremely sad and depressing. At Paris the presence of the King of Saxony made some diversion; but the Empress appeared more unhappy than ever, which gave rise to numerous conjectures, but as for me, I knew only too well the cause of it all. The Emperor's brow became more furrowed with care each day, until the 30th of November arrived.

On that day the dinner was more silent than ever. The Empress had wept the whole day; and in order to conceal as far as possible her pallor, and the redness of her eyes, wore a large white hat tied under her chin, the brim of which concealed her face entirely. The Emperor sat in silence, his eyes fastened on his plate, while from time to time convulsive movements agitated his countenance; and if he happened to raise his eyes, glanced stealthily at the Empress with unmistakable signs of distress. The officers of the household, immovable as statues, regarded

this painful and gloomy scene with sad anxiety; while
the whole repast was simply a form, as their Majesties
touched nothing, and no sound was heard but the regular movement of plates placed and carried away, varied
sadly by the monotonous tones of the household officers,
and the tinkling sound made by the Emperor's striking
his knife mechanically on the edge of his glass. Once
only his Majesty broke the silence by a deep sigh, followed by these words addressed to one of the officers:
"What time is it?" An aimless question of the Emperor's, it seemed, for he did not hear, or at any rate
did not seem to hear, the answer; but almost immediately
he rose from the table, and the Empress followed him
with slow steps, and her handkerchief pressed against her
lips as if to suppress her sobs. Coffee was brought, and,
according to custom, a page presented the waiter to the
Empress that she might herself pour it out; but the Emperor took it himself, poured the coffee in the cup, and
dissolved the sugar, still regarding the Empress, who remained standing as if struck with a stupor. He drank,
and returned the cup to the page; then gave a signal that
he wished to be alone, and closed the door of the saloon.
I remained outside seated by the door; and soon no one
remained in the dining-room except one of the prefects
of the palace, who walked up and down with folded arms,
foreseeing, as well as I, terrible events. At the end of
a few moments I heard cries, and sprang up; just then the
Emperor opened the door quickly, looked out, and saw
there no one but us two. The Empress lay on the floor,
screaming as if her heart were breaking: "No; you will
not do it! You would not kill me!" The usher of the

room had his back turned. I advanced **towards him;** he understood, **and went out.** His Majesty ordered the person who was with **me to** enter, and the door was again closed. I have since learned **that the Emperor requested** him to assist **him in** carrying **the Empress to** her apartment. "She has," **he said,** "**a** violent nervous attack, and her condition requires most prompt attention." M. de B—— with **the** Emperor's assistance raised the Empress in his arms; and the Emperor, taking a lamp **from the** mantel, lighted M. **de B——** along the passage from which ascended the little **staircase** leading **to** the apartments of the **Empress.** This staircase was so narrow, **that** a man with such **a burden** could not go down without great risk of falling; and M. de **B——, having called his** Majesty's attention **to this, he summoned** the keeper of the **portfolio,** whose duty it was **to** be always at the door of the Emperor's cabinet which opened on this staircase, and **gave** him the light, which **was no** longer needed, as the lamps had just been lighted. His Majesty passed in front of the keeper, who still held the light, and carrying the feet of the Empress himself, descended the staircase safely with M. de **B——; and they thus reached** the bedroom. The Emperor **rang for** her women, and when they entered, retired **with tears in his eyes and** every sign of **the deepest emotion.** This scene affected him so deeply that he said to M. de **B——** in a trembling, broken tone, some words which he **must never reveal** under any circumstances. **The** Emperor's agitation must **have been** very **great** for **him to** have informed **M. de B——** of the cause of her Majesty's despair, and **to** have told him that the interests of France and of the Imperial Dynasty had done violence to his heart, and the divorce had become a duty, deplorable and painful, but none the less a duty.

Queen Hortense and M. Corvisart soon reached the Empress, who passed a miserable night. The Emperor also did not sleep, and rose many times to ascertain Josephine's condition. During the whole night her Majesty did not utter a word. I have never witnessed such grief.

Immediately after this, the King of Naples, the King of Westphalia, the King of Würtemberg, and the king and princesses of the Imperial family, arrived at Paris to be present at the *fêtes* given by the city of Paris to his Majesty in commemoration of the victories and the pacification of Germany, and at the same time to celebrate the anniversary of the coronation. The session of the legislative corps was also about to open. It was necessary, in the interval between the scene which I have just described and the day on which the decree of divorce was signed, that the Empress should be present on all these occasions, and attend all these *fêtes*, under the eyes of an immense crowd of people, at a time when solitude alone could have in any degree alleviated her sorrow; it was also necessary that she should cover up her face with rouge in order to conceal her pallor and the signs of a month passed in tears. What tortures she endured, and how much she must have bewailed this elevation, of which nothing remained to her but the necessity of concealing her feelings!

On the 3d of December their Majesties repaired to Notre Dame, where a *Te Deum* was sung; after which the Imperial *cortège* marched to the palace of the Corps Législatif, and the opening of the session was held with unusual magnificence. The Emperor took his place amidst inexpressible enthusiasm, and never had his appearance excited such bursts of applause: even the Empress was more cheerful for an instant, and seemed to enjoy these proofs of affection for one who was soon to be no longer her husband; but when he began to speak she relapsed into her gloomy reflections.

It was almost five o'clock when the *cortège* returned to the Tuileries, and the Imperial banquet was to take place at half-past seven. During this interval, a reception of the ambassadors was held, after which the guests passed on to the gallery of Diana.

The Emperor held a grand dining in his coronation robes, and wearing his plumed hat, which he did not remove for an instant. He ate more than was his custom, notwithstanding the distress under which he seemed to be laboring, glanced around and behind him every moment, causing the grand chamberlain continually to bend forward to receive orders which he did not give. The Empress was seated in front of him, most magnificently dressed in an embroidered robe blazing with diamonds; but her face expressed even more suffering than in the morning.

On the right of the Emperor was seated the King of Saxony, in a white uniform with red facings, and collar richly embroidered in silver, wearing a false cue of prodigious length.

By the side of the King of Saxony was the King of Westphalia, Jérôme Bonaparte, in a white satin tunic, and girdle ornamented with pearls and diamonds, which reached almost up to his arms. His neck was bare and white, and he wore no whiskers and very little beard;

MARIE LOUISA.

a collar of magnificent lace fell over his shoulders; and a black velvet cap ornamented with white plumes, which was the most elegant in the assembly, completed this costume. Next him was the King of Würtemberg with his enormous stomach, which forced him to sit some distance from the table; and the King of Naples, in so magnificent a costume that it might almost be considered extravagant, covered with crosses and stars, who played with his fork, without eating or drinking.

On the right of the Empress was Madame Mère, the Queen of Westphalia, the Princess Borghèse, and Queen Hortense, pale as the Empress, but rendered only more beautiful by her sadness, her face presenting a striking contrast on this occasion to that of the Princess Pauline, who never appeared in better spirits. Princess Pauline wore an exceedingly handsome toilet; but this did not increase the charms of her person nearly so much as that worn by the Queen of Holland, which, though simple, was elegant and full of taste.

Next day a magnificent *fête* was held at the Hôtel de Ville, where the Empress displayed her accustomed grace and kind consideration. This was the last time she appeared on occasions of ceremony.

A few days after all these rejoicings, the Vice-king of Italy, Eugène de Beauharnais, arrived, and learned from the lips of the Empress herself the terrible measure which circumstances were about to render necessary. This news overcame him: agitated and despairing, he sought his Majesty; and, as if he could not believe what he had just heard, asked the Emperor if it was true that a divorce was about to take place. The Emperor made a sign in the

affirmative, and, with deep grief depicted on his **counte-**
nance, held out his **hand to** his adopted son. "Sire, allow
me to quit your **service."**—"What!"—"Yes, Sire; the **son .**
of one who **is** no longer Empress cannot remain vice-king.
I wish to accompany my mother to her retreat, and console
her." — "Do you wish **to** leave me, Eugène? You? Ah,
you do not know how imperious are the reasons which force
me to pursue such a course. And if I obtain this son, the
object of my most cherished wishes, this son who is so
necessary to me, who will take my place with him when I
shall be absent? Who will be a father to him when I die?
Who will rear him, and who will make **a** man **of** him?"
Tears filled the Emperor's eyes as he pronounced these
words; he again **took** Eugène's hand, **and** drawing him
to his arms, embraced him tenderly. I did not hear the
remainder of this interesting conversation.

At last the fatal day arrived; it was the 16th cf December. **The** Imperial family were assembled in ceremonial **costume, when the** Empress entered in a simple white
dress, entirely devoid of ornament; she was pale, but
calm, and leaned on the arm of Queen Hortense, who was
equally **as** pale, and much more agitated than her august
mother. The Prince de Beauharnais stood beside the Emperor, and trembled so violently that it was thought he
would fall every moment. When the Empress entered,
Count Regnaud de Saint-Jean d'Angely[1] read the act of
separation.

This was heard in the midst of profound silence, and
the deepest concern was depicted **on** every face. The
Empress appeared calmer than any one else in the assem-

---

[1] Born at St. Fargeau, 1762; counselor of state, 1800; died 1819.—TRANS.

blage, although tears incessantly flowed from her eyes. She was seated in an armchair in the midst of the saloon, resting her elbow on a table, while Queen Hortense stood sobbing behind her. The reading of the act ended, the Empress rose, dried her eyes, and in a voice which was almost firm, pronounced the words of assent, then seated herself in a chair, took a pen from the hand of M. Regnaud de Saint-Jean d'Angely, and signed the act. She then withdrew, leaning on the arm of Queen Hortense; and Prince Eugène endeavored to retire at the same moment through the cabinet, but his strength failed, and he fell insensible between the two doors. The cabinet usher immediately raised him up, and committed him to the care of his *aide-de-camp*, who lavished on him every attention which his sad condition demanded.

During this terrible ceremony the Emperor uttered not a word, made not a gesture, but stood immovable as a statue, his gaze fixed and almost wild, and remained silent and gloomy all day. In the evening, when he had just retired, as I was awaiting his last orders, the door opened, and the Empress entered, her hair in disorder, and her countenance showing great agitation. This sight terrified me. Josephine (for she was now no more than Josephine) advanced towards the Emperor with a trembling step, and when she reached him, paused, and weeping in the most heartrending manner, threw herself on the bed, placed her arms around the Emperor's neck, and lavished on him most endearing caresses. I cannot describe my emotions. The Emperor wept also, sat up and pressed Josephine to his heart, saying to her, "Come, my good Josephine, be more reasonable! Come, courage, courage; I will always be your friend." Stifled by her sobs, the Empress could not reply; and there followed a silent scene, in which their tears and sobs flowed together, and said more than the tenderest expressions could have done. At last his Majesty, recovering from this momentary forgetfulness as from a dream, perceived that I was there, and said to me in a voice choked with tears, " Withdraw, Constant." I obeyed, and went into the adjoining saloon; and an hour after Josephine passed me, still sad and in tears, giving me a kind nod as she passed. I then returned to the sleeping-room to remove the light as usual; the Emperor was silent as death, and so covered with the bedclothes that his face could not be seen.

The next morning when I entered the Emperor's room he did not mention this visit of the Empress; but I found him suffering and dejected, and sighs which he could not repress issued from his breast. He did not speak during the whole time his toilet lasted, and as soon as it was completed entered his cabinet. This was the day on which Josephine was to leave the Tuileries for Malmaison, and all persons not engaged in their duties assembled in the vestibule to see once more this dethroned empress whom all hearts followed in her exile. They looked at her without daring to speak, as Josephine appeared, completely veiled, one hand resting on the shoulder of one of her ladies, and the other holding a handkerchief to her eyes. A concert of inexpressible lamentations arose as this adored woman crossed the short space which separated her from her carriage, and entered it without even a glance at the palace she was quitting forever; the blinds were immediately lowered, and the horses set off at full speed.

CHAPTER XXIV.

Anecdotes anterior to the Emperor's second marriage. — The Empress Josephine's jealousy of Madame Gazani. — The Emperor's interference. — Change of *rôles*. — Madame Gazani attacked by the Emperor and defended by the Empress. — Furnishers shown to the door. — Female conclave surprised by the Emperor. — Milliner sent to Bicêtre. — Great scandal. — The Emperor's indifference. — Audacity of a dressmaker. — The Emperor censured to his face. — Constant's fear. — Precipitate retreat. — The Emperor needing Constant's presence. — The Emperor wishing Constant to write at his dictation. — Constant's refusal. — Special permission to hunt granted to Constant. — Gun given Constant by the Emperor. — The Emperor's preference for the guns of Louis XVI. — Louis XVI. an excellent shot. — Napoleon's opinion of Louis XVI. — Diplomatic breakfasts. — The saloon and family portraits. — Constant's cousin at the theater of Saint-Cloud. — Curiosity and delight. —Provincial prudery. — Constant's cousin on guard against pickpockets at the court theater. — Petitions presented to the Emperor by Constant. — Poor success of petition from the family of Cerf-Berr. — Complete success of Constant's petition for General Lemarrois. — Disgrace of Constant's uncle unintentionally caused by Marshal Bessières. — The marshal's reparation. — A woman's imprudence, and a husband's misfortune.

THE marriage of the Emperor to Marie Louise was the first step in a new career. He flattered himself that it would be as glorious as that he had just brought to a close, but it was to be far otherwise. Before entering on a recital of the events of the year 1810, I shall narrate some recollections, jotted down at random, which, although I can assign them no precise date, were, nevertheless, anterior to the period we have now reached.

The Empress Josephine had long been jealous of the beautiful Madame Gazani, one of her readers, and treated her coldly; and when she complained to the Emperor, he spoke to Josephine on the subject, and requested her to show more consideration for her reader, who deserved it on account of her attachment to the person of the Empress, and added that she was wrong in supposing that there was between Madame Gazani and himself the least *liaison*. The Empress, without being convinced by this last declaration of the Emperor, had nevertheless become much more cordial to Madame Gazani, when one morning the Emperor, who apparently was afraid the beautiful Genoese might obtain some ascendency over her, suddenly entered the Empress's apartment, and said to her, " I do not wish to see Madame Gazani here longer; she must return to Italy." This time it was the good Josephine who defended her reader. There were already rumors of a divorce; and the Empress remarked to his Majesty, " You know well, my friend, that the best means of being rid of Madame Gazani's presence is to allow her to remain with me. Let me keep her, then. We can weep together; she and I understand each other well."

From this time the Empress was a firm friend of Madame Gazani, who accompanied her to Malmaison and Navarre. What increased the kind feelings of the Empress for this lady was that she thought her distressed by the Emperor's inconstancy. For my part, I have always believed that Madame Gazani's attachment to the Emperor was sincere, and her pride must have suffered when she was dismissed; but she had no difficulty in consoling herself in the midst of the homage and adoration which naturally surrounded such a pretty woman.

The name of the Empress Josephine recalls two anecdotes which the Emperor himself related to me. The outrageous extravagance in the Empress's household was a continual vexation to him, and he had dismissed several furnishers of whose disposition to abuse Josephine's ready credulity he had ample proof.

One morning he entered the Empress's apartments unannounced, and found there assembled several ladies holding a secret toilet council, and a celebrated milliner making an official report as to all the handsomest and most elegant novelties. She was one of the very persons whom the Emperor had expressly forbidden to enter the palace, and he did not anticipate finding her there. Yet he made no outburst; and Josephine, who knew him better than any one else, was the only one who understood the irony of his look as he retired, saying, "Continue ladies; I am sorry to have disturbed you." The milliner, much astonished that she was not put rudely out of the door, hastened to retire; but when she reached the last step of the stairs leading to the apartments of her Majesty the Empress, she encountered an agent of the police, who requested her as politely as possible to enter a cab which awaited her in the Court of the Carrousel. In vain she protested that she much preferred walking; the agent, who had received precise instructions, seized her arm in such a manner as to prevent all reply, and she was obliged to obey, and to take in this unpleasant company the road to Bicêtre.

Some one related to the Emperor that this arrest had caused much talk in Paris, and that he was loudly accused of wishing to restore the Bastile; that many persons had visited the prisoner, and expressed their sympathy, and there was a procession of carriages constantly before the prison.

His Majesty took no notice of this, and was much amused by the interest excited in this seller of topknots, as he called her. "I will," said his Majesty on this subject, "let the gossips talk, who think it a point of honor to ruin themselves for gewgaws; but I want this old Jewess to learn that I put her inside because she had forgotten that I told her to stay outside."

Another celebrated milliner also excited the surprise and anger of his Majesty one day by observations which no one in France except this man would have had the audacity to make. The Emperor, who was accustomed, as I have said, to examine at the end of every month the accounts of his household, thought the bill of the milliner in question exorbitant, and ordered me to summon him. I sent for him; and he came in less than ten minutes, and was introduced into his Majesty's apartment while he was at his toilet. "Monsieur," said the Emperor, his eyes fixed on the account, "your prices are ridiculous, more ridiculous, if possible, than the silly, foolish people who think they need your goods. Reduce this to a reasonable amount or I will do it myself." The merchant, who held in his hand the duplicate of his bill, began to explain article by article the price of his goods, and concluded the somewhat long narration with a mild surprise that the sum total was no more. The Emperor, whom I was dressing during all this harangue, could hardly restrain his impatience; and I had already foreseen that this singular scene would end unpleasantly, when the milliner filled up the measure of his assurance by taking the unparalleled liberty of remarking to his Majesty that the sum allowed for her Majesty's toilet was insufficient, and that there were simple citizens' wives

who spent more than that. I must confess that at this
last impertinence I trembled for the shoulders of this imprudent person, and watched the Emperor's movements
anxiously. Nevertheless, to my great astonishment, he contented himself with crumpling in his hand the bill of the
audacious milliner, and, his arms folded on his breast,
made two steps towards him, pronouncing this word only,
" Really!" with such an accent and such a look that the
merchant rushed to the door, and took to his heels without waiting for a settlement.

The Emperor did not like me to leave the château, as
he wished always to have me within call, even when my
duties were over and he did not need me; and I think it
was with this idea of detaining me that his Majesty several
times gave me copying to do. Sometimes, also, the Emperor wished notes to be taken while he was in bed or in
his bath, and said to me, " Constant, take a pen and write;"
but I always refused, and went to summon M. de Méneval.
I have already stated that the misfortunes of the Revolution had caused my education to be more imperfect than it
should have been; but even had it been as good as it is
defective, I much doubt whether I would ever have been
able to write from the Emperor's dictation. It was no easy
thing to fill this office, and required that one should be
well accustomed to it; for he spoke quickly, all in one
breath, made no pause, and was impatient when obliged to
repeat.

In order to have me always at hand, the Emperor gave
me permission to hunt in the Park of Saint-Cloud, and was
kind enough to remark that since I was very fond of hunting, in granting me this privilege he was very glad to have

combined my pleasure with his need of me. I was the only person to whom permission was given to hunt in the park. At the same time the Emperor made me a present of a handsome double-barreled gun which had been presented to him at Liège, and which I have still in my possession. His Majesty himself did not like double-barreled guns, and used in preference the simple, small guns which had belonged to Louis XVI., and on which this monarch, who was an excellent gunsmith, had worked, it is said, with his own hands.

The sight of these guns often led the Emperor to speak of Louis XVI., which he never did except in terms of respect and pity. "That unfortunate prince," said the Emperor, "was good, wise, and learned. At another period he would have been an excellent king, but he was worth nothing in a time of revolution. He was lacking in resolution and firmness, and could resist neither the foolishness nor the insolence of the Jacobins. The courtiers delivered him up to the Jacobins, and they led him to the scaffold. In his place I would have mounted my horse, and, with a few concessions on one side, and a few cracks of my whip on the other, I would have reduced things to order."

When the diplomatic corps came to pay their respects to the Emperor at Saint-Cloud (the same custom was in use at the Tuileries), tea, coffee, chocolate, or whatever these gentlemen requested, was served in the saloon of the ambassadors. M. Colin, steward controller, was present at this collation, which was served by the domestics of the service.

There was at Saint-Cloud an apartment which the Emperor fancied very much; it opened on a beautiful avenue

of chestnut-trees in the private park, where he could walk
at any hour without being seen. This apartment was surrounded with full-length portraits of all the princesses of
the Imperial family, and was called the family salon. Their
Highnesses were represented standing, surrounded by their
children; the Queen of Westphalia only was seated. She
had, as I have said, a very fine bust, but the rest of her
figure was ungraceful. Her Majesty the Queen of Naples
was represented with her four children; Queen Hortense
with only one, the oldest of her living sons; the Queen of
Spain with her two daughters; Princess Eliza with hers,
dressed like a boy; the Vice-Queen alone, having no child
at the time this portrait was made; Princess Pauline was
also alone.

The theater and hunting were my chief amusements
at Saint-Cloud. During my stay at this château I received
a visit from a distant cousin whom I had not seen for many
years. All that he had heard of the luxury which surrounded the Emperor, and the magnificence of the court,
had vividly excited his curiosity, which I took pleasure in
gratifying; and he was struck with wonder at every step.
One evening when there was a play at the château, I took
him into my box, which was near the pit; and the view
which the hall offered when filled so delighted my cousin,
that I was obliged to name each personage in order to sat-
isfy his insatiable curiosity, which took them all in succession, one by one. It was a short time before the marriage
of the Emperor to the Archduchess of Austria, and the
court was more brilliant than ever. I showed my cousin
in succession their Majesties, the King and Queen of Westphalia, the King and Queen of Naples, the Queen of

Holland, King of Bavaria, their Highnesses the Grand Duchess of Tuscany, Prince and Princess Borghèse, the Princess of Baden, the Grand Duke of Würzburg, etc., besides the numerous dignitaries, princes, marshals, ambassadors, etc., by whom the hall was filled. My cousin was in ecstasy, and thought himself at least a foot taller from being in the midst of this gilded multitude, and consequently paid no attention to the play, being much more interested in the interior of the hall; and when we left the theater could not tell me what piece had been played. His enthusiasm, however, did not carry him so far as to make him forget the incredible tales that had been related to him about the pickpockets of the capital, and the recommendations which had been made to him on this subject. In the promenades at the theater, in every assemblage whatever, my cousin watched with anxious solicitude over his purse, watch, and handkerchief; and this habitual prudence did not abandon him even at the court theater, for just as we were leaving our box, to mingle with the brilliant crowd which came out of the pit and descended from the boxes, he said to me with the utmost coolness, covering with his hand his chain and the seals of his watch, "After all, it is well to take precautions; one does not know every one here."

At the time of his marriage the Emperor was more than ever overwhelmed with petitions, and granted, as I shall relate farther on, a large number of pardons and petitions.

All petitions sent to the Emperor were handed by him to the *aide-de-camp* on duty, who carried them to his Majesty's cabinet, and received orders to make a report on them the next day; and not even as many as ten times did I find any petitions in his Majesty's pockets, though I always examined them carefully, and even these rare instances were owing to the fact that the Emperor had no *aide-de-camp* near him when they were presented. It is then untrue, as has been so often said and written, that the Emperor placed in a private pocket, which was called the good pocket, the petitions he wished to grant, without even examining them. All petitions which deserved it received an answer, and I remember that I personally presented a large number to his Majesty; he did not put these in his pocket, and in almost every instance I had the happiness of seeing them granted. I must, however, make an exception of some which I presented for the Cerf-Berr brothers, who claimed payment for supplies furnished the armies of the republic; for to them the Emperor was always inexorable. I was told that this was because Messieurs Cerf-Berr had refused General Bonaparte a certain sum which he needed during the campaign of Italy.

These gentlemen interested me deeply in their cause; and I several times presented their petition to his Majesty, and in spite of the care I took to place it in his Majesty's hands only when he was in good humor, I received no reply. I nevertheless continued to present the petition, though I perceived that when the Emperor caught a glimpse of it he always became angry; and at length one morning, just as his toilet was completed, I handed him as usual his gloves, handkerchief, and snuff-box, and attached to it again this unfortunate paper. His Majesty passed on into his cabinet, and I remained in the room attending to my duties, and while busied with these saw the Emperor re-enter, a paper in his hand. He said to me,

"Come, Constant, read this; you will see that you are mistaken, and the government owes nothing to the Cerf-Berr brothers; so say nothing more to me about it; they are regular Arabs." I threw my eyes on the paper, and read a few words obediently; and though I understood almost nothing of it, from that moment I was certain that the claim of these gentlemen would never be paid. I was grieved at this, and knowing their disappointment, made them an offer of services which they refused. The Cerf-Berr brothers, notwithstanding my want of success, were convinced of the zeal I had manifested in their service, and thanked me warmly. Each time I addressed a petition to the Emperor, I saw M. de Méneval, whom I begged to take charge of it. He was very obliging, and had the kindness to inform me whether my demands could hope for success; and he told me that as for the Cerf-Berr brothers, he did not think the Emperor would ever compensate them.

In fact, this family, at one time wealthy, but who had lost an immense patrimony in advances made to the Directory, never received any liquidation of these claims, which were confided to a man of great honesty, but too much disposed to justify the name given him.[1]

Madame Théodore Cerf-Berr on my invitation had presented herself several times with her children at Rambouillet and Saint-Cloud, to beseech the Emperor to do her justice. This respectable mother of a family whom nothing could dismay, again presented herself with the eldest of her daughters at Compiègne. She awaited the Emperor

---

[1] M. de Fermon, counselor of state, director of general liquidation, was usually called "Fermons-la-Caisse."—CONSTANT.

in the forest, and throwing herself in the midst of the horses, succeeded in handing him her petition; but this time what was the result? Madame and Mademoiselle Cerf-Berr had hardly re-entered the hotel where they were staying, when an officer of the secret police came and requested them to accompany him. He made them enter a mean cart filled with straw, and conducted them under the escort of two gens d'armes to the prefecture of police at Paris, where they were forced to sign a contract never to present themselves again before the Emperor, and on this condition were restored to liberty.

About this time an occasion arose in which I was more successful. General Lemarrois, one of the oldest of his Majesty's *aides-de-camp*, a soldier of well-known courage, who won all hearts by his excellent qualities, was for some time out of favor with the Emperor, and several times endeavored to obtain an audience with him; but whether it was that the request was not made known to his Majesty, or he did not wish to reply, M. Lemarrois received no answer. In order to settle the matter he conceived the idea of addressing himself to me, entreating me to present his petition at an opportune moment. I did this, and had the happiness to succeed; and in consequence M. Lemarrois obtained an audience with such gratifying results that a short time after he obtained the governorship of Magdeburg.

The Emperor was absent-minded, and often forgot where he had put the petitions which were handed to him, and thus they were sometimes left in his coats, and when I found them there I carried them to his Majesty's cabinet and handed them to M. de Méneval or M. Fain; and

often, too, the papers for which he was hunting were found
in the apartments of the Empress. Sometimes the Emperor gave me papers to put away, and those I placed in
a box of which I alone had the key. One day there was
a great commotion in the private apartments over a paper
which could not be found. These were the circumstances:
Near the Emperor's cabinet was a small room in which
the secretaries stayed, furnished with a desk, on which
notes or petitions were often placed. This room was
usually occupied by the cabinet usher, and the Emperor
was accustomed to enter it if he wished to hold a private
conversation without being overheard by the secretaries.
When the Emperor entered this room the usher withdrew and remained outside the door; he was responsible
for everything in this room, which was never opened
except by express orders from his Majesty.

Marshal Bessières had several days before presented
to the Emperor a request for promotion from a colonel of
the army which he had warmly supported. One morning
the marshal entered the little room of which I have just
spoken, and finding his petition already signed lying on
the desk, he carried it off, without being noticed by my
wife's uncle who was on duty. A few hours after, the
Emperor wished to examine this petition again, and was
very sure he had left it in this small room; but it was not
there, and it was thought that the usher must have allowed
some one to enter without his Majesty's orders. Search
was made everywhere in this room and in the Emperor's
cabinet, and even in the apartments of the Empress, and
at last it was necessary to announce to his Majesty that
the search had been in vain; whereupon the Emperor gave

way to one of those bursts of anger which were so terrible though fortunately so rare, which terrified the whole château, and the poor usher received orders never to appear in his sight again. At last Marshal Bessières, having been told of this terrible commotion, came to accuse himself. The Emperor was appeased, the usher restored to favor, and everything forgotten; though each one was more careful than ever that nothing should be disturbed, and that the Emperor should find at his finger's end whatever papers he needed.

The Emperor would not allow any one to be introduced without his permission, either into the Empress's apartments or his own; and this was the one fault for which the people of the household could not expect pardon. Once, I do not exactly remember when, the wife of one of the Swiss Guard allowed one of her lovers to enter the apartments of the Empress; and this unfortunate woman, without the knowledge of her imprudent mistress, took in soft wax an impression of the key of the jewel-box which I have already mentioned as having belonged to Queen Marie Antoinette, and, by means of a false key made from this impression, succeeded in stealing several articles of jewelry. The police soon discovered the author of the robbery who was punished as he deserved, though another person was also punished who did not deserve it, for the poor husband lost his place.

CHAPTER XXV.

AFTER his divorce from the Empress Josephine, the Emperor appeared much preoccupied; and as it was known that he thought of marrying again, all persons at the château and in his Majesty's service were greatly concerned about this marriage, though all our conjectures concerning the princess destined to share the Imperial crown proved to be wrong. Some spoke of a Russian princess, while others said the Emperor would marry none but a French woman; but no one thought of an Austrian archduchess. When the marriage had been decided, nothing was spoken of at the court but the youth, grace, and native goodness of the new Empress. The Emperor

was very gay, and paid more attention to his toilet, giving
me orders to renew his wardrobe, and to order better fitting
coats, made in a more modern style. The Emperor also
sat for his portrait, which the Prince de Neuchâtel carried
to Marie Louise; and the Emperor received at the same
time that of his young wife, with which he appeared delighted.

The Emperor, in order to win Marie Louise's affection,
did more undignified things than he had ever done for any
woman. For instance, one day when he was alone with
Queen Hortense and the Princess Stéphanie, the latter mis-
chievously asked him if he knew how to waltz; and his
Majesty replied that he had never been able to go beyond the first lesson, because after two or three turns he
became so dizzy that he was compelled to stop. "When I
was at *l'École Militaire*," added the Emperor, "I tried
again and again to overcome dizziness which waltzing
produced, but I could not succeed. Our dancing-master
having advised us, in learning to waltz, to take a chair
in our arms instead of a lady, I never failed to fall with
the chair, which I pressed so lovingly that it broke; and
thus the chairs in my room, and that of two or three of
my companions, were destroyed, one after the other."
This tale told in the most animated and amusing manner
by his Majesty excited bursts of laughter from the two
princesses.

When this hilarity had somewhat subsided, Princess
Stéphanie returned to the charge, saying, "It really is a
pity that your Majesty does not know how to waltz, for
the Germans are wild over waltzing, and the Empress will
naturally share the taste of her compatriots; she can have

no partner but the Emperor, and thus she will be deprived
of a great pleasure through your Majesty's fault." — "You
are right!" replied the Emperor; "well, give me a lesson, and you will have a specimen of my skill." Whereupon he rose, took a few turns with Princess Stéphanie,
humming the air of the Queen of Prussia; but he could
not take more than two or three turns, and even this he
did so awkwardly that it increased the amusement of these
ladies. Then the Princess of Baden stopped, saying,
"Sire, that is quite enough to convince me that you will
never be anything but a poor pupil. You were made to
give lessons, not to take them."

Early in March the Prince de Neuchâtel set out for
Vienna commissioned to officially request the hand of the
Empress in marriage. The Archduke Charles, as proxy
of the Emperor, married the Archduchess Marie Louise,
and she set out at once for France, the little town of
Braunau, on the frontier between Austria and Bavaria,
having been designated as the place at which her Majesty
was to pass into the care of a French suite. The road
from Strasburg was soon filled with carriages conveying to
Braunau the household of the new Empress, composed of
the following persons: —

The Prince Aldobrandini Borghèse, first equerry, in
place of General Ordener, appointed governor of the château of Compiègne; the Count de Beauharnais, chevalier of
honor.

Lady of honor, Madame de Montebello; lady of attire,
the Countess de Luçay.

Ladies of the palace, Mesdames the Duchess de Bassano and de Rovigo, and Mesdames the Countess de Mont-

morenci, de Mortemart, de Talhouet, de Lauriston, de Duchâtel, de Bouillé, de Montalivet, de Perron, de Lascaris, de Noailles, de Brignolle, de Gentile, and de Canisy (afterwards Duchess of Vicenza[1]).

Most of these ladies had passed from the household of the Empress Josephine into that of Marie Louise.

The Emperor wished to see for himself if the trousseau and wedding presents intended for his new wife were worthy of him and of her, consequently all the clothing and linen were brought to the Tuileries, spread out before him, and packed under his own eyes. The good taste and elegance of each article were equaled only by the richness of the materials. The furnishers and modistes of Paris had worked according to models sent from Vienna; and when these models were presented to the Emperor he took one of the shoes, which were remarkably small, and with it gave me a blow on the cheek in the form of a caress. "See, Constant," said his Majesty, "that is a shoe of good augury. Have you ever seen a foot like that? This is made to be held in the hand."

Her Majesty the Queen of Naples had been sent to Braunau by the Emperor to receive the Empress. Queen Caroline, of whom the Emperor once said that she was a man among her sisters, as Prince Joseph was a woman among his brothers, mistook, it is said, the timidity of Marie Louise for weakness, and thought that she would only have to speak and her young sister-in-law would hasten to obey. On her arrival at Braunau the formal transfer was solemnly made; and the Empress bade farewell to all her Austrian

---

[1] See the recital of the disgrace of Madame de La Rochefoucault.— CONSTANT.

household, retaining in her service only her **first lady of honor**, Madame **de** Lajanski, who had **reared** her and never been absent from **her.** Etiquette required that the household **of** the **Empress should be** entirely French, and the orders of the Emperor **were** very precise in this regard; but **I do not know** whether **it is** true, **as** has been stated, that the Empress had demanded **and** obtained from the Emperor permission to retain for a year this lady **of** honor. However that may be, the Queen of Naples thought it to **her** interest to remove a person whose influence over the mind **of the Empress** she **so much** feared; and as the ladies of the household **of her** Imperial Majesty were themselves eager **to be rid of the rivalry** of Madame de Lajanski, and endeavored **to excite still more** the **jealousy of** her Imperial highness, a positive order was demanded from the Emperor, and Madame **de** Lajanski **was** sent **back** from Munich to **Vienna.** The Empress obeyed without complaint, **but** knowing who had instigated the blow, cherished a **profound** resentment against her Majesty **the** Queen of Naples. The **Empress** traveled **only by** short stages, and was **welcomed by** *fêtes* in each **town through** which she passed. Each day **the Emperor sent her a letter** from his own hand, **and she replied** regularly. The first letters of the Empress were **very** short, and probably cold, for the Emperor said nothing about them; but afterwards **they grew** longer and gradually more affectionate, and the Emperor read them in transports of delight, **awaiting the arrival of** these letters with the impatience **of a** lover twenty years of age, and always **saying the couriers** traveled **slowly,** although they broke down their **horses.**

The Emperor returned from the chase one day holding

in his hands two pheasants which he had himself killed, and followed by footmen bearing in their hands the rarest flowers from the conservatory of Saint-Cloud. He wrote a note, and immediately said to his first page, " In ten minutes be ready to enter your carriage. You will find there this package which you will give with your own hand to her Majesty the Empress, with the accompanying letter. Above all do not spare the horses ; go as fast as possible, and fear nothing. The Duke of Vicenza shall say nothing to you." The young man asked nothing better than to obey his Majesty; and strong in this authority, which gave him perfect liberty, he did not grudge drink money to the postilions, and in twenty-four hours had reached Strasburg and delivered his message.

I do not know whether he received a reprimand from the grand equerry on his return; but if there was any cause for this, the latter would not have failed to bestow it, in spite of the Emperor's assurance to the first page. The Duke of Vicenza had organized and kept in admirable order the service of the stables, where nothing was done except by his will, which was most absolute ; and it was only with the greatest difficulty that the Emperor himself could change an order which the grand equerry had given. For instance, his Majesty was one day *en route* to Fontainebleau, and being very anxious to arrive quickly, gave orders to the outrider who regulated the gait of the horses, to go faster. This order he transmitted to the Duke of Vicenza whose carriage preceded that of the Emperor; and finding that the grand equerry paid no attention to this order, the Emperor began to swear, and cried to the outrider through the door, " Let my carriage pass in front, since those in front will not go on." The outriders and postilions were about to execute this maneuver when the grand equerry also put his head out of the door and exclaimed, "Keep to a trot, the first man who gallops I will dismiss on arriving." It was well known that he would keep his word, so no one dared to pass, and his carriage continued to regulate the pace of the others. On reaching Fontainebleau the Emperor demanded of the Duke of Vicenza an explanation of his conduct. "Sire," replied the duke to his Majesty, "when you allow me a larger sum for the expenses of the stables, you can kill your horses at your pleasure."

The Emperor cursed every moment the ceremonials and *fêtes* which delayed the arrival of his young wife. A camp had been formed near Soissons for the reception of the Empress. The Emperor was now at Compiègne, where he made a decree containing several clauses of benefits and indulgences on the occasion of his marriage, setting at liberty many condemned, giving Imperial marriage dowries to six thousand soldiers, amnesties, promotions, etc. At length his Majesty learned that the Empress was not more than ten leagues from Soissons, and no longer able to restrain his impatience, called me with all his might, "Ohé ho, Constant! order a carriage without livery, and come and dress me." The Emperor wished to surprise the Empress, and present himself to her without being announced; and laughed immoderately at the effect this would produce. He attended to his toilet with even more exquisite care than usual, if that were possible, and with the coquetry of glory dressed himself in the gray redingote he had worn at Wagram; and thus arrayed, the Emperor entered a carriage with the King of Naples. The circumstances of this first meeting of their Imperial Majesties are well known.

In the little village of Courcelles, the Emperor met the last courier, who preceded by only a few moments the carriages of the Empress; and as it was raining in torrents, his Majesty took shelter on the porch of the village church. As the carriage of the Empress was passing, the Emperor made signs to the postilions to stop; and the equerry, who was at the Empress's door, perceiving the Emperor, hastily lowered the step, and announced his Majesty, who, somewhat vexed by this, exclaimed, "Could you not see that I made signs to you to be silent?" This slight ill-humor, however, passed away in an instant; and the Emperor threw himself on the neck of Marie Louise, who, holding in her hand the picture of her husband, and looking attentively first at it, then at him, remarked with a charming smile, "It is not flattered." A magnificent supper had been prepared at Soissons for the Empress and her *cortège;* but the Emperor gave orders to pass on, and drove as far as Compiègne, without regard to the appetites of the officers and ladies in the suite of the Empress.

CHAPTER XXVI.

Arrival of their Majesties at Compiègne. — The Emperor's jealousy. — Injustice done by his Majesty to M. de Beauharnais. — Forgetfulness of ceremonial. — The Emperor's coquetry. — First nocturnal visit of his Majesty to the Empress. — The Emperor's opinion of Germans. — **The** Emperor's gayety. — His devoted attentions to Marie Louise. — Report denied. — Description of the Empress Marie Louise. — Instructions to the Empress. — Comparison between the wives of the Emperor. — Differences **and points** of resemblance **between the two Empresses.** — The **memorial of Saint** Helena. — Preference **of the Emperor for the second wife.** — Economy of the Empress Marie **Louise.** — Her **want of taste.** — **The Emperor an excellent husband. — The Emperor's words contradicted by** Constant. — **Remembrance of Josephine not effaced** by Marie Louise. — Prejudice **of Marie Louise** against **her household** and the Emperor's. — Return of Constant **from** the Russian campaign. — Consideration **of** the Emperor and of Queen Hortense. — Disdainful coldness **of the** Empress. — Excessive consideration of **the** Empress Josephine. — Intrigues among the ladies of the Empress. — Order restored by the **Emperor.** — The Emperor's watchfulness **over the** Empress. — Harshness towards the ladies of the Empress. — Anecdote refuted.

ON their Majesties' arrival at Compiègne, the Emperor presented his hand to the Empress, and conducted her to her apartment. He wished that no one should approach or touch his young wife before himself; and his jealousy was so extreme on this point that he himself forbade the senator de Beauharnais, the Empress's chevalier of honor, to present his hand to her Imperial Majesty, although this was one of the requirements of his position. According to the programme, the Emperor should have occupied a different residence from the Empress, and have slept at the hotel of the Chancellerie; but he did nothing of the sort, since after a long conversation with the Empress, he returned to his room, undressed, perfumed himself with cologne, and wearing only a nightdress returned secretly to the Empress.

The next morning the Emperor asked me at his toilet if any one noticed the change he had made in the programme; and I replied that I thought not, though at the risk of falsehood. Just then one of his Majesty's intimate friends entered who was unmarried, to whom his Majesty, pulling his ears, said, "My dear fellow, marry a German. They are the best wives in the world; gentle, good, artless, and fresh as roses." From the air of satisfaction with which the Emperor said this, it was easy to see that he was painting a portrait, and it was only a short while since the painter had left the model. After making his toilet, the Emperor returned to the Empress, and towards noon had breakfast sent up for her and him, and served near the bed by her Majesty's women. Throughout the day he was in a state of charming gayety, and contrary to his usual custom, having made a second toilet for dinner, wore the coat made by the tailor of the King of Naples; but next day he would not allow it to be put on again, saying it was much too uncomfortable.

The Emperor, as may be seen from the preceding details, loved his new wife most tenderly. He paid her constant attentions, and his whole conduct was that of a lover deeply enamoured. Nevertheless, it is not true, as some one has said, that he remained three months almost without working, to the great astonishment of his ministers; for work was not only a duty with the Emperor, it was both a necessity and an enjoyment, from which no other pleasure, however great, could distract him; and on this occasion, as

on every other, he knew perfectly well how to combine
the duties he owed to his empire and his army with those
due to his charming wife.

The Empress Marie Louise was only nineteen years
old at the period of her marriage. Her hair was blond,
her eyes blue and expressive, her carriage noble, and her
figure striking, while her hand and foot might have served
as models; in fact, her whole person breathed youth,
health, and freshness. She was diffident, and maintained a
haughty reserve towards the court; but she was said to be
affectionate and friendly in private life, and one fact I
can assert positively is that she was very affectionate
toward the Emperor, and submissive to his will. In their
first interview the Emperor asked her what recommendations were made to her on her departure from Vienna.
" To be entirely devoted to you, and to obey you in all
things," which instructions she seemed to find no difficulty
in obeying.

No one could resemble the first Empress less than
the second, and except in the two points of similarity of
temperament, and an extreme regard for the Emperor, the
one was exactly the opposite of the other; and it must be
confessed the Emperor congratulated himself on this dif-
ference, in which he found both novelty and charm. He
himself drew a parallel between his two wives in these
terms : —

" The one [Josephine] was all art and grace; the other
[Marie Louise] innocence and natural simplicity. At no
moment of her life were the manners or habits of the former
other than agreeable and attractive, and it would have been
impossible to take her at a disadvantage on these points;

for it was her special object in life to produce only advantageous impressions, and she gained her end without allowing this effort to be seen. All that art can furnish to supplement attractions was practiced by her, but so skillfully that the existence of this deception could only be suspected at most. On the contrary, it never occurred to the mind of the second that she could gain anything by innocent artifices. The one was always tempted to infringe upon the truth, and her first emotion was a negative one. The other was ignorant of dissimulation, and every deception was foreign to her. The first never asked for anything, but she owed everywhere. The second did not hesitate to ask if she needed anything, which was very rarely, and never purchased anything without feeling herself obliged to pay for it immediately. To sum it all up, both were good, gentle wives, and much attached to their husband." Such, or very nearly these, were the terms in which the Emperor spoke of his Empresses. It can be seen that he drew the comparison in favor of the second; and with this idea he gave her credit for qualities which she did not possess, or at least exaggerated greatly those really belonging to her.

The Emperor granted Marie Louise 500,000 francs for her toilet, but she never spent the entire amount. She had little taste in dress, and would have made a very inelegant appearance had she not been well advised. The Emperor was present at her toilet those days on which he wished her to appear especially well, and himself tried the effect of different ornaments on the head, neck, and arms of the Empress, always selecting something very handsome. The Emperor was an excellent husband, of which he gave proof

in the case of both his wives. He adored his son, and
both as father and husband might have served as a model
for all his subjects; yet in spite of whatever he may have
said on the subject himself, I do not think he loved Marie
Louise with the same devoted affection as Josephine. The
latter had a charming grace, a kindness, an intelligence,
and a devotion to her husband which the Emperor knew
and appreciated at its full value; and though Marie Louise
was younger, she was colder, and had far less grace of manner. I think she was much attached to her husband; but
she was reserved and reticent, and by no means took the
place of Josephine with those who had enjoyed the happiness of being near the latter.

Notwithstanding the apparent submission with which
she had bidden farewell to her Austrian household, it is
certain that she had strong prejudices, not only against
her own household, but also against that of the Emperor,
and never addressed a gracious word to the persons in
the Emperor's personal service. I saw her frequently, but
not a smile, a look, a sign, on the part of the Empress
showed me that I was in her eyes anything more than a
stranger. On my return from Russia, whence I did not
arrive until after the Emperor, I lost no time in entering
his room, knowing that he had already asked for me, and
found there his Majesty with the Empress and Queen Hortense. The Emperor condoled with me on the sufferings
I had recently undergone, and said many flattering things
which proved his high opinion of me; and the queen, with
that charming grace of which she is the only model since
the death of her august mother, conversed with me for
some time in the kindest manner. The Empress alone

kept silence; and noticing this the Emperor said to her, "Louise, have you nothing to say to poor Constant?" —"I had not perceived him," said the Empress. This reply was most unkind, as it was impossible for her Majesty not to have "*perceived*" me, there being at that moment present in the room only the Emperor, Queen Hortense, and I.

The Emperor from the first took the severest precautions that no one, and especially no man, should approach the Empress, except in the presence of witnesses.

During the time of the Empress Josephine, there were four ladies whose only duty was to announce the persons received by her Majesty. The excessive indulgence of Josephine prevented her repressing the jealous pretensions of some persons of her household, which gave rise to endless debates and rivalries between the ladies of the palace and those of announcement. The Emperor had been much annoyed by all these bickerings, and, in order to avoid them in future, chose, from the ladies charged with the education of the daughters of the Legion of Honor in the school at Écouen, four new ladies of announcement for the Empress Marie Louise. Preference was at first given to the daughters or widows of generals; and the Emperor decided that the places becoming vacant belonged by right to the best pupils of the Imperial school of Écouen, and should be given as a reward for good conduct. A short time after, the number of these ladies now being as many as six, two pupils of Madame de Campan were named, and these ladies changed their titles to that of first ladies of the Empress.

This change, however, excited the displeasure of the

ladies of the palace, and again aroused their clamors around the Emperor; and he consequently decided that the ladies of announcement should take the title of *first ladies of the chamber.* Great clamor among the ladies of announcement in their turn, who came in person to plead their cause before the Emperor; and he at last ended the matter by giving them the title of *readers* to the Empress, in order to reconcile the requirements of the two belligerent parties.

These ladies of announcement, or first ladies of the chamber, or readers, as the reader may please to call them, had under their orders six *femmes de chambre*, who entered the Empress's rooms only when summoned there by a bell. These latter arranged her Majesty's toilet and hair in the morning; and the six first ladies took no part in her toilet except the care of the diamonds, of which they had special charge. Their chief and almost only employment was to follow the steps of the Empress, whom they left no more than her shadow, entering her room before she arose, and leaving her no more till she was in bed. Then all the doors opening into her room were closed, except that leading into an adjoining room, in which was the bed of the lady on duty, and through which, in order to enter his wife's room, the Emperor himself must pass.

With the exception of M. de Méneval, secretary of orders of the Empress, and M. Ballouhai, superintendent of expenses, no man was admitted into the private apartments of the Empress without an order from the Emperor; and the ladies even, except the lady of honor and the lady of attire, were received only after making an appointment with the Empress. The ladies of the private apartments were required to observe these rules, and were responsible for their execution; and one of them was required to be present at the music, painting, and embroidery lessons of the Empress, and wrote letters by her dictation or under her orders.

The Emperor did not wish that any man in the world should boast of having been alone with the Empress for two minutes; and he reprimanded very severely the lady on duty because she one day remained at the end of the saloon while M. Biennais, court watchmaker, showed her Majesty a secret drawer in a portfolio he had made for her. Another time the Emperor was much displeased because the lady on duty was not seated by the side of the Empress while she took her music-lesson with M. Paër.

These facts prove conclusively the falsity of the statement that the milliner Leroy was excluded from the palace for taking the liberty of saying to her Majesty that she had beautiful shoulders. M. Leroy had the dresses of the Empress made at his shop by a model which was sent him; and they were never tried on her Majesty, either by him, or any person of her Majesty's household, and necessary alterations were indicated by her *femmes de chambre.* It was the same with the other merchants and furnishers, makers of corsets, the shoemaker, glovemaker, etc.; not one of whom ever saw the Empress or spoke to her in her private apartments.

CHAPTER XXVII.

Religious ceremony of the marriage of their Majesties. — The day after their marriage. — Magnificent *fêtes.* — The temples of glory and of hymen. — Present of the city of Paris to the Empress. — Journey to the departments of the North. — Recollections of Josephine. — Triumph and isolation. — Arrival at Antwerp. — Coolness between the King of Holland and the Emperor. — Mutual distrust in the midst of the *fêtes.* — Rage of the Emperor. — The two sovereigns and the two brothers. — Some traits in the character of Prince Louis. — Error in regard to him. — Boat-race at Flushing. — A storm. — Danger incurred by the Emperor. — Her Majesty's anxiety. — Critical situation of an usher on duty. — A word from the Emperor. — Rapid progress. — Fondness of the Empress for balls and the stage. — Continued festivities. — Burning of the residence of the Prince of Schwartzenberg. — Fortunate presence of mind of the Emperor and the Vice-king of Italy. — The Emperor's words. — The three capitals of the French Empire.

THEIR Majesties' civil marriage was celebrated at Saint-Cloud on Sunday, the 1st of April, at two o'clock in the afternoon. The religious ceremony was solemnized the next day in the grand gallery of the Louvre. A very singular circumstance in this connection was the fact that Sunday afternoon at Saint-Cloud the weather was beautiful, while the streets of Paris were flooded with a heavy shower lasting some time, and on Monday there was rain at Saint-Cloud, while the weather was magnificent in Paris, as if the fates had decreed that nothing should lessen the splendor of the *cortège*, or the brilliancy of the wonderful illuminations of that evening. "The star of the Emperor," said some one in the language of that period, "has borne him twice over equinoctial winds."

On Monday evening the city of Paris presented a scene that might have been taken from the realms of enchantment: the illuminations were the most brilliant I have ever witnessed, forming a succession of magic panorama in which houses, hotels, palaces, and churches, shone with dazzling splendor, the glittering towers of the churches appeared like stars and comets suspended in the air. The hotels of the grand dignitaries of the empire, the ministers, the ambassadors of Austria and Russia, and the Duke d'Abrantes, rivaled each other in taste and beauty. The Place Louis XV. was like a scene from fairyland; from the midst of this Place, surrounded with orange-trees on fire, the eye was attracted in succession by the magnificent decorations of the Champs-Élysées, the Garde Meuble, the Temple of Glory, the Tuileries, and the Corps· Législatif. The palace of the latter represented the Temple of Hymen, the transparencies on the front representing Peace uniting the august spouses. Beside them stood two figures bearing shields, on which were represented the arms of the two empires; and behind this group came magistrates, warriors, and the people presenting crowns. At the two extremities of the transparencies were represented the Seine and the Danube, surrounded by children — image of fecundity. The twelve columns of the peristyle and the staircase were illuminated; and the columns were united by garlands of colored lights, the statues on the peristyle and the steps also bearing lights. The bridge Louis XV., by which this Temple of Hymen was reached, formed in itself an avenue, whose double rows of lamps, and obelisks and more than a hundred columns, each surmounted by a star and connected

by spiral festoons of colored lights, produced an effect
so brilliant that it was almost unendurable to the naked
eye. The cupola of the dome of Saint Geneviève was
also magnificently lighted, and each side outlined by a
double row of lamps. At each corner were eagles, ciphers
in colored glass, and garlands of fire suspended between
torches of Hymen. The peristyle of the dome was lighted
by lamps placed between each column, and as the columns
were not lighted they seemed as if suspended in the air.
The lantern tower was a blaze of light; and all this mass
of brilliancy was surmounted by a tripod representing the
altar of Hymen, from which shot tongues of flame, produced by bituminous materials. At a great elevation
above the platform of the observatory, an immense star,
isolated from the platform, and which from the variety of
many-colored glasses composing it sparkled like a vast
diamond, under the dome of night. The palace of the
senate also attracted a large number of the curious; but
I have already extended too far the description of this
wonderful scene which unfolded itself at every step before us.

The city of Paris did homage to her Majesty the
Empress by presenting her with a toilet set even more
magnificent than that formerly presented to the Empress
Josephine. Everything was in silver gilt, even the armchair and the cheval glass. The paintings on the exquisite
furniture had been made by the first artists, and the elegance and finish of the ornaments surpassed even the richness of the materials.

About the end of April their Majesties set out together
to visit the departments of the North; and the journey was

an almost exact repetition of the one I made in 1804 with the Emperor, only the Empress was no longer the good, kind Josephine. While passing again through all these towns, where I had seen her welcomed with so much enthusiasm, and who now addressed the same adoration and homage to a new sovereign, and while seeing again the châteaux of Lacken, Brussels, Antwerp, Boulogne, and many other places where I had seen Josephine pass in triumph, as at present Marie Louise passed, I thought with chagrin of the isolation of the first wife from her husband, and the suffering which must penetrate even into her retreat, as she was told of the honors rendered to the one who had succeeded her in the Emperor's heart and on the Imperial throne.

The King and Queen of Westphalia and Prince Eugène accompanied their Majesties. We saw a vessel with eighty cannon launched at Antwerp, which received, before leaving the docks, the benediction of M. de Pradt, Archbishop of Malines. The King of Holland, who joined the Emperor at Antwerp, felt most unkindly towards his Majesty, who had recently required of him the cession of a part of his states, and soon after seized the remainder. He was, however, present in Paris at the marriage *fêtes* of the Emperor, who had even sent him to meet Marie Louise; but the two brothers had not ceased their mutual distrust of each other, and it must be admitted that that of King Louis had only too good foundation. What struck me as very singular in their altercations was that the Emperor, in the absence of his brother, gave vent to the most terrible bursts of rage, and to violent threats against him, while if they had an interview they treated each other in the

most amicable **and** familiar and brotherly **manner.   Apart**
they were, the one, Emperor of the French, **the other, King**
of Holland, **with opposite** interests and views; together
they were no more than, if I may be permitted **to so ex-**
press myself, Napoleon and Louis, companions and friends
from childhood.

Prince Louis **was** habitually sad and melancholy.   The
annoyances he experienced on the throne, where **he** had
been placed against his will, added to his domestic troubles,
made him evidently very unhappy, and all who knew him
pitied him **sincerely; for King** Louis was **an** excellent
master, and an honest **man** of much merit.   **It has been**
said that **when the** Emperor **had** decided **on the** union
of **Holland and France, King Louis** resolved to defend
himself in the town of Amsterdam to the last extremity,
and to break the dikes **and inundate** the **whole** country
if necessary, in order to arrest the invasion **of the** French
troops.   I do not **know** whether this is true; but from
what I have seen **of** this prince's **character, I am very sure**
that, while having enough personal **courage to expose his**
own person **to** all the chances **of this** desperate alternative,
his naturally **kind** heart and his **humanity** would have
prevented **the** execution of **this** project.

At Middleburg the Emperor embarked **on board** the
Charlemagne to **visit the** mouth **of** the Scheldt and the
port and island **of Flushing.   During** this excursion **we**
were assailed **by a** terrible tempest, **three** anchors were
broken in **succession; we met with other** accidents, and
encountered great **dangers.**

The Emperor was made **very sick, and every** few moments threw himself **on his** bed, making **violent** but unsuc-

cessful efforts to vomit, which rendered his sickness more distressing. I was fortunate enough not to be at all inconvenienced, and was thus in a position to give him all the attention he required; though all the persons of his suite were sick, and my uncle, who was usher on duty, and obliged to remain standing at the door of his Majesty's cabin, fell over continually, and suffered agony. During this time of torment, which lasted for three days, the Emperor was bursting with impatience. "I think," said he, "that I would have made a pretty admiral."

A short time after our return from this voyage, the Emperor wished her Majesty the Empress to learn to ride on horseback; and for this purpose she went to the riding-hall of Saint-Cloud. Several persons of the household were in the gallery to see her take her first lesson, I among the number; and I noticed the tender solicitude of the Emperor for his young wife, who was mounted on a gentle, well-broken horse, while the Emperor held her hand and walked by her side, M. Jardin, Sr., holding the horse's bridle. At the first step the horse made, the Empress screamed with fright, whereupon the Emperor said to her, "Come, Louise, be brave. What have you to fear? Am I not here?" And thus the lesson passed, in encouragement on one side and fright on the other. The next day the Emperor ordered the persons in the gallery to leave, as they embarrassed the Empress; but she soon overcame her timidity, and ended by becoming a very good horsewoman, often racing in the park with her ladies of honor and Madame the Duchess of Montebello, who also rode with much grace. A coach with some ladies followed the Empress, and Prince Aldobrandini, her equerry, never left her in her rides.

The Empress was at an age in which one enjoys balls and *fêtes;* but the Emperor feared above all things her becoming tired, and consequently rejoicings and amusements were given up at the court and in the city. A *fête* given in honor of their Majesties by the Prince of Schwartzenberg, ambassador from Austria, ended in a frightful accident.

The prince occupied the former Hôtel de la Montesson in the rue de la Chaussée d'Antin; and in order to give this ball had added to this residence a broad hall and wooden gallery, decorated with quantities of flowers, banners, candelabra, etc. Just as the Emperor, who had been present at the *fête* for two or three hours, was about to retire, one of the curtains, blown by the breeze, took fire from the lights, which had been placed too near the windows, and was instantly in flames. Some persons made ineffectual efforts to extinguish the fire by tearing down the drapery and smothering the flames with their hands; but in the twinkling of an eye the curtains, papers, and garlands caught, and the wood-work began to burn.

The Emperor was one of the first to perceive the rapid progress of the fire, and foresee the results. He approached the Empress, who had already risen to join him, and got out with her, not without some difficulty, on account of the crowd which rushed towards the doors; the Queens of Holland, Naples, Westphalia, the Princess Borghèse, etc., following their Majesties, while the Vice-queen of Italy, who was pregnant, remained in the hall, on the platform containing the Imperial boxes. The vice-king, fearing the crowd as much as the fire for his wife, took her out through a little door that had been cut in the platform in order to serve refreshments to their Majesties. No one had thought of this opening before Prince Eugène, and only a few persons went out with him. Her Majesty the Queen of Westphalia did not think herself safe, even when she had reached the terrace, and in her fright rushed into the rue Taitbout, where she was found by a passer-by.

The Emperor accompanied the Empress as far as the entrance of the Champs-Élysées, where he left her to return to the fire, and did not re-enter Saint-Cloud until four o'clock in the morning. From the time of the arrival of the Empress we were in a state of terrible apprehension, and every one in the château was a prey to the greatest anxiety in regard to the Emperor. At last he arrived unharmed, but very tired, his clothing all in disorder, and his face blackened with smoke, his shoes and stockings scorched and burned by the fire. He went directly to the chamber of the Empress to assure himself if she had recovered from the fright she had experienced; and then returned to his room, and throwing his hat on the bed, dropped on a sofa, exclaiming, "Mon Dieu! What a *fête!*" I remarked that the Emperor's hands were all blackened, and he had lost his gloves at the fire. He was much dejected, and while I was undressing him, asked if I had attended the prince's *fête*, and when I replied in the negative, deigned to give me some details of this deplorable event. The Emperor spoke with an emotion which I saw him manifest only two or three times in his life, and which he never showed in regard to his own misfortunes. "The fire," said his Majesty, "has to-night devoured a heroic woman. The sister-in-law of the Prince of Schwartzenberg, hearing from the burning hall cries which she thought were uttered by her eldest daughter, threw herself into the midst of the flames, and the floor, already nearly burned through, broke under her feet, and she disappeared. After all the poor mother was mistaken, and all her children were out of danger. Incredible efforts were made, and at last she was recovered from the flames; but she was entirely dead, and all the attentions of the physicians have been unsuccessful in restoring her to life." The emotion of the Emperor increased at the end of this recital. I had taken care to have his bath in readiness, foreseeing he would need it on his return; and his Majesty now took it, and after his customary rubbing, found himself in much better condition. Nevertheless, I remember his expressing fear that the terrible accident of this night was the precursor of some fatal event, and he long retained these apprehensions. Three years after, during the deplorable campaign of Russia, it was announced to the Emperor one day, that the army-corps commanded by the Prince of Schwartzenberg had been destroyed, and that the prince himself had perished; afterwards he found fortunately that these tidings were false, but when they were brought to his Majesty, he exclaimed as if replying to an idea that had long preoccupied him, " Then it was *he* whom the bad omen threatened."

Towards morning the Emperor sent pages to the houses of all those who had suffered from the catastrophe with his compliments, and inquiries as to their condition. Sad answers were brought to his Majesty. Madame the Princess de la Layen, niece of the Prince Primate, had died from her wounds; and the lives of General Touzart, his wife, and daughter were despaired of, — in fact, they died that same day. There were other victims of this disaster; and among a number of persons who recovered after long-continued sufferings were Prince Kourakin and Madame Durosnel, wife of the general of that name.

Prince Kourakin, always remarkable for the magnificence as well as the singular taste of his toilet, wore at the ball a coat of gold cloth, and it was this which saved his life, as sparks and cinders slipped off his coat and the decorations with which he was covered like a helmet; yet, notwithstanding this, the prince was confined to his bed for several months. In the confusion he fell on his back, was for some time trampled under foot and much injured, and owed his life only to the presence of mind and strength of a musician, who raised him in his arms and carried him out of the crowd.

General Durosnel, whose wife fainted in the ball-room, threw himself in the midst of the flames, and reappeared immediately, bearing in his arms his precious burden. He bore Madame Durosnel into a house on the boulevard, where he placed her until he could find a carriage in which to convey her to his hotel. The Countess Durosnel was painfully burned, and was ill more than two years. In going from the ambassador's hotel to the boulevard he saw by the light of the fire a robber steal the comb from the head of his wife who had fainted in his arms. This comb was set with diamonds, and very valuable.

Madame Durosnel's affection for her husband was equal to that he felt for her; and when at the end of a bloody combat, in the second campaign of Poland, General Durosnel was lost for several days, and news was sent to France that he was thought to be dead, the countess in despair fell ill of grief, and was at the point of death. **A short time after it was** learned that the general was badly but **not** mortally wounded, **and that** he had been found, **and his wounds would** quickly **heal.** When Madame Durosnel **received this** happy **news her** joy amounted almost to delirium; and in the court of her hotel she made a pile of her mourning clothes **and those of her people, set** fire to them, and saw this gloomy pile turn to ashes amid wild transports **of joy** and delight.

Two days after the burning of the hotel of the Prince of Schwartzenberg,[1] the Emperor received the **news of** the abdication of his **brother** Louis, by which event his Majesty seemed at first much chagrined, and said to some one who entered **his room just** as he had been **informed of it, "I foresaw this madness** of Louis, but I did **not** think he **would** be in such haste." Nevertheless, the Emperor soon decided what course to take; **and** a few days afterwards his Majesty, who during the toilet had not opened his mouth, came suddenly out of his preoccupation just as I handed him his coat, and gave me two or three of his familiar taps. "Monsieur Constant," said he, " do you know what are the three capitals of the **French** Empire?" and without giving me time to answer, the Emperor continued, " Paris, Rome, and Amsterdam. **That sounds** well, does it not?"

---

[1] Prince Karl Philipp von Schwartzenberg, an Austrian field-marshal, born **at Vienna,** 1771. Commanded the Austrian forces under Napoleon in the **Russian** campaign, and was commander-in-chief of the allied army against **him in** 1813 and 1814. He was several **times** ambassador, and negotiated the **marriage** of Marie Louise. Died 1820. — TRANS.

CHAPTER XXVIII.

IN the latter part of July large crowds visited the Church of the Hôtel des Invalides, in which were placed the remains of General Saint-Hilaire and the Duke de Montebello, the remains of the marshal being placed near the tomb of Turenne. The mornings were spent in the celebration of several masses, at a double altar which was raised between the nave and the dome; and for four days there floated from the spire of the dome a long black banner or flag edged with white.

The day the remains of the marshal were removed from the Invalides to the Pantheon, I was sent from Saint-Cloud to Paris with a special message for the Emperor. After this duty was attended to, I still had a short time of leisure, of which I availed myself to witness the sad ceremony and bid a last adieu to the brave warrior whose death I had witnessed. At noon all the civil and military authorities assembled at the Invalides; and the body was transferred from the dome into the church, and placed on a catafalque in the shape of a great Egyptian pyramid, raised on an elevated platform, and approached through four large arches, the posts of which were entwined with garlands of laurels interlaced with cypress. At the corners were statues in the attitude of grief, representing Force, Justice, Prudence, and Temperance, virtues characteristic of the hero. This pyramid ended in a funeral urn surmounted by a crown of fire. On the front of the pyramid were placed the arms of the duke, and medallions commemorating the most remarkable events of his life borne by genii. Under the obelisk was placed the sarcophagus containing the remains of the marshal, at the corners of which were trophies composed of banners taken from his enemies, and innumerable silver candelabra were placed on the steps by which the platform was reached. The oaken altar, in the position it occupied before the Revolution, was double, and had a double tabernacle, on the doors of which were the commandments, the whole surmounted by a large cross, from the intersection of which was suspended a shroud. At the corners of the altar were the statues of St. Louis and St. Napoleon. Four large candelabra were placed on pedestals at the corners of the steps, and the pavement of the choir and that of the nave were covered with a black carpet. The pulpit, also draped in black and decorated with the Imperial eagle, and from which was pronounced the funeral oration over the marshal, was situated on the left in front of the bier; on the right was a seat of ebony decorated with Imperial arms, bees, stars, lace, fringes, and other ornaments in silver, which was intended for the prince archchancelor of the Empire, who presided at the ceremony. Steps were erected in the arches of the aisles, and corresponded to the tribunes which were above; and in front of these steps were seats and benches for the civil and military authorities, the cardinals, archbishops, bishops, etc. The arms, decorations, baton, and laurel crown of the marshal were placed on the bier.

All the nave and the bottom of the aisles were covered with black with a white bordering, as were the windows also, and the draperies displayed the marshal's arms, baton, and cipher.

The organ was entirely concealed by voluminous hangings which in no wise lessened the effect of its mournful tones. Eighteen sepulchral silver lamps were suspended by chains from lances, bearing on their points flags taken from the enemy. On the pilasters of the nave were fastened trophies of arms, composed of banners captured in the numerous engagements which had made the marshal's life illustrious. The railing of the altar on the side of the esplanade was draped in black, and above this were the arms of the duke borne by two figures of Fame holding palms of victory; above was written: "*Napoleon to the Memory of the Duke of Montebello, who died gloriously on the field of Essling, 22d May, 1809.*"

The conservatory of music executed a mass composed of selections from the best of Mozart's sacred pieces. After the ceremony the body was carried as far as the door of the church and placed on the funeral car, which was ornamented with laurel and four groups of the banners captured from the enemy by his army-corps in the numerous battles in which the marshal had taken part, and was preceded by a military and religious procession, followed by one of mourning and honor. The military *cortège* was composed of detachments from all branches of the army, — cavalry, and light infantry, and the line, and artillery both horse and foot; followed by cannon, caissons, sappers, and miners, all preceded by drums, trumpets, bands, etc.; and the general staff, with the marshal, Prince of Wagram, at its head, formed of all the general officers, with the staff of the division and of the place.

The religious procession was composed of children and old men from the hospitals, clergy from all the parishes and from the metropolitan church of Paris, bearing crosses and banners, with singers and sacred music, and his Majesty's chaplain with his assistants. The car on which was placed the marshal's body followed immediately after. The marshals, Duke of Conegliano,[1] Count Serrurier,[2] Duke of Istria,[3] and Prince of Eckmuhl,[4] bore the corners of the pall. On each side of the car two of the marshal's *aides-de-camp* bore a standard, and on the bier were fastened the baton of the marshal and the decorations of the Duke of Montebello.

After the car came the *cortège* of mourning and of honor; the marshal's empty carriage, with two of his *aides-de-camp* on horseback at the door, four mourning carriages for the marshal's family, the carriages of the princes, grand dignitaries, marshals, ministers, colonel-generals, and chief inspectors. Then came a detachment of cavalry preceded by trumpets, and bands on horseback followed the carriages and ended the procession. Music accompanied the chants,

---

[1] Marshal Moncey.   [2] Marshal Serrurier.   [3] Marshal Bessières.   [4] Marshal Davoust. —TRANS.

all the bells of the churches tolled, and thirteen cannon thundered at intervals.

On arriving at the subterranean entrance of the church of Saint-Geneviève, the body was removed from the car by grenadiers who had been decorated and wounded in the same battles as the marshal. His Majesty's chaplain delivered the body to the archpriest. The Prince of Eckmuhl addressed to the new Duke of Montebello the condolences of the army, and the prince archchancelor deposited on the bier the medal destined to perpetuate the memory of these funeral honors of the warrior to whom they were paid, and of the services which so well merited them. Then all the crowd passed away, and there remained in the church only a few old servants of the marshal, who honored his memory as much and even more by the tears which they shed in silence than did all this public mourning and imposing ceremony. They recognized me, for we had been together on the campaign. I remained some time with them, and we left the Pantheon together.

During my short excursion to Paris, their Majesties had left Saint-Cloud for Rambouillet, so I set out to rejoin them with the equipages of the marshal, Prince de Neuchâtel, who had left court temporarily to be present at the obsequies of the brave Duke of Montebello.

It was, if I am not mistaken, on arriving at Rambouillet that I learned the particulars of a duel which had taken place that day between two gentlemen, pages of his Majesty. I do not recall the subject of the quarrel; but, though very trivial in its origin, it became very serious from the course of conduct to which it led. It was a dispute between school-boys; but these school-boys wore swords, and regarded each other, not without reason, as more than three-fourths soldiers, so they had decided to fight. But for this fight, two things were necessary, — time and secrecy; as to their time, it was employed from four or five in the morning till nine in the evening, almost constantly, and secrecy was not maintained.

M. d'Assigny, a man of rare merit and fine character, was then sub-governor of the pages, by whom his faithfulness, kindness, and justice had caused him to be much beloved. Wishing to prevent a calamity, he called before him the two adversaries; but these young men, destined for army service, would hear of no other reparation than the duel. M. d'Assigny had too much tact to attempt to argue with them, knowing that he would not have been obeyed; but he offered himself as second, was accepted by the young men, and being given the selection of arms, chose the pistol, and appointed as the time of meeting an early hour next morning, and everything was conducted in the order usual to such affairs. One of the pages shot first, and missed his adversary; the other discharged his weapon in the air, upon which they immediately rushed into each other's arms, and M. d'Assigny took this opportunity of giving them a truly paternal lecture. Moreover, the worthy sub-governor not only kept their secret, but he kept his own also; for the pistols loaded by M. d'Assigny contained only cork balls; a fact of which the young men are still ignorant.

Some persons saw the 25th of August, which was the *fête* day of the Empress, arrive with feelings of curiosity. They thought that from a fear of exciting the memories of the royalists, the Emperor would postpone this solemnity to another period of the year, which he could easily have done

DUROC.

by *fêting* his august spouse under the name of Marie. But
the Emperor was not deterred by such fears, and it is also
very probable that he was the only one in the château to
whom no such idea occurred. Secure in his power, and the
hopes that the French nation then built upon him, he knew
well that he had nothing to dread from exiled princes, or
from a party which appeared dead without the least chance
of resurrection. I have heard it asserted since, and very
seriously too, that his Majesty was wrong to *fête* Saint
Louis, which had brought him misfortune, etc.; but these
prognostications, made afterwards, did not then occupy the
thoughts of any one, and Saint Louis was celebrated in
honor of the Empress Marie Louise with almost unparalleled pomp and brilliancy.

A few days after these rejoicings, their Majesties held
in the Bois de Boulogne a review of the regiments of the
Imperial Guard of Holland, which the Emperor had recently ordered to Paris. In honor of their arrival his
Majesty had placed here and there in the walks of the
Bois casks of wine with the heads knocked in, so that
each soldier could drink at will; but this imperial muni-
ficence had serious results which might have become fatal.
The Holland soldiery more accustomed to strong beer than
to wine, nevertheless found the latter much to their taste,
and imbibed it in such great quantities, that in consequence their heads were turned to an alarming extent.
They began at first with some encounters, either among
themselves or with the curious crowd who observed them
too closely. Just then a storm arose suddenly, and the
promenaders of Saint-Cloud and its environs hastened to
return to Paris, passing hurriedly through the Bois de

Boulogne; and these Hollanders, now in an almost complete state of intoxication, began fighting with each other in the woods, stopping all the women who passed, and threatening very rudely the men by whom most of them were accompanied. In a flash the Bois resounded with cries of terror, shouts, oaths, and innumerable combats. Some frightened persons ran as far as Saint-Cloud, where the Emperor then was; and he was no sooner informed of this commotion, than he ordered squad after squad of police to march on the Hollanders and bring them to reason. His Majesty was very angry, and said, " Has any one ever seen anything equal to these big heads? See them turned topsy-turvy by two glasses of wine ! " but in spite of this jesting, the Emperor was not without some anxiety, and placed himself at the grating of the park, opposite the bridge, and in person gave directions to the officers and soldiers sent to restore order. Unfortunately the darkness was too far advanced for the soldiers to see in what direction to march; and there is no knowing how it would have ended if an officer of one of the patrol guards had not conceived the happy idea of calling out, " The Emperor! there is the Emperor! " And the sentinels repeated after him, " There is the Emperor," while charging the most mutinous Hollanders. And such was the terror inspired in these soldiers by the simple name of his Majesty, that thousands of armed men, drunken and furious, dispersed before this name alone, and regained their quarters as quickly and secretly as they could. A few were arrested and severely punished.

I have already said that the Emperor often superintended the toilet of the Empress, and even that of her ladies. In fact, he liked all the persons surrounding him to be well and even richly dressed.

But about this time he gave an order the wisdom of which I much admired. Having often to hold at the baptismal font the children of his grand officers, and foreseeing that the parents would not fail to dress their new-born babes in magnificent toilets, the Emperor ordered that children presented for baptism should wear only a simple long linen robe.

This prudent measure spared at the same time the purse and the vanity of the parents. I remarked during this ceremony that the Emperor had some trouble in paying the necessary attention to the questions of the officiating priest. The Emperor was usually very absent-minded during the services at church, which were not long, as they never lasted more than ten or fifteen minutes; and yet I have been told that his Majesty asked if it were not possible to perform them in less time. He bit his nails, took snuff oftener than usual, and looked about him constantly, while a prince of the church uselessly took the trouble to turn the leaves of his Majesty's book, in order to follow the service.

CHAPTER XXIX.

Pregnancy of Marie Louise. — What was thought of it in public. — **Beginning** of her illness. — All the palace in commotion. — M. Dubois. — **The Emperor's** agitation. — He is summoned from the bath-hall. — The Emperor's words. — He goes up to the apartment of Marie Louise. — **The** instruments. — Marie Louise's words. — The Emperor listens in **agony at** the **door of the** room. — Madame de Montesquieu. — The King **of Rome comes into** the world. — Paternal joy of the Emperor. — What he said **to** me. — Booming of cannon. — Appearance of the streets of Paris. — The twenty-second discharge. — Madame Blanchard. — Pages serving as couriers. — Paris **to the** sixth and seventh stories. — Poets. — Goods. — The **ceremony of anointing.** — Again Madame Blanchard. — The balloon falls. — **A whole** village lamenting **the death of an aeronaut who is in** Paris **in perfect health.** — Doubts **as to** Marie Louise's pregnancy. — **Napoleon** accused of libertinage. — **His love for his** children. — My **son dies of** croup. — The Emperor's words. — **My wife** at Malmaison. — Kind **act of** Josephine — Consolation.

THE pregnancy of Marie Louise had been free from accident, and promised a happy deliverance, which was awaited by the Emperor with an impatience in which France had joined for a long while. It was a curious thing to observe the state of the public mind, while the people formed all sorts of conjectures, and made unanimous and ardent prayers that the child should be a son, who might receive the vast inheritance of Imperial glory. The 19th of March, at seven o'clock in the evening, the Empress was taken ill; and from that moment the whole palace was in commotion. The Emperor was informed, and sent immediately for M. Dubois, who had been staying constantly at the château for some time past, and whose attentions were so valued at such a time.

All the private household of the Empress, as well as Madame de Montesquieu, were gathered in the apartment, the Emperor, his mother, sisters, Messieurs Corvisart, Bourdier, and Yvan in an adjoining room.

The Emperor came in frequently, and encouraged his young wife. In the interior of the palace, the attention was eager, impassioned, clamorous; and each vied with the other as to who should first have the news of the birth of the child. At five o'clock in the morning, as the situation of the Empress continued the same, the Emperor ordered every one to retire, and himself withdrew in order to take his bath; for the anxiety he had undergone made a moment of repose very necessary to him in his great agitation. After fifteen minutes spent in the bath he was hastily summoned, as the condition of the Empress had become both critical and dangerous. Hastily throwing on his dressing-gown, he returned to the apartment of the Empress, and tenderly encouraged her, holding her hand. The physician, M. Dubois, informed him that it was improbable both mother and child could be saved; whereupon he cried, "Come, M. Dubois, keep your wits about you! Save the mother, think only of the mother, I order you."

As the intense suffering continued, it became necessary to use instruments; and Marie Louise, perceiving this, exclaimed with bitterness, "Is it necessary to sacrifice me because I am an Empress?" The Emperor overcome by his emotions had retired to the dressing-room, pale as death, and almost beside himself. At last the child came into the world; and the Emperor immediately rushed into the apartment, embracing the Empress with extreme tender-

ness, without glancing at the child, which was thought to
be dead; and in fact, it was seven minutes before he gave
any signs of life, though a few drops of brandy were blown
into his mouth and many efforts made to revive him. At
last he uttered a cry.

The Emperor rushed from the Empress's arms to embrace this child, whose birth was for him the last and
highest favor of fortune, and seemed almost beside himself with joy, rushing from the son to the mother, from
the mother to the son, as if he could not sufficiently feast
his eyes on either. When he entered his room to make
his toilet, his face beamed with joy; and, seeing me, he
exclaimed, "Well, Constant, we have a big boy! He is
well made to pinch ears for example; " announcing it thus
to every one he met. It was in these effusions of domestic
bliss that I could appreciate how deeply this great soul,
which was thought impressible only to glory, felt the joys
of family life.

From the moment the great bell of Notre Dame and
the bells of the different churches of Paris sounded in
the middle of the night, until the hour when the cannon announced the happy delivery of the Empress, an extreme agitation was felt throughout Paris. At break of
day the crowd rushed towards the Tuileries, and filled the
streets and quays, all awaiting in anxious suspense the first
discharge of the cannon. But this curious sight was not
only seen in the Tuileries and neighboring districts, but
at half-past nine in streets far removed from the chateau,
and in all parts of Paris, people could be seen stopping to
count with emotion the discharges of the cannon.

The twenty-second discharge which announced the birth

of a boy was hailed with general acclamations. To the silence of expectation, which had arrested as if by enchantment the steps of all persons scattered over all parts of the city, succeeded a burst of enthusiasm almost indescribable. In this twenty-second [1] boom of the cannon was a whole dynasty, a whole future, and simultaneously hats went up in the air; people ran over each other, and embraced those to whom they were strangers amid shouts of " *Vive l'Empereur!* " Old soldiers shed tears of joy, thinking that they had contributed by their labors and their fatigues to prepare the heritage of the King of Rome, and that their laurels would wave over the cradle of a dynasty.

Napoleon, concealed behind a curtain at one of the windows of the Empress's room, enjoyed the sight of the popular joy, and seemed deeply touched. Great tears rolled from his eyes, and overcome by emotion he came again to embrace his son. Never had glory made him shed a tear; but the happiness of being a father had softened this heart on which the most brilliant victories and the most sincere testimonials of public admiration seemed hardly to make an impression. And in truth Napoleon had a right to believe in his good fortune, which had reached its height on the day when an archduchess of Austria made him the father of a king, who had begun as a cadet in a Corsican family. At the end of a few hours the event which was awaited with equal impatience by France and Europe had become the personal joy of every household.

At half-past ten Madame Blanchard set out from *L'École Militaire* in a balloon for the purpose of carrying

---

[1] It had been announced in the papers that if it was a girl a salute of twenty-one guns would be fired; if a boy, one hundred guns. — TRANS.

into all the towns and villages through which she passed, the news of the birth of the King of Rome.

The telegraph carried the happy news in every direction; and at two o'clock in the afternoon replies had already been received from Lyons, Lille, Brussels, Antwerp, Brest, and many other large towns of the Empire, which replies, as may well be imagined were in perfect accord with the sentiments entertained at the capital.

In order to respond to the eagerness of the crowd which pressed continually around the doors of the palace to learn of the welfare of the Empress and her august child, it was decided that one of the chamberlains should stand from morning till evening in the first saloon of the state apartments, to receive those who came, and inform them of the bulletins which her Majesty's physicians issued twice a day. At the end of a few hours, special couriers were sent on all roads leading to foreign courts, bearing the news of the delivery of the Empress; the Emperor's pages being charged with this mission to the Senate of Italy, and the municipal bodies of Milan and Rome. Orders were given in the fortified towns and ports that the same salutes should be fired as at Paris, and that the fleets should be decorated. A beautiful evening favored the special rejoicings at the capital where the houses were voluntarily illuminated. Those who seek to ascertain by external appearances the real feelings of a people amid events of this kind, remarked that the topmost stories of houses in the faubourgs were as well lighted as the most magnificent hotels and finest houses of the capital. Public buildings, which under other circumstances are remarkable from the darkness of the surrounding houses, were scarcely seen amid this profusion of lights with which public gratitude had lighted every window. The boatmen gave an impromptu *fête* which lasted part of the night, and to witness which an immense crowd covered the shore, testifying the most ardent joy. This people, who for thirty years had passed through so many different emotions, and who had celebrated so many victories, showed as much enthusiasm as if it had been their first *fête*, or a happy change in their destiny. Verses were sung or recited at all the theaters; and there was no poetic formula, from the ode to the fable, which was not made use of to celebrate the event of the 20th of March, 1811. I learned from a well-informed person that the sum of one hundred thousand francs from the private funds of the Emperor was distributed by M. Dequevauvilliers, secretary of the treasury of the chamber, among the authors of the poetry sent to the Tuileries; and finally, fashion, which makes use of the least events, invented stuffs called *roi-de-Rome*, as in the old régime they had been called *dauphin*.

On the evening of the 20th of March at nine o'clock the King of Rome was anointed in the chapel of the Tuileries. This was a most magnificent ceremony. The Emperor Napoleon, surrounded by the princes and princesses of his whole court, placed him in the center of the chapel on a sofa surmounted by a canopy with a *Prie-Dieu.* Between the altar and the balustrade had been placed on a carpet of white velvet a pedestal of granite surmounted by a handsome silver gilt vase to be used as a baptismal font. The Emperor was grave; but paternal tenderness diffused over his face an expression of happiness, and it might have been said that he felt himself half relieved of the burdens of the Empire on seeing the august child who seemed destined to receive it one day from the hands of his father. When he approached the baptismal font to present the child to be anointed there was a moment of silence and religious contemplation, which formed a touching contrast to the vociferous gayety which at the same moment animated the crowd outside, whom the spectacle of the brilliant fireworks had drawn from all parts of Paris to the Tuileries.

Madame Blanchard, who as I have said had set out in her balloon an hour after the birth of the King of Rome, to carry the news into all places she passed, first descended at Saint-Tiebault near Lagny, and from there, as the wind had subsided, returned to Paris. Her balloon rose after her departure, and fell at a place six leagues farther on, and the inhabitants, finding in this balloon only clothing and provisions, did not doubt that the intrepid aeronaut had been killed; but fortunately just as her death was announced at Paris, Madame Blanchard herself arrived and dispelled all anxiety.

Many persons had doubted Marie Louise's pregnancy. Some believed it assumed, and I never could comprehend the foolish reasons given by these persons on this subject which malevolence tried to disseminate. But a very singular fact which carries its own proof is, that among the great number of these evil-thinking, suspicious persons, one part accused the Emperor of being a libertine, supposing him the father of many natural children, and the other thought him incapable of obtaining children even by a young princess only nineteen years of age, their hatred thus blinding their judgment. If Napoleon had natural children, why could he not have legitimate ones, especially with a young wife who was known to be in most flourishing health. Besides, it was not the first, as it was not the last, shaft of malice aimed at Napoleon; for his position was too high, his glory too brilliant, not to inspire exaggerated sentiments whether of joy or hatred.

There were also some ill-wishers who took pleasure in saying that Napoleon was incapable of tender sentiments, and that the happiness of being a father could not penetrate this heart so filled with ambition as to exclude all else. I can cite, among many others in my knowledge, a little anecdote which touched me exceedingly, and which I take much pleasure in relating, since, while it triumphantly answers the calumnies of which I have spoken, it also proves the special consideration with which his Majesty honored me, and consequently, both as a father and a faithful servant, I experience a mild satisfaction in placing it in these *Memoirs.* Napoleon was very fond of children; and having one day asked me to bring mine to him, I went to seek him. Meanwhile Talleyrand was announced to the Emperor; and as the interview lasted a long time, my child grew weary of waiting, and I carried him back to his mother. A short time after he was taken with croup, which cruel disease, concerning which his Majesty had made a special appeal to the faculty of Paris,[1] snatched many children from their families. Mine died at Paris. We were then at the château of Compiègne, and I received the sad news just as I was preparing to go to the toilet. I was too much overcome by my loss to perform my duties; and when the Emperor asked what prevented my coming, and was told that I had just heard of the death of my son, said kindly, "Poor

---

[1] On the occasion of the death from croup in 1807 of his heir presumptive, the young son of the King of Holland.—TRANS.

Constant! what a terrible sorrow! We fathers alone can know what it is!"

A short time after, my wife went to see the Empress Josephine at Malmaison; and this lovely princess deigned to receive her alone in the little room in front of her bedroom. There she seated herself beside her, and tried in touching words of sympathy to console her, saying that this stroke did not reach us alone, and that her grandson, too, had died of the same disease. As she said this she began to weep; for this remembrance reopened in her soul recent griefs, and my wife bathed with tears the hands of this excellent princess. Josephine added many touching remarks, trying to alleviate her sorrow by sharing it, and thus restore resignation to the heart of the poor mother. The remembrance of this kindness helped to calm our grief, and I confess that it is at once both an honor and a consolation to recall the august sympathy which the loss of this dear child excited in the hearts of Napoleon and Josephine. The world will never know how much sensibility and compassion Josephine felt for the sorrows of others, and all the treasures of goodness contained in her beautiful soul.

CHAPTER XXX.

Marie Louise and Josephine. — The young Empress' simplicity. — She thinks herself ill. — Pills of bread and sugar. — German expressions of Marie Louise. — Napoleon's tenderness. — Severe etiquette. — Cordial welcomes of the Empress. — Caen. — An act of kindness. — Cherbourg. — A descent into the basin of Cherbourg. — Baptism of the King of Rome. — Souvenirs of the *fête.* — The Emperor presents his son to those present. — Banquet and concert at the Hôtel de Ville. — Kind words. — The Tiber at Paris. — The balloonist Garnerin. — The provinces. — The Puy-de-Dôme in flames. — The sea on fire in the port of Flushing. — Other *fêtes.* — The road to Saint-Cloud. — Fountains of barley-water and currant wine. — Shrubs for lamp-posts. — Madame Blanchard. — The air-balloon. — The great star and the smaller stars. — Fairyland. — The doves. — The storm. — The Emperor and the mayor of Lyons. — The courtiers. — The musicians. — Prince Aldobrandini. – The Prince and Princess Borghèse. — The men of bad omen. — Women without shoes. — No carriages. — Act of gallantry and kindness of M. de Rémusat.

NAPOLEON was accustomed to compare Marie Louise with Josephine, attributing to the latter all the advantages of art and grace, and to the former all the charms of simplicity, modesty, and innocence. Sometimes, however, this simplicity had in it something childish, an instance of which I received from good authority. The young Empress, thinking herself sick, consulted M. Corvisart, who, finding that her imagination alone was at fault, and that she was suffering simply from the nervousness natural to a young woman, ordered, as his only prescription, a box of pills composed of bread and sugar, which the Empress was to take regularly; after doing which Marie Louise found herself better, and thanked M. Corvisart, who did not think

proper, as may well be believed, to enlighten her as to his
little deception.   Having been educated in a German court,
and having learned French only from masters, Marie Louise
spoke the language with the difficulty usually found in
expressing one's self in a foreign tongue.   Among the awkward expressions she often used, but which in her graceful
mouth were not without a certain charm, the one which
struck me especially, because it often recurred, was this:
" *Napoléon qu'est ce que veux-tu?* "   The Emperor showed
the deepest affection for his young wife, and at the same
time made her conform to all the rules of etiquette, to
which the Empress submitted with the utmost grace.   In
the month of May, 1811, their Majesties made a journey
into the departments of Calvados and La Manche, where
they were received with enthusiasm by all the towns; and
the Emperor made his stay at Caen memorable by his
gifts, favors, and acts of benevolence.   Many young men
belonging to good families received sub-lieutenancies, and
one hundred and thirty thousand francs were devoted
to various charities.   From Caen their Majesties went to
Cherbourg.   The day after their arrival the Emperor set
out on horseback early in the morning, visited the heights
of the town, and embarked on several vessels, while the populace pressed around him crying, " *Vive l'Empereur!* "   The
following day his Majesty held several Councils, and in the
evening visited all the marine buildings, and descended to
the bottom of the basin which is cut out of the solid rock in
order to allow the passage of vessels of the line, and which
was to be covered with fifty-five feet of water.   On this
brilliant journey the Empress received her share of the enthusiasm of the inhabitants, and in return, at the different

receptions which took place, gave a graceful welcome to the authorities of the country. I dwell purposely on these details, as they prove that joy over the birth of the King of Rome was not confined to Paris alone, but, on the contrary, the provinces were in perfect sympathy with the capital.

The return of their Majesties to Paris brought with them a return of rejoicings and *fêtes* on the occasion of the baptismal ceremony of the King of Rome, and the *fêtes* by which it was accompanied were celebrated at Paris with a pomp worthy of their object. They had as spectators the entire population of Paris, increased by a prodigious crowd of strangers of every class.

At four o'clock the Senate left its palace; the Council of State, the Tuileries; the Corps Législatif, its palace; the Court of Cassation, the Court of Accounts, the Council of the University, and the Imperial Court, the ordinary places of their sittings; the municipal corps of Paris and the deputations from the forty-nine good towns, the Hôtel de Ville. On their arrival at the Metropolitan Church these bodies were placed by the master of ceremonies with his aides, according to their rank, on the right and left of the throne, reaching from the choir to the middle of the nave. The diplomatic corps at five o'clock took their place on the platform erected for this purpose.

At half-past five cannon announced the departure of their Majesties from the Tuileries. The Imperial procession was dazzlingly magnificent; the fine bearing of the troops, the richness and elegance of the carriages, the brilliant costumes, made up a ravishing spectacle. The acclamations of the people which resounded on their Majesties' route, the houses hung with garlands and drapery, the banners streaming from the windows, the long line of carriages, the trappings and accouterments of which progressively increased in magnificence, following each other as in the order of a hierarchy, this immense paraphernalia of a *fête* which inspired true feeling and hopes for the future — all this is profoundly engraved on my memory, and often occupies the long leisure hours of the old servitor of a family which has disappeared. The baptismal ceremony took place with unusual pomp and solemnity. After the baptism the Emperor took his august son in his arms, and presented him to the clergy present. Immediately the acclamations, which had been repressed till then from respect to the ceremony and the sanctity of the place, burst forth on all sides. The prayers being ended, their Majesties, at eight o'clock in the evening, went to the Hôtel de Ville, and were there received by the municipal corps. A brilliant concert and a sumptuous banquet had been tendered them by the city of Paris. The decorations of the banquet hall showed the arms of the forty-nine good cities, — Paris, Rome, Amsterdam, being placed first, and the forty-six others in alphabetical order. After the banquet their Majesties took their places in the concert hall; and at the conclusion of the concert they repaired to the throne room, where all invited persons formed a circle. The Emperor passed round this circle, speaking affably, sometimes even familiarly, to most of the persons who composed it, each of whom responded in the most cordial manner.

At last, before retiring, their Majesties were invited to pass into the artificial garden which had been made in the court of the Hôtel de Ville, the decorations of which were very elegant. At the bottom of the garden, the Tiber was represented by flowing water, the course of which was directed most artistically, and diffused a refreshing coolness. Their Majesties left the Hôtel de Ville about half-past eleven, and returned to the Tuileries by the light of most beautiful illuminations and luminous emblems, designed in most exquisite taste. Perfect weather and a delightful temperature favored this memorable day.

The aeronaut Garnerin left Paris at half-past six in the evening, and descended the morning of the next day at Maule, in the department of Seine-et-Oise. After resting there a short while, he re-entered his balloon and continued his journey.

The provinces vied in magnificence with the capital in celebrating the *fêtes* of the birth and baptism of the King of Rome. Every imaginable device, both in emblems and illuminations, had been made use of in order to add still more pomp to these *fêtes;* and each town had been governed in the form of homage it rendered to the new king, either by its geographical position or by its especial industry. For instance, at Clermont-Ferrand an immense fire had been lighted at ten o'clock in the evening on the summit of the Puy-de-Dôme, at a height of more than five thousand feet; and several departments could enjoy during the whole night this grand and singular sight. In the port of Flushing the vessels were covered with flags and banners of all colors. In the evening the whole squadron was illuminated; thousands of lanterns hung from the masts, yards, and rigging, forming a beautiful scene. Suddenly, at the signal of a gun fired from the admiral's vessel, all the vessels sent forth at once tongues of flame, and it seemed as if the most brilliant day succeeded to the darkest night, outlining magnificently those imposing masses reflected in the water of the sea as in a glass.

We passed so continually from one *fête* to another it was almost confusing. The rejoicings over the baptism were followed by a *fête* given by the Emperor in the private park of Saint-Cloud, and from early in the morning the road from Paris to Saint-Cloud was covered with carriages and men on foot. The *fête* took place in the inclosed park and the orangery, all the boxes of which and the front of the château were decorated with rich hangings, while temples and kiosks rose in the groves, and the whole avenue of chestnut-trees was hung with garlands of colored glass. Fountains of barley water and currant wine had been distributed so that all persons attending the *fête* might refresh themselves, and tables, elegantly arranged, had been placed in the walks. The whole park was illuminated by *pôts à feu* concealed among the shrubbery and groups of trees.

Madame Blanchard had received orders to hold herself in readiness to set out at half-past nine at a given signal.

At nine o'clock, the balloon being filled, she entered the basket, and was carried to the end of the basin of the swans, in front of the château; and until the moment of departure she remained in this position, above the height of the tallest trees, and thus for more than half an hour could be seen by all the spectators present at the *fête*. At half-past nine, a gun fired from the château having given the expected signal, the cords which held the balloon were cut; and immediately the intrepid aeronaut could be seen rising majestically into the air before the eyes of the crowd assembled in the throne room. Having arrived at a certain height, she set off an immense star constructed around the basket, the center of which she thus occupied; and this star for seven or eight moments threw from its points and angles numerous other small stars, producing a most extraordinary effect. It was the first time a woman had been seen to rise boldly into the air surrounded by fireworks, and she appeared as if sailing in a chariot of fire at an immense height. I imagined myself in fairyland.

The whole of the garden which their Majesties traversed presented a view of which it is impossible to give an idea. The illuminations were designed in perfect taste; there were a variety of amusements, and numerous orchestras concealed amid the trees added yet more to the enchantment. At a given signal three doves flew from the top of a column surmounted with a vase of flowers, and offered to their Majesties numerous and most ingenious devices. Farther on German peasants danced waltzes on a charming lawn, and crowned with flowers the bust of her Majesty the Empress, and shepherds and nymphs from the opera executed dances. Finally, a theater had been erected in the midst of the trees, on which was represented a village *fête*, a comedy composed by M. Étienne, and set to music by Nicolo. The Emperor and Empress were seated under a dais during this play, when suddenly a heavy shower fell, throwing all the spectators into commotion. Their Majesties did not notice the rain at first, protected as they were by the dais, and the Emperor being engaged in conversation with the mayor of the town of Lyons. The latter was complaining of the sales of the cloths of that town, when Napoleon, noticing the frightful rain which was falling, said to this functionary, " I answer for it that to-morrow you will have large orders."

The Emperor kept his position during most of the storm, while the courtiers, dressed in silk and velvet, with uncovered heads, received the rain with a smiling face. The poor musicians, wet to the skin, at last could no longer draw any sound from their instruments, of which the rain had snapped or stretched the cords, and it was time to put an end to this state of affairs. The Emperor gave the signal for departure, and they retired.

On that day Prince Aldobrandini, who in his quality of first equerry of Marie Louise accompanied the Empress, was very happy to find and borrow an umbrella in order to shelter Marie Louise; but there was much dissatisfaction in the group where this borrowing was done because the umbrella was not returned. That evening the Prince Borghèse and Princess Pauline nearly fell into the Seine in their carriage while returning to their country house at Neuilly. Those persons who took pleasure in finding omens, and those especially (a very small number) who saw with chagrin the rejoicings of the Empire, did not fail to remark that every *fête* given to Marie Louise had been attended by some accident. They spoke affectedly of the ball given by the Prince of Schwartzenberg on the occasion of the espousals, and of the fire which consumed the dancing-hall, and the tragic death of several persons, notably of the sister of the prince. They drew from this coincidence bad auguries; some from ill-will, and in order to undermine the enthusiasm inspired by the high fortunes of Napoleon; others from a superstitious credulity, as if there could have been any serious connection between a fire which cost the lives of several persons, and the very usual accident of a storm in June, which ruined the toilets, and wet to the skin thousands of spectators.

It was a very amusing scene for those who had no finery to spoil, and who ran only the risk of taking cold, to see these poor women drenched with the rain, running in every direction, with or without a cavalier, and hunting for shelter which could not be found.

A few were fortunate enough to find modest umbrellas; but most of them saw the flowers fall from their heads, beaten down by the rain, or their finery dripping with water, dragging on the ground, in a pitiable state. When it was time to return to Paris the carriages were missing, as the coachmen, thinking that the *fête* would last till daylight, had prudently thought that they would not take the trouble to wait all night. Those persons with carriages could not use them, as the press was so great that it was almost impossible to move. Several ladies got lost, and returned to Paris on foot; others lost their shoes, and it was a pitiable sight to see the pretty feet in the mud. Happily there were few or no accidents, and the physician and the bed repaired everything. But the Emperor laughed heartily at this adventure, and said that the merchants would gain by it.

M. de Rémusat, so good and ready to render a service, always forgetting himself for others, had succeeded in procuring an umbrella, when he met my wife and mother-in-law, who were escaping like the others, took them on his arm, and conducted them to the palace without their having received the least injury. For an hour he traveled back and forth from the palace to the park, and from the park to the garden, and had the happiness to be useful to a great number of ladies whose toilets he saved from entire ruin. It was an act of gallantry which inspired infinite gratitude, because it was performed in a manner evincing such kindness of heart.

CHAPTER XXXI.

THIS seemed to be a year of *fêtes*, and I dwell upon it with pleasure because it preceded one filled with misfortunes. The years 1811 and 1812 offered a striking contrast to each other. All those flowers lavished on the *fêtes* of the King of Rome and his august mother covered an abyss, and all this enthusiasm was changed to mourning a few months later. Never were more brilliant *fêtes* followed by more overwhelming misfortunes. Let us, then, dwell a little longer upon the rejoicings which preceded 1812. I feel that I need to be fortified before entering upon reminiscences of that time of unprofitable sacrifices, of bloodshed without preserving or conquering, and of glory without result. On the 25th of August, the Empress's *fête* was celebrated at Trianon; and from early in the morning the road from Paris to Trianon was covered with an immense number of carriages and people on foot, the same sentiment attracting the court, the citizens, the people, to the delightful place at which the *fête* was held. All ranks were mingled, all went pell-mell; and I have never seen a crowd more singularly variegated, or which presented a more striking picture of all conditions of society. Ordinarily the multitude at *fêtes* of this kind is composed of little more than one class of people and a few modest bourgeois — that is all; very rarely of people with equipages, more rarely still people of the court; but here there were all, and there was no one so low that he could not have the satisfaction of elbowing a countess or some other noble inhabitant of the Faubourg St. Germain, for all Paris seemed to be at Versailles. That town so beautiful, but yet so sadly beautiful, which seemed since the last king to be bereft of its inhabitants, those broad streets in which no one was to be seen, those squares, the least of which could hold all the inhabitants of Versailles, and which could hardly contain the courtiers of the Great King, this magnificent solitude which we call Versailles, had been populated suddenly by the capital. The private houses could not contain the crowd which arrived from every direction. The park was inundated with a multitude of promenaders of every sex and all ages; in these im-

mense avenues one walked on foot, one needed air on this
vast plateau which was so airy, one felt cramped on this
theater of a great public *fête*, as at balls given in those
little saloons of Paris built for about a dozen persons, and
where fashion crams together a hundred and fifty.

Great preparations had been made for four or five days
in the delightful gardens of Trianon; but the evening before,
the sky became cloudy, and many toilets which had been
eagerly prepared were prudently laid aside; but the next
day a beautiful blue sky reassured every one, and they
set out for Trianon in spite of the recollections of the storm
which had dispersed the spectators at the *fête* of Saint
Cloud. Nevertheless, at three o'clock a heavy shower made
every one fear for a short while that the evening might
end badly. "Afternoon shower making its obeisance," as
the proverb says; but, on the contrary, this only made the
fête pleasanter, by refreshing the scorching air of August,
and laying the dust which was most disagreeable. At six
o'clock the sun had reappeared, and the summer of 1811
had no softer or more agreeable evening.

All the outlines of the architecture of the Grand Trianon were ornamented with lamps of different colors. In
the gallery could be seen six hundred women, brilliant
with youth and adornments; and the Empress addressed
gracious words to several among them, and all were
charmed by the cordial and affable manners of a young
princess who had lived in France only fifteen months.

At this *fête*, as at all the *fêtes* of the Empire, there were
not wanting poets to sing praises of those in whose honor
they were given. There was a play which had been composed for the occasion, the author of which I remember

perfectly was M. Alissan de Chazet; but I have forgotten
the title. At the end of the piece, the principal artists of
the opera executed a ballet which was considered very fine.
When the play was over, their Majesties commenced a
promenade in the park of the Petit-Trianon, the Emperor,
hat in hand, giving his arm to the Empress, and being followed by all his court. They first visited the Isle of Love,
and found all the enchantments of fairyland and its il-
lusions there united. The temple, situated in the midst of
the lake, was splendidly illuminated, and the water reflected
its columns of fire. A multitude of beautiful boats furrowed this lake, which seemed on fire, manned by a
swarm of Cupids, who appeared to sport with each other
in the rigging. Musicians concealed on board played melo-
dious airs; and this harmony, at once gentle and mysterious,
which seemed to spring from the bosom of the waves, added
still more to the magic of the picture and the charms of the
illusion. To this spectacle succeeded scenes of another
kind, taken from rural life, — a Flemish living picture, with
its pleasant-faced, jolly people, and its rustic ease; and
groups of inhabitants from every province of France,
giving an impression that all parts of the Empire were
convened at this *fête*. In fine, a wonderful variety of attractions in turn arrested the attention of their Majesties.
Arrived at the saloon of Polhymnie, they were welcomed
by a charming choir, the music composed, I think, by Paër,
and the words by the same M. Alissan de Chazet. At last,
after a magnificent supper, which was served in the grand
gallery, their Majesties retired at one o'clock in the morning.

There was only one opinion in this immense assembly

as to the grace and perfect dignity of Marie Louise. This young princess was really charming, but with peculiarities rather than traits of character. I recall some occurrences in her domestic life which will not be without interest to the reader.

Marie Louise talked but little with the people of her household; but whether this arose from a habit brought with her from the Austrian court, whether she feared to compromise her dignity by her foreign accent before persons of inferior condition, or whether it arose from timidity or indifference, few of these persons could remember a word she had uttered. I have heard her steward say that in three years she spoke to him only once.

The ladies of the household agreed in saying that in private she was kind and agreeable. She did not like Madame de Montesquieu. This was wrong; since there were no cares, endearments, attentions of all sorts, which Madame de Montesquieu did not lavish on the King of Rome.

The Emperor, however, appreciated highly this excellent lady who was so perfect in every respect. As a man he admired the dignity, perfect propriety, and extreme discretion of Madame de Montesquieu; and as a father he felt an infinite gratitude for the cares she lavished on his son. Each one explained in his own way the coolness which the young Empress showed to this lady; and there were several reasons assigned for this, all more or less untrue, though the leisure moments of the ladies of the palace were much occupied with it. What appeared to me the most likely solution, and most in accordance with the artless simplicity of Marie Louise, was this: The Empress had as lady of honor Madame de Montebello, a charming woman of perfect manners. Now, there was little friendship between Madame de Montesquieu and Madame de Montebello, as the latter feared it is said to have a rival in the heart of her august friend; and, in fact, Madame de Montesquieu would have proved a most dangerous rival for this lady, as she combined all those qualities which please and make one beloved. Born of an illustrious family, she had received a distinguished education, and united the tone and manners of the best society with a solid and enlightened piety. Never had calumny dared to attack her conduct, which was as noble as discreet. I must admit that she was somewhat haughty; but this haughtiness was tempered by such elegant politeness, and such gracious consideration, that it might be considered simple dignity. She was attentive and assiduous in her devotion to the King of Rome, and was entitled to the deep gratitude of the Empress; for she afterwards, actuated by the most generous devotion, tore herself from her country, her friends, her family, to follow the fate of a child whose every hope was blasted.

Madame de Montebello was accustomed to rise late. In the morning when the Emperor was absent, Marie Louise went to converse with her in her room; and in order not to go through the saloon where the ladies of the palace were assembled, she entered the apartment of her lady of honor through a very dark closet, and this conduct deeply wounded the feelings of the other ladies. I have heard Josephine say that Madame de Montebello was wrong to initiate the young Empress into the scandalous adventures, whether true or false, attributed to some of these ladies, and which a young, pure, simple woman like Marie Louise should not have known; and that this was one cause of her coldness towards the ladies of her court, who on their side did not like her, and confided their feelings to their neighbors and friends.

Josephine tenderly loved Madame de Montesquieu, and when they were parted wrote to her often; this correspondence lasted till Josephine's death. One day Madame de Montesquieu received orders from the Emperor to take the little king to Bagatelle, where Josephine then was. She had obtained permission to see this child, whose birth had covered Europe with *fêtes*. It is well known how disinterested Josephine's love for Napoleon was, and how she viewed everything that could increase his glory and render it more durable; and there entered into the prayers she made for him since the burning disgrace of the divorce, even the hope that he might be happy in his private life, and that his new wife might bear this child, this first-born of his dynasty, to him whom she herself could not make a father.

This woman of angelic goodness, who had fallen into a long swoon on learning her sentence of repudiation, and who since that fatal day had dragged out a sad life in the brilliant solitude of Malmaison; this devoted wife who had shared for fifteen years the fortunes of her husband, and who had assisted so powerfully in his elevation, — was not the last to rejoice at the birth of the King of Rome. She was accustomed to say that the desire to leave a posterity, and to be represented after our death by beings who owe their life and position to us, was a sentiment deeply engraved in the heart of man; that this desire, which was so natural, and which she had felt so deeply

as wife and mother, this desire to have children to sur-
vive and continue us on earth, was still more augmented
when we had a high destiny to transmit to them; that in
Napoleon's peculiar position, as founder of a vast empire,
it was impossible he should long resist a sentiment which
is at the bottom of every heart, and which, if it is true
that this sentiment increases in proportion to the inheritance we leave our children, no one could experience more
fully than Napoleon, for no one had yet possessed so
formidable a power on the earth; that the course of nature having made her sterility a hopeless evil, it was her
duty to be the first to sacrifice the sentiments of her heart
to the good of the state, and the personal happiness of
Napoleon — sad but powerful reasoning, which policy in-
voked in aid of the divorce, and of which this excellent
princess in the illusion of her devotion thought herself
convinced in the depths of her heart.

The royal child was presented to her. I know nothing
in the world which could be more touching than the joy
of this excellent woman at the sight of Napoleon's son.
She at first regarded him with eyes swimming in tears;
then she took him in her arms, and pressed him to her
heart with a tenderness too deep for words. There were
present no indiscreet witnesses to take pleasure in indul-
ging irreverent curiosity, or observe with critical irony
the feelings of Josephine, nor was there ridiculous etiquette
to freeze the expression of this tender soul ; it was a scene
from private life, and Josephine entered into it with all her
heart. From the manner in which she caressed this child,
it might have been said that it was some ordinary child,
and not a son of the Cæsars, as flatterers said, not the

son of a great man, whose cradle was surrounded with so
many honors, and who had been born a king. Josephine
bathed him with her tears, and said to him some of those
baby words with which a mother makes herself understood
and loved by her new born. It was necessary at last to
separate them. The interview had been short, but it had
been well employed by the loving soul of Josephine. In
this scene one could judge from her joy of the sincerity
of her sacrifice, while at the same time her stifled sighs
testified to its extent. Madame de Montesquieu's visits
were made only at long intervals, which distressed Josephine greatly; but the child was growing larger, an indiscreet word lisped by him, a childish remembrance, the
least thing, might offend Marie Louise, who feared Josephine. The Emperor wished to avoid this annoyance,
which would have affected his domestic happiness; so
he ordered that the visits should be made more rarely,
and at last they were stopped. I have heard Josephine
say that the birth of the King of Rome repaid her for all
sacrifices, and surely never was the devotion of a woman
more disinterested or more complete.

Immediately after his birth the King of Rome was
confided to the care of a nurse of a healthy, robust constitution, taken from among the people. This woman
could neither leave the palace nor receive a visit from
any man; the strictest precautions were observed in this
respect. She was taken out to ride for her health in a
carriage, and even then she was accompanied by several
women.

These were the habits of Marie Louise with her son.
In the morning about nine o'clock the king was brought

to his mother; she took him in her arms and caressed him a few moments, then returned him to his nurse, and began to read the papers. The child grew tired, and the lady in charge took him away. At four o'clock the mother went to visit her son; that is to say, Marie Louise went down into the king's apartments, carrying with her some embroidery, on which she worked at intervals. Twenty minutes after she was informed that M. Isabey or M. Prudhon had arrived for the lesson in painting or drawing, whereupon the Empress returned to her apartments.

Thus passed the first months which followed the birth of the King of Rome. In the intervals between *fêtes*, the Emperor was occupied with decrees, reviews, monuments, and plans, constantly employed, with few distractions, indefatigable in every work, and still not seeming to have anything to occupy his powerful mind, and happy in his private life with his young wife, by whom he was tenderly beloved. The Empress led a very simple life, which suited her disposition well. Josephine needed more excitement; her life had been also more in the outside world, more animated, more expansive; though this did not prevent her being very faithful to the duties of her domestic life, and very tender and loving towards her husband, whom she knew how to render happy in her own way.

One day Bonaparte returned from a hunt worn out with fatigue, and begged Marie Louise to come to him. She came, and the Emperor took her in his arms and gave her a sounding kiss on the cheek. Marie Louise took her handkerchief and wiped her cheek. "Well, Louise, you are disgusted with me?"—"No," replied the Empress,

"I did it from habit; I do the same with the King of Rome." The Emperor seemed vexed. Josephine was very different; she received her husband's caresses affectionately, and even met him half way. The Emperor sometimes said to her, "Louise, sleep in my room."—"It is too warm there," replied the Empress. In fact, she could not endure the heat, and Napoleon's apartments were constantly warmed. She had also an extreme repugnance to odors, and in her own rooms allowed only vinegar or sugar to be burnt.

END OF VOLUME TWO.